In Presence of
My Foes

Part 1

Chapter 1

The pretty girl, holding a white feather behind her back, nudged her friend, and nodded at a young couple approaching them along the path. 'There's one coming now! He's asking for it. Get ready.' Her friend, older, plainer, and standing alongside a pram, gave a nervous giggle.

The path was full of pedestrians. West Park in Hull was a popular place and the early autumn sunlight had brought the townsfolk out to enjoy it and forget for a few hours their anxieties and fears. Soldiers on leave threw cheeky or hopeful glances at women dressed in their Sunday finery. In turn women averted their eyes, half-smiled, or returned looks of brazen willingness according to their virtue or their temperament. The air was full of chatter, the shouts of children, and the brassy strains of a distant band.

But the two girls' eyes were fixed on the young couple approaching them. The man, Harry Miles, hatless and wearing a civilian suit, was in his middle twenties, slim but wiry with a sensitive face and dark, curly hair. His wife, Mary, who was wearing a pale grey costume and carrying a light coat, was the same age with an excellent figure, clear blue eyes and a warm and generous mouth. Although she was wearing a wide-brimmed flowered

3

hat, it could not contain the long blonde hair that, when loosened from its pins, reached down to her waist. Clearly in love, the two were engrossed with one another and did not notice the pair ahead of them.

They were almost level with the girls when the younger one suddenly ran forward and jabbed the white feather into the lapel of Harry's jacket. Standing back, she gave a loud cry of scorn. 'That's for being a coward! They ought to stick a pinny on creatures like you. You'd make a better woman than any of us.'

Her gibe, carrying far down the path, caused men and women to turn. Here and there soldiers could be seen wincing but a number of women laughed and one gave a cheer of approval.

For a moment both Harry and Mary stood frozen. Then Mary ran forward. 'How dare you? How dare you insult my husband like that?'

The girl turned and sneered at her. 'Why not? He deserves it. My young man's in France, fighting for the likes of him.'

Mary was breathless with anger. For a moment it seemed she might strike the girl. 'My husband has been wounded twice in France and been given the Military Medal for bravery. So how dare you insult him in this way?'

The girl's defiance turned to sulleness. 'I don't believe you. They all say that.'

Harry, who had recovered by this time, caught Mary's arm before she could react further. 'Come along, love. It doesn't matter.'

'Doesn't matter? You fight for your country and then get insulted like this!' Wrenching away her arm, Mary swung back on the discomforted girl. 'You little wretch! I ought to put the police on you. Get away from here before I slap your face.'

4

Sobered now, the sullen girl ran after her companion who had already moved away. Noticing an empty bench under a nearby tree, Harry drew Mary towards it. 'Let's sit down a minute, love. You're trembling like a leaf.'

For a moment she resisted him as she stood staring down the path after the shaken girl. Then she followed him to the bench and sank down beside him. 'I could have killed her, Harry. I wanted to.'

He gave her a grin. 'You made that obvious enough, love. But you'd no need to take it that seriously.'

She was still trembling from reaction. 'No need? Harry, that girl was calling you a coward. My God, I'm beginning to wonder if people here are worth fighting for. Have you been given white feathers before?'

His lips quirked humorously. 'Once or twice.'

She gave a shudder of disgust. 'How can you keep so calm about it after all you've done?'

He smiled again. 'What's the use? As that girl said, to her I'm a scrounger who's dodging his duty while her lad's over there risking his life for us. Seen that way, you can't blame people.'

Shaking her head, she took a deep breath. 'I'm not as forgiving as you, Harry. I hate them. Even if they were right, it would still be unforgivable to shame a man like that.'

He was about to answer when the strident cries of a newsboy interrupted him. Turning, he saw people crowding round the boy. He rose to his feet, curious, and when the boy broke free, waved him over.

The panting boy, his grimy face sweat-streaked, dug into his canvas bag and thrust out a paper 'It's the Ruskies, mister. They're chucking it in.'

Harry gave a start as the headlines leapt up at him. RUSSIA IN REVOLUTION. ALLIES FACE MASSIVE GERMAN OFFENSIVE. Fumbling in his pocket he dropped a coin into the boy's grubby hand.

As the boy ran off, Mary turned her startled face to Harry. 'Do you think it's true?'

He lowered the newspaper. 'I wouldn't be surprised. Things have been going badly for them during the last two years.'

'But if it's true, it's going to mean all the Germans who've been fighting over there will now be able to fight on the Western Front, doesn't it?'

He knew there was no point in lying to her. 'Yes, it probably does.'

By this time her cheeks were pale. 'That's terrible. Only won't the Americans make up the difference?'

He frowned. 'They will eventually. But Jerry will know they won't have enough men in France until next summer or even later. So he's certain to get his Eastern Armies over as quickly as possible.'

'Perhaps Russia won't sue for peace,' she said hopefully. 'She's been a good ally so far, hasn't she?'

'She will if the Bolsheviks get their way,' he said. 'They've got no reason to fight for Capitalism.'

A shudder ran through her. 'Thank God you're no longer over there.'

He did not answer her. Instead he changed the subject. 'Your mother's going to the doctor tomorrow afternoon, isn't she? What's wrong with her?'

'Her elbow's swollen. I think it's only rheumatism but she says its quite painful.'

'What about Elizabeth? Will your mother be back in time to collect her from school?'

'She doesn't think so. I wondered if you could collect her? You are travelling in this area tomorrow, aren't you?'

He nodded. 'Yes, that's no problem. I can be there at four o'clock.'

She hesitated, then turned to him. 'You don't think we're pampering her by taking and fetching her from school like this, do you? After all, it's only five minutes walk away. Quite a few mothers let their children go by themselves.'

He knew she was thinking about his own working-class background where mothers were too busy scraping a living for their children to provide them with an escort. He smiled. 'No. Don't forget she's much younger than most of the other children.'

'She might be younger in years but not in any other way,' Mary said. 'Have you noticed how differently she speaks compared with the other children? Sometimes I think it's a little old woman talking instead of a child.'

'That's through being with your mother all day. I suppose it's inevitable she picks up some of her ways.'

She wondered if it were a criticism. 'That's something I haven't been able to avoid, Harry. At least not while you were away in France.'

He was quick to reassure her. 'I didn't mean it that way. I know you had no choice. But it is making her grow up more quickly than if she had you to talk to and play with.'

She could not deny it. 'The only answer to that, now that you're back, is for me to give up work and spend more time with her. But unless we rent a house or buy a very cheap one, we're all going to have to stay at No. 57 and in that case Elizabeth will still remain under Mother's influence.'

He gave a wry grin. 'In other words, heads she wins and tails we lose.'

Knowing how he longed for their own home again after their first house had been destroyed in a Zeppelin raid, and how he worried about Elizabeth, she had half expected him to jump at her suggestion. Curious, she

7

gave him a second chance. 'As you're the one who gets most of her tongue, it's only fair you decide. Do you want to leave or can you stand it a while longer?'

He gave another wry shrug. 'I think I can stand it. At least I'll try. But she can lay it on a bit, can't she? Do you think she'd be this way if you'd married someone of your own class, as she would put it?'

His question made her wince. No, she thought. She'd have caused trouble and conflict because she is that kind of woman. But the snob in her would not have found such an apt cause to spread its poison. She avoided the direct answer. 'I don't know what she has to be so uppity about. We were poor ourselves once when Dad was struggling to start his business. But instead of it giving her sympathy for working-class people, it's had just the opposite effect on her.'

Harry nodded. 'She's ashamed of it. So she dislikes people who remind her what it was like. It's not unusual.'

She felt for his hand. 'It's never had that effect on you, has it, my love?'

He laughed. 'That's because I'm the genuine article. One of the great unwashed. That's what Gareth used to call us. Did I ever tell you that?'

She had always loved his sense of humour and laughed with him. 'No, you didn't. And don't tell Mother either or it'll give her another stick to beat you with.'

A silence fell between them. On the far side of the path the autumnal leaves of a row of oaks were ablaze in the slanting sunlight. As she sat admiring them, a single golden leaf fluttered down to the grass. Without warning she suddenly felt sad and immediately chastised herself. What right had she of all women to be sad when the man she loved had been brought back from the horrors of war? To shake off the mood she turned to

Harry, only to find him gazing down at the newspaper again. Feeling her eyes on him, he looked up and gave a wry laugh. 'I'll tell you who will be happy if the Germans launch a big offensive in the spring. Chadwick will be in his element.'

The name sent a chill through her. 'Don't talk about him, Harry. That's all over now. Try to forget him.'

Forget Chadwick, he thought? The perfect soldier, the dashing hero of a hundred boy's magazines? The charismatic, handsome, fearless leader of fighting men? The young officer with breeding, education, wealth and position? Forget Michael Chadwick and what he did to Gareth? Better ask me to forget myself.

He heard her voice again. 'What is it, Harry? What are you thinking?'

He turned to her. 'Nothing, love. Except how good it is to get away from the house for a while.'

She nodded eagerly. 'Yes, isn't it? And what a beautiful day.'

As they fell silent again she noticed how the crowds were thinning out and remembered the war news. With their chatter subdued, people were making towards the park gates where a second newsboy was selling his papers as fast as he could pull them from his bag. Only the children were unaffected but even they were now being called to heel. As she watched them running after their parents, a large cloud crossed the sun and stole the glory from the trees opposite.

The sudden chill made her shiver and reach for her coat. Catching his eye, she smiled brightly. 'You can tell it's autumn, can't you? The moment the sun goes in, it feels cold.' When he nodded she glanced at her watch. 'We'll have to start back soon, Harry, or Mother might get into another of her moods.'

He nodded again but lit a cigarette. Conscious of his

9

reluctance to leave, she waited patiently. A gust of wind, accompanying the cloud, rustled the dry branches above them. Down the path, now thin with pedestrians, she could see a man sweeping up dead leaves. A minute passed and then Harry crushed out his cigarette and turned to her. 'You're right. We'd better go. We'll take a tram back, if you like. It'll save us fifteen minutes or so.'

Chapter 2

Ethel Hardcastle was at the door of No. 57 Ellerby Road only a few seconds after Mary rang the bell, convincing Mary her mother had been watching out for them through the lace-curtained front room window. Ethel was a woman in her late forties, of medium height, with handsome features and thick brown hair piled up and held in position by whalebone combs. She carried her head very erect and with her expensive and conservative clothes she gave a first impression of being a woman in full command of herself. At the moment, however, she was frowning and gave a tut of annoyance as she drew aside for the couple to enter. 'You're late, aren't you? Elizabeth's been complaining for the last half hour how hungry she is.'

Seeing the storm signals flying, Mary did her best to be conciliatory 'I'm sorry, Mother, but we don't usually eat as early as this, do we?'

'I told you I was going round to Mrs Bellmore's after dinner. And you know how early she goes to bed. Also Molly wanted to get off early tonight. As things are we won't have eaten and cleared up before seven or even later.'

'I'll clear up for you,' Mary said, removing her coat. 'I thought you wanted us to go out this afternoon so that you and Elizabeth could work on that jigsaw you bought her? You can get away straight after we've eaten. I'll see to the dishes.'

'And what about Molly?'

'She can go whenever suits you.' When Ethel gave her characteristic sniff of disapproval, Mary went on: 'Be fair, Mother. You did say we could go out today. And Harry and I don't get out that often together, do we?'

No one was better at counter-attacking from an indefensible position than Ethel. 'What's that supposed to mean? I hope you're not blaming me because you both go out to work. In my day a man earned the income and his wife stayed home to take care of the house and family. It's not my fault if you do things differently today.'

Harry, who had not said a word since entering the house, gave Mary a look and walked into the front room. Angry now, Mary closed the door and turned to Ethel. 'There you go again, Mother. You can't say half a dozen words without sniping at Harry, can you? You know the reasons we both have to work. It's to keep Dad's business alive, the business that brings you and Connie an income. And we both have to work because neither of us takes a decent wage out, knowing the business can't afford it at this time. You should be grateful to Harry for all he does for you. If we'd to depend on Willis, as we had to do when Harry was in France, we'd have no business left by this time.'

Ethel had the look now of a woman who knew she was in the wrong but would die rather than admit it. She sniffed again. 'Mr Willis seems to take the blame for everything these days. But even he can't be blamed for your getting home late for dinner.'

Mary was angry with the tears that suddenly stung her eyes. 'You always have to do this, don't you, Mother?

We've had a lovely afternoon but you have to spoil it for us. Can't you bear to see anyone happy?'

Ethel half opened her mouth, then closed it again. Tossing her head, she opened the door to the kitchen. 'I'm going to help Molly get the dinner out or the poor girl will never get away. You'd better go and pacify Elizabeth.'

Drying her eyes and checking in the hall mirror that no traces of her distress remained, Mary entered the sitting room. It was a large room containing a piano, a small organ, and a beautiful ornate oak sideboard that reached almost from wall to wall. It was a room that reflected an easily forgivable side of her deceased father's character. Estranged from his own father and the family's druggist business by a quarrel whose origins Mary did not know, William had started a rival business and made a success of it by hard work and honest trading. He had been a generous and tolerant man, if a bluff one, but had possessed the need to prove his worth by his possessions. As a result No. 57 was a house that lacked few of the amenities available in the early decades of the twentieth century. The sideboard, with its carved figurines, had always fascinated Mary and was an item left her in William's will. At present it was awaiting the time when she and Harry could afford a house big enough to contain it.

A large settee stood in front of the sideboard. A small girl was sitting on it, with Harry alongside her. With neat, regular features and long blonde hair, the girl was almost a miniature facsimile of Mary but at the moment she was looking petulant. 'I'm hungry, Mummy. Why have you been so long?'

'We haven't been long, darling. You never eat this early.'

'Yes, I do. And you are late, Grannie said so.'

13

Mary's face tightened. 'Then Grannie's wrong. What have you been doing this afternoon?'

'Just playing with my new jigsaw,' the girl muttered. 'The one Grannie bought me this week. Where have you been?'

'We've had a walk in West Park. You should have come with us. There were lots of children playing there.'

'I didn't want to come. I wanted to finish the jigsaw with Grannie.'

Mary looked round. 'Where is it?'

'On a tray in my room.' The girl's tone changed. 'We finished it. It's a picture of a big ship. Grannie did most of it. She's ever so good at jigsaws.'

Mary nodded and picked up a book that was lying alongside the girl. 'Is this what you were reading when we came back?'

Elizabeth nodded. 'Yes. Grannie was reading it to me until she went into the front room.'

Mary glanced at Harry. 'Then why doesn't Daddy read it to you while I go and help Grannie with the dinner?'

Harry nodded and picked up the book. 'That's a good idea. Can you show me where Grannie got to, love?'

To Mary's dismay the child took the book away from him. 'No. It's Grannie's book. She gave it to me.'

'If Grannie gave it to you, then it's your book,' Mary said. 'So why shouldn't Daddy read from it?'

'Because she wouldn't like it, that's why.'

As she noticed Harry's expression, Mary's voice turned sharp. 'That's ridiculous. Let Daddy read to you.'

The child's lips began to tremble. 'I don't want Daddy to read to me. I want Grannie to read. After we've had supper.'

Mary found herself breathing hard. 'You're making

14

me very angry, Elizabeth. Give the book to Daddy.'

The child jumped to her feet. 'I won't! I won't! It's my book and I want Grannie to read it to me.'

With Harry unable to hide his distress, Mary's temper broke. 'Don't you dare to argue like this. Go upstairs and wash your hands and face. I'll come up and talk to you in a minute.'

Elizabeth sobbed and ran out of the room. Harry's eyes followed her, then turned to Mary. 'We're losing her, aren't we? At least I am. More and more every day.'

She dropped on the settee and put her arms around him. 'It's only because you've been away so long in France, darling. It'll be all right once you've been back a few more weeks.'

He shook his head. 'You know better than that. Your mother's buying her away from us. Present by present.'

Before she could reply, Ethel's raised voice could be heard through the closed kitchen door. 'Stop snivelling, Molly. It's not my fault you're late. Put the blame where it belongs, on those who're too inconsiderate to care about other people's feelings.'

Harry turned away. 'She never lets up, does she?'

'She never will,' Mary said, watching him. 'Not so long as we live with her.'

He seemed about to reply, then sighed and shook his head. 'I'm going upstairs to have a talk with Elizabeth. I must try to get closer to her.'

The weather had changed and the sky was a uniform grey when Harry turned his bicycle into the lane that ran behind No. 57 the following day. Trees and bushes, their leaves yellow and russet, hid the gardens that backed on to the lane. As he rode past a huge chestnut tree, a gate appeared ahead. Beyond it stood a two-storeyed warehouse and a sign proclaiming THE

15

HARDCASTLE DRUGGIST COMPANY.

Harry never saw the warehouse without being reminded of its founder. A formidable figure with his huge build, walrus moustache, and good broadcloth suits, William Hardcastle had first employed him when he was a mere urchin seeking a job during school holidays to help out his widowed mother. It had not been a popular choice with Ethel, who had seen him as nothing but a little hooligan, and in the end it had been she who had brought about his dismissal.

However it had not been the end of his involvement with William's business. Seven years later, when out of work, he had run into Mary again and she had suggested to her father that he became a salesman for the company. William, who had always had a soft spot for Harry as a young lad, had agreed to give him a chance.

It was an arrangement that had prospered to the extent that William, who had been given two daughters but no son, had begun to see Harry as his natural successor. He had welcomed the deepening relationship between Harry and Mary, his favourite daughter, in spite of Ethel's almost fanatical opposition, and it had been he who, after their marriage, had helped them buy their first house. In turn Harry had come to see the gruff but kindly William as a surrogate father and when William had died unexpectedly in 1917 his loss had equalled that of Mary, who had worshipped her father.

It was now that the matter of William's will had come into prominence. More and more aware that Ethel lacked any kind of business sense, William had made out a new will that, although making ample provision for Ethel and his elder daughter, Connie, had left the business itself to Mary. Proud of his creation, William had believed that in this way its future would be secure.

Before giving the will to his solicitor, William had

shown it to Mary to obtain her consent. Aware of the effect it would have on her mother, Mary had been reluctant to accept the bequest until William had pointed out that under Ethel's control his life's work would be in jeopardy. Put that way she had felt unable to refuse and William had slipped the new will into a drawer to await his solicitor's return from holiday.

It had proved a fatal delay. After William's heart attack a few days later the new will could not be found. From Ethel's behaviour at the reading of the original will, neither Harry nor Mary doubted that Ethel had found the new will and destroyed it. Nevertheless, without proof, the old will remained valid and so the young couple had been left not only at Ethel's mercy in No. 57 but also under her suzerainty at work.

It would all have been different if William had lived, Harry thought, as he dismounted and opened the gate. William had been the one man who could control Ethel. When he was alive he had only to rear his huge bulk from his armchair and express his Edwardian anger and Ethel would drop her complaints and hastily retire into the kitchen.

Harry had never been able to decide where the full power of William's control over her had lain. Part of it had been undoubtedly due to her own upbringing, the teaching that a husband was and should be the master of his house. But although Harry had found it hard to believe a loving heart beat behind the armoured breastplate of Ethel's bosom, Mary had assured him she had loved William deeply.

This was probably the answer to the puzzle, Harry thought. Ethel would not be the first woman of her kind who, while a tyrant elsewhere, could be dominated by the man she loved and who bedded her well. And with both Harry and Mary knowing William had kept a secret mistress, there was good cause to believe he had been a virile man.

Harry pushed his bicycle across the yard to the warehouse, acknowledging on the way the greeting of a man of fifty-five or so who was carrying a crate from one of the sheds that lined the yard. With war losses mounting by the day, the few young men once employed in the warehouse had long gone and conscription was now inducting men in their forties.

Leaning his bicycle against the warehouse wall, Harry ran up the steps to the top floor where Mary had her office. He found her sitting at her desk by the window with a small pile of invoices in front of her. Giving her a kiss, he laid his order book on the desk and dropped into the chair opposite. He grimaced as she picked up the book. 'You won't find much in there, love. They're always cautious on Mondays. Has Willis got back yet?'

She shook her head. Willis was the flabby, middle-aged Londoner whom William had been forced to take on as a traveller after Harry had joined the Colours. A lazy man and a libertine who was taking all the sexual advantage he could from the lonely women among his customers, Mary had wanted to discharge him on Harry's return but Ethel, who thought him a gentleman, had so far refused. 'No. Not that I want him back yet,' Mary said. 'He's so slow on his bicycle he doesn't cover half the shops you do.'

Harry grinned. 'He hates having to cycle, doesn't he? I'd have loved to see his face when they stopped our petrol ration.'

She laughed with him. 'You'd have thought it was the end of the world. I know it sounds awful but I think I was pleased. He looked so pompous when he was driving the Ford about. And I'm sure he took his girl friends out in it.'

'He probably did,' Harry said. He turned to glance at the round-faced clock over the doorway. 'I'd better go and fetch Elizabeth. Shall I bring her back here or take her home?'

'I should take her straight home. I haven't much more to do tonight and I'll come back as soon as I've seen to Willis.'

Nodding, he ran down the steps and cycled off to Elizabeth's small private school. Down a street only four blocks away from No. 57, it was a large converted house that had once belonged to a successful lawyer. Somewhat pretentious in appearance, with two turreted attics to distinguished it from its less illustrious neighbours, it boasted three crab apple trees in its front garden, all of which were shedding their leaves in a rising wind.

A small crowd of adults was assembled on the pavement in front of the school when he dismounted. Most were young mothers although here and there an elderly man could be seen among them. Leaning his bicycle against a wall, Harry lit a cigarette and waited.

He was halfway through it when he heard the muffled sound of a bell. A jabber of young voices sounded almost immediately afterwards, followed by a rush of children on to the pavement.

He caught sight of Elizabeth thirty seconds later, talking animatedly with a girl of her own age. Pushing his bicycle forward, he gave a shout. 'Elizabeth! Over here, love.'

The child turned and saw him. For a moment he imagined her face fell. Then, with a last word to her friend, she walked towards him. 'Hello, Daddy. Where's Grannie?'

He kissed her, then began buttoning up her coat against the wind. 'She had to go to the doctor this afternoon. Didn't she tell you?'

19

The girl showed immediate alarm. 'No. She's not going to die, is she?'

Harry stared down at her. 'Die? Of course she's not going to die. She's got a bit of rheumatism, that's all. Whatever gave you that idea?'

The child looked close to tears. 'She says she will die one day. And when she does I have to take flowers to her grave once a week, just as we do to Grandpa's.'

'You needn't worry about Grannie dying,' Harry said, with feeling. 'She'll probably live to be a hundred.' He patted the saddle of his bicycle. 'If you like, you can sit up here and I'll push you home.'

When the girl gave an eager nod, he swung her up into the saddle and began pushing the bicycle along the pavement. He had not gone five yards when he paused. 'How long has Grannie being taking you to Grandpa's grave?'

'I don't remember,' she told him. 'But it's a long time.'

'What do you do there?'

'We put flowers into a vase. Then we pray for him.'

'And you say you go there every week?'

'Yes.' The child was growing impatient. 'Why are you asking me all this, Daddy?'

Pushing the bicycle again, Harry changed the subject. 'What lessons have you had this afternoon?'

'We had a reading lesson. And then Miss Knowles talked to us about birds and things.'

'Birds?' Harry said.

'Yes. Mostly skylarks.' The girl looked up. 'Mummy says you used to like skylarks once.'

'That's right. I still do. I like listening to them singing.'

'Mummy says you once had a fight with a boy who shot one. Is that right, Daddy?'

'Yes,' he said after a short pause.

The girl's curiosity was growing. 'Was it a bad fight, Daddy?'

20

If a bad fight means a fight that makes a man an enemy for life, then it was a very bad fight, Harry thought. 'No, love. Just two silly schoolboys hitting one another, that's all.'

'But Mummy says it was the squire's son that you fought with. Someone called Cha . . .'

'Chadwick,' Harry said.

'Was he really the squire's son?'

'Yes.'

'But wasn't the squire angry, Daddy?'

The squire had been very angry, Harry thought. But with his son, Michael, not with me. No man who puts his son into a boxing ring to settle a quarrel likes to hear him taunt his opponent who is hopelessly outmatched. And because Michael, with all his faults, has a deep respect for his father, he has never forgiven me for his father's disgust with him. 'No, the squire wasn't angry, love. He's a fair-minded man.'

'Is he still alive, Daddy.'

'Sir Henry? Oh yes, very much alive. But why are you asking me all these questions about him?'

'Miss Knowles was talking about dukes and squires and people like that this morning. That's when I remembered what Mummy had said.'

Harry, whose instincts were egalitarian, was not impressed by this aspect of the child's private education. 'I hope you'll always remember not to judge people on the money or the rank they have, love. It's the person himself that counts. Do you understand what I mean?'

The child's forehead furrowed. 'I think so. You were poor once, weren't you, Daddy?'

'Yes. Very poor. But who told you that?'

'Grannie. She said you had nothing before you came and worked for Grandpa. Was it horrible being poor?'

'It wasn't much fun,' he said dryly. 'What else did Grannie say?'

'Nothing much. Except you'd different ideas to her in some things.'

'Did she say what things?'

'No. She just said I'd understand one day.'

They were now passing a row of shops on the main road. As they reached a confectioner's, Elizabeth tugged at Harry's arm. 'Will you buy me some sweets, Daddy? Grannie always does.'

'Every day?' Harry asked. When the child nodded vigorously, he went on: 'Does Mummy know about this?'

'There was a long pause before the girl shook her head. Harry stared at her. 'Don't you offer some to Mummy when you get home? You've always been told to share things, haven't you?'

Shame turned the child sullen. 'Grannie says they're only for me. She wouldn't buy them if I gave them away.'

'But that's being selfish. When do you eat them? Surely not on your way home?' Unable to hear the child's muttered reply, he frowned and leaned closer to her. 'What did you say?'

'I said I ate them in bed.' The girl was both tearful and indignant now, 'Why are you looking like that? It's not wrong to eat sweets, is it?'

'It's wrong if you don't tell Mummy about them. Sweets rot your teeth, particularly if you eat them just before going to sleep. If you'd told Mummy about them, she'd have explained that to you.'

The girl gave a resentful sob. 'Are you saying Grannie can't give me sweets any more?'

'No, but you mustn't eat them in bed. And you must share things with Mummy. She shares things with you, doesn't she?'

22

'But Grannie buys them just for me!'

Harry could feel his temper rising. 'Then Grannie should be ashamed of herself. She should teach you to be generous, not to hide things from your Mummy and Daddy.'

The girl's question made him start. 'Why don't you like Grannie?'

Harry chose his words with great care. 'I never said I didn't like Grannie, love. What I said was that she shouldn't ask you to keep things from Mummy. Mummy should know everything because she knows what's best for you.'

'But why shouldn't Grannie know what's best for me? She's older than Mummy.'

Harry was trying to find a suitable reply when a plackard outside a newsagent caught his eye. Headed Late Extra News, it read RUSSIAN CRISIS WORSENS. Lifting Elizabeth down from the saddle, he leaned the bicycle against a lamp post, then bent down to speak to the child. 'Wait here for a moment while I buy a paper. Don't go on the road. I'll only be a moment.'

When he returned she was playing with one of the pedals of his bicycle. As she turned to him, he handed her a bag of sweets. 'Here,' he said. 'Take these. But only on condition you offer some to both Grannie and Mummy tonight.'

The child brightened at once, only for her face to drop when she opened the bag. 'They're just toffees. Grannie always gets me Liquorice-All-Sorts.'

Shaking his head, Harry took the bag back to the shop and returned with another. 'The shopkeeper says you're lucky to get these. They're in short supply these days.'

The girl pointed to another confectioner across the road. 'That's where Grannie gets hers. They always keep some for her. Do you want one, Daddy?'

There was no answer from Harry. Turning, the girl saw him gazing down at the open newspaper. 'Daddy! I said do you want a sweet?'

For a long moment Harry did not respond. Then, frowning, he lowered the paper.

The impatient girl turned curious. 'What are you looking like that for? What's happened?'

Folding the newspaper, Harry gave her a smile. 'Nothing's happened, love. At least nothing you need worry about. Let's get home, shall we, or Mummy will be there before us.'

Chapter 3

Although he was lying motionless so as not to disturb her, Mary knew Harry was not asleep. In the silence she heard the clang of a bell and the muffled screech of metal wheels as a tram made for the depot. Once she moved closer to him but he did not stir. Finally she raised her head. 'What is it, Harry? What's troubling you?'

He turned towards her. 'Have I kept you awake? Sorry. I tried not to.'

'Never mind about that. What are you thinking about? The sweets Mother's been buying Elizabeth?'

He shifted restlessly. 'I suppose so. But not only that. I don't like this business of Ethel taking her to your father's grave every week and making her promise to attend hers one day. It's damned morbid for a child. Hasn't Elizabeth mentioned it to you before?'

'No. Not a word.'

'I don't like any of it,' he muttered. 'It's not only morbid. She's being taught to be deceitful and to keep things from us.'

Mary knew she would never get a better chance to have things out with him. 'Then let's leave, Harry,' she said fiercely. 'Let mother keep her threat to sell the business if she wants to. We'll manage somehow. At least we've enough for a down payment on a house with

25

the £300 Dad left me. We can't afford to wait and let her turn Elizabeth against us.'

She waited expectantly for his response. He sighed before he answered her. 'There are a lot of things to consider, love. What about Elizabeth's school? Even if I was lucky enough to get a job, it's not likely I'd make enough to keep her there.'

She did not believe what she was hearing. 'Surely you of all people would rather she went to a State school than stay with mother and have her turned into a spoiled little princess?'

His laugh had a bitter sound. 'Would I? After the education I got? Are you sure?'

'What do you mean, am I sure? It never did you any harm, did it? And in any case we could always send her back when things improved.'

He shifted restlessly but made no comment. Her suspicion of his behaviour was growing so acute now that she was afraid to voice it. In the silence that followed she heard the distant chiming of a clock. Then, aware she must face the truth, she laid a hand on his arm. 'These aren't the real reasons you feel we shouldn't move out at this time, are they, Harry?'

He gave a start. In the few seconds it took him to reply she felt she already had her answer. 'What do you mean by that?'

'I think you know. You've never really settled down since you returned home, have you? And this news about Russia has made it worse, hasn't it?'

He sat up sharply. 'What the hell are you talking about?'

His outburst, so unlike him, confirmed her belief. 'I'm saying that you want to go back to France. And because of it you don't want Elizabeth and me to rough it in shabby accommodation with perhaps only soldier's pay to live on while you're away. Isn't that it?'

His laugh was scathing and yet unconvincing. 'You must have had a nightmare to get ideas like that! Stop talking nonsense and go to sleep.'

She struggled to a sitting position alongside him. 'It might be a nightmare, Harry, but it's real enough. You haven't denied it, have you?'

He gave an impatient exclamation and reached out for his cigarettes. 'I don't have to deny a daft thing like that.'

She opened her mouth to reply, then closed it again. His match scratched and in its flare she caught sight of his face, resentful and brooding. As he exhaled smoke a sudden thought came like a reprieve. 'Then has it anything to do with the white feathers you've been given? If so, with a war record like yours, it's ridiculous.'

He exhaled smoke again. 'Of course it hasn't. It don't give a tinker's damn what they give me.'

'Then what is it, Harry?' The last thing in the world she wanted to do was influence him with tears and yet she felt they were not far away. 'If you don't tell me I shall start thinking it's my fault.'

He turned sharply towards her. 'Your fault? How can it be your fault?'

'Why shouldn't it be? Like you, I worry what Mother might be doing to Elizabeth and it makes me tired and irritable. Also, when we're making love I imagine she might be listening and it inhibits me. So I could be disappointing you as a wife.'

Anger returned to his voice. 'For God's sake, I owe all the happiness I've known in my life to you. Surely you must know that.'

This time her tears did come, if only silently, and she had to pause to steady her voice. 'Then what is it, Harry? You must see that I need to know.'

His cigarette glowed as he dropped back on his pillow.

27

The silence that followed was deep enough for her to hear the pulse of blood in her ears. He drew in smoke twice before giving a wry, embarrassed laugh. 'You know, it's a funny thing, love. War's a foul, dirty, bloody and obscene business and yet . . .'

With every muscle taut, she felt she was listening to some guilty, long-held secret. 'And yet what?'

His laugh, a complex of emotions, came again. 'In another way it's very honest. Your enemies wear grey to warn you they're your enemies. Your friends wear khaki to tell you they're your friends. And they *are* friends. They'll cuss and swear at you and sometimes pinch your equipment if they lose theirs but they'll share their last tin of bully beef with you if you're hungry and their last tot of rum if you're scared. And if you catch a bullet out in No Man's Land, they'll risk their very lives to bring you in.'

She knew she must crush this romanticism at birth. 'That's only because they need one another. It always happens when people face a common enemy.'

Again he shifted restlessly. 'I don't deny it. But once you're experienced it, it's much more difficult to live in a world where men smile in your face and stick a dagger in your back.'

'You're talking about Mother, aren't you?' she said. 'Not everyone's like her, thank God.'

He shook his head. 'No, it's not just her. The war's changed people back home. I see it when I'm travelling. People pretend sympathy for the lads out there but you get the feeling they don't really give a damn how long the war lasts providing they aren't called up and can go on making money out of it. They sing patriotic songs and then put in a bid for another fat Army contract.'

She felt it wiser not to argue with him. 'I know what you mean and I get disgusted with them myself sometimes, like the other afternoon. But it won't always be like this. When the war's over, people will start behaving like normal human beings again.'

His laughter was bitter this time. 'What are normal human beings? Perhaps the war has just torn off the pretty wrappings and shown us what we really are.'

His words were chilling her. 'Harry, war is destruction, mutilation and killing. How can anything be worse than that?'

His cigarette glowed again. 'There are many ways of dying, love. And many ways of killing too.'

Her fear was growing by the minute. 'Surely things aren't that bad here. Surely you're exaggerating.'

'If I am, I'm not alone. I've heard dozens of the lads say how people back home have changed. I even know a couple who came back before their leave ended.'

Her fear turned into anger. 'Then they were selfish fools. Didn't they stop to think about their wives or sweethearts? Are you saying it's better to die than to live?'

Suddenly he sounded weary. 'I don't know what I'm saying. Go to sleep and forget all about it.'

'Forget it? When you've as good as admitted you want to go back to France? Because you do, don't you?'

She felt as if she were on the rack as she awaited his reply. He muttered something, stubbed out his cigarette, then turned and took hold of one of her chilled hands. 'It hasn't anything to do with my life with you, love. You must believe that. It's just something I must do. I wish I could explain it but I can't.'

She jerked her hand away as if he had struck her. 'But you have explained! You prefer life in the trenches with your friends to building a future here for me, Elizabeth, and the other children I was hoping to have.'

His face was near enough now for her to see its torment through the darkness. 'No. I was only talking to see if I could find out the reason. But I can't.'

'Are you saying you want to go back to that hell but don't know why?'

'Yes. I knows it must sound like madness but it's true. Do you think I'm going crazy?'

Feeling heat radiating from him, she realised he was sweating freely. Believing the reason could only be shame that he would not be with his comrades when the German offensive began, she felt her hostility die. 'Of course you're not crazy. But, Harry, you're forgetting what it was like for you. You're the man who hated fighting so much that it nearly destroyed you. After your last wound you were so ashamed of the killing you'd done that you didn't want to come home. Surely you can't have forgotten that?'

His voice was startled. 'Who told you? The doctors?'

'No. Nicole Levrey, the doctor's wife you were billetted with in France. She felt I ought to know why you were so long coming home and wrote me a letter.'

He dropped back on his pillow. 'Nicole wrote to you! I never knew.'

'I didn't see any pointing in bringing it all back to you. But now it looks as if you need reminding. You hated killing, Harry. It nearly destroyed you. So how can you want to go back? I hope it's not patriotism. Because you've done more than enough for your country.'

His laugh made her wince. 'Patriotism? All that went down the sewer when they executed Gareth.'

'Then is it your friends? Do you feel bad because you won't be with them if the German offensive comes?'

'What friends?' he said. 'I'd lost nearly all of them before I came back.' She shuddered as he went on with forced lightness: 'Unless you're thinking of Chadwick, that is.'

30

She seized on the name. 'That's another reason why you mustn't think of going back. Think of the hell he put you through.'

He exhaled smoke slowly. 'He's a good soldier, love. That's one thing you can't fault him on.'

'I don't give a damn how good a soldier he is! All I know is he nearly destroyed your mind. You don't want to face all that again, do you?' When he did not reply, she knew that to keep him she would have to fight with every weapon at her disposal, fair or foul. 'It's silly even to think of going back. You were discharged because of your war wounds, so you couldn't go if you tried.'

His reply shocked her. 'Chadwick could probably get me back. His father has influence in the War Office.'

Chadwick! Oh God, she had forgotten. Whatever the differences between the two men, she knew Chadwick had the highest respect for him as a soldier and so would welcome his return. If she was to hold him she would have to appeal to his heart, not his mind. She lowered herself to one elbow to be closer to him. 'Harry, have you thought what would happen to us if you went back?'

He shifted uncomfortably. 'You've managed before, love. You know more about the druggist trade than I do.'

'I can't work in the office and go out and get orders too, can I?'

'You've got Willis,' he muttered.

'Willis? Chatting with pretty women all day? You've said yourself what a useless salesman he is.'

His brusqueness betrayed his state of mind. 'Then kick his backside and *make* him work!' Then his voice softened. 'I know how hard it would be for you, love. But couldn't you manage just a little longer? One way or the other the war must end next year.'

With his life in peril, she dared not give an inch. 'You

can't go back to France on an impulse you don't even understand, Harry. What about Elizabeth and me? If you were killed, we might have to stay with Mother for the rest of our lives. Is that what you want for us?'

He murmured something and she could feel him sweating again. Remembering the acute concussion he had received during his last action in France, she was now convinced the reason for his wish to return was trapped in some padlocked cell of his mind. She ached with pity but knew the stakes were too high for a retreat now. 'You've already seen what Mother's doing to Elizabeth. I need your help to fight her, Harry. I can't do it alone.'

Another long silence followed. Then, with a sigh, he sat up, stubbed out his cigarette, and turned to her. 'All right,' he said, with a return of his dry humour. 'You win. I'll stay and fight with your mother instead of the Germans. Do you feel happier now?'

She could not decide whether she felt shame or victory as she threw herself into his arms. 'Thank God for that, Harry. You frightened me. I couldn't have borne it if you'd gone back and I'd lost you. You're my world, you know. I couldn't live without you.'

They kissed for a full minute before his need to be understood made him draw back. 'It isn't that I want to go, love. It would be hell leaving you both. No man in his right mind could feel anything else. And yet . . .'

Alarmed again, she tried to read his expression in the darkness. 'Yet what, darling?'

He shook his head impatiently. 'Nothing. That shell must have scrambled my brains. Just forget and forgive me, will you?'

She pressed against him, her lips moving urgently over his cheeks and mouth. 'I could forgive you anything, Harry. No matter what you did. But, oh God, how glad I am you're not going back to France.'

Chapter 4

The train, hauling its long line of wagons and carriages, chugged slowly across the snow-covered countryside. As it panted under its load, its coal-tainted breath drifted into the packed carriages and mingled with the stench of wet uniforms and stale tobacco smoke.

Harry was wedged into one of the carriages along with a motley collection of uniformed men. He was gazing out through a grimy window at flat fields held in the icy grip of winter. In the distance the haulage wheels of two mine shafts rose starkly against the yellow-grey sky. Here and there small farmhouses and barns stood huddled against the bitter wind and he saw a single horse-drawn cart making its way down a muddy lane. A crow wheeled towards the train and began flapping alongside it, seeking crumbs of food that the cold was denying it elsewhere. Yet these signs of life did nothing to lessen the air of desolation. The land looked stricken by the holocaust that was being enacted only thirty miles away.

The melancholy of the scene sank into Harry as the slow miles dragged by. What madness had drawn him back to this purgatory? In spite of his wounds, a miracle of chance had allowed him to return home to his wife, his child, and his work. Moreover he had eventually recovered to be sound in wind and limb, whereas on the long

33

battle fronts that stretched from the Channel to the Alps, from Riga to Czernowitz, millions and millions of lice-ridden soldiers would gladly barter an arm or a leg for the bounty he had been given.

Then what in God's name was this obsession that had eventually defeated both him and Mary and made her agree to his return?

He had loved Mary Hardcastle almost as long as he could remember. Their first meeting had been in 1904 when as a grubby urchin he had come to the Hardcastle Druggist Company searching for work. On his way down the lane he had found Mary being frightened by a large dog. Having a way with animals, he had soon pacified the dog and led the girl safely away. He had not known at the time she was William Hardcastle's daughter, only that she was the loveliest and most animated creature he had ever seen. In turn, as she had often laughingly told him, she had seen him as her shining and intrepid Galahad.

With such a relationship between them, he was even more mystified that he could accept Mary's agreeing to his return when he had been fully aware what that submission had cost her.

His thoughts went back to the beginning of the war. Taught non-violence by his deeply-religious mother, he had not joined the rush to the Colours. Instead he had worked on with William until Ethel's taunts and the escalation of the war had driven him to enlist and to serve in France.

How different then to now, he thought. Then the act of killing fellow human beings seemed a crime against God. Yet today, freed from the necessity, I have chosen to return, which means in all likelihood I will kill many more. How is it possible I can have changed so much?

A tap on his shoulder interrupted his thoughts.

34

Turning, he saw a skinny soldier gazing at him. 'Got a light, Sarge?'

'A what?'

The Cockney, whose uniform looked two sizes too big for him, lifted a nicotine-stained hand to display the stub of a cigarette. 'A light, mate! For me fag.'

Fumbling in his greatcoat pocket, Harry handed him a box of matches. The man cupped his hand, sucked in his cheeks, then exhaled smoke luxuriously. 'That's better!' He handed back the matches. 'You been on leave then, Sarge?'

With a lie seeming less trouble than the truth, Harry nodded.

The Cockney sucked in smoke again. It's hell goin' back, ain't it? You married, Sarge?'

'Yes.'

'Any kids?'

'One. A girl.' Harry hesitated, then went on: 'What about you?'

'Nah. We 'adn't been spliced long enough when the bastards called me up.' The soldier grinned. 'Mind you, there could be one up the spout now.'

'How did you find it back home? Were you dis-appointed?'

The soldier looked surprised. 'Disappointed? Nah, 'course I wasn't. Why?'

'You didn't find people had changed? Grown more selfish?'

The Cockney glanced round at a second, equally skinny soldier squashed on the seat alongside him. 'I'd no time to find out, mate. Me and Millie only got outa bed to go shoppin' and that kind of fing. We'd a lot of catchin' up to do, you see.'

The second soldier gave a coarse laugh. Inhaling smoke again, the Cockney cursed as the stub burned his fingers. Grinding it out under his boot, he turned to Harry again. 'How'd your missus take it, Sarge?'

'Take what?'

'You goin' back. My Millie cried her bloomin' heart out. It's rough on women, ain't it?'

'Yes, it is.'

The remark was reminding Harry of Mary's expression when she had waved him goodbye at Paragon Station the previous day. He had left her to face not only the fear that he might not return but also her mother's enmity. For although Ethel had stopped at nothing to make him enlist, in the way of her kind she had been equally vitriolic on learning he was going back to France. Now he was a deserter, not only running away from his family responsibilities but also taking his revenge because the business had been left to her and not to Mary. It was, she had told Mary, the kind of behaviour one could only expect from a Socialist.

Harry, who in truth had always considered himself a pale-pink Socialist (a view endorsed by his life-long friend Gareth Evans) had often wondered in his lighter moments – and his resilient nature had plenty of those – to what heights Ethel's dislike of him would have risen had she known his father. Arthur Miles had been a quietly-spoken, self-educated man but one who had fought for the rights of his fellow workers in every job he had found. With employers deciding they wanted no trouble-making Socialists in their work-forces, jobs had become fewer and fewer until finally Arthur had found himself working for a builder who had paid rock bottom wages and broken every safety regulation in the statute book.

The inevitable had happened. Arthur had fallen thirty feet to his death from an unsecured scaffold. As compensation Polly Miles, Harry's mother, had been sent a

36

five pound note and a short letter of regret from his employer.

The tragedy had not changed her. A gentle, religious woman who had taught her two children from birth the virtues of non-violence and forgiveness, she had taken on the role of breadwinner and worked herself into an early grave.

In his early days Harry had lived up to his mother's code, although his quiet resistance to injustice had convinced some, Sir Henry Chadwick and his son among them, that the sense of egalitarianism in Harry's family had not come to an end with his father's death. Certainly it had made him stand up to the titled family when he was a mere boy, an act that had earned him Sir Henry's respect but Michael's bitter animosity.

The war had given that animosity full rein. With Michael Chadwick and Harry of almost identical age, they had joined the 16th Battalion of the East Yorks Regiment within a few weeks of one another. Chadwick had been given a commission while Harry and Gareth had gone into the ranks. When Harry was found to be an excellent shot, Chadwick, fully aware of Harry's religious upbringing, had arranged that he and Gareth should join the machine-gun section that he was to command. Conscious that the machine-gun was adding a new dimension to wartime slaughter, Harry was only too aware of Chadwick's purpose in making the move.

The battalion had gone over to France and into action. It was soon clear to Harry that Gareth's nerves were suspect under shell fire. The fact had not escaped Chadwick who had taken pleasure in telling Harry what he would do to his friend if the Welshman were ever to shirk his duty.

On top of this Harry found the slaughter he was having to inflict was causing him acute distress. He was also conscious of a psychological fear. Throughout his life he had disliked men of Chadwick's mould, with their aggressive, blood-letting instincts. Yet now, when he felt relief and exultation after repelling an enemy attack, he would wonder if he and Chadwick were more alike than he had realised.

It had been this fear, coupled with his battle sickness, that had evoked the sympathy of Nicole Levrey when he had visited her after a particularly bloody engagement. He and Gareth had been billetted with Nicole on first arriving in France and had won her heart by the attention they had given her small daughter. He could see Nicole now, a tall, slim woman with brown expressive eyes. Sensing his state of mind, she had given him cognac and then, when the floodgates of his despair had burst open, had taken him into her arms to offer him physical solace.

At this point his religious faith, although shaken, had been still intact. Its disintegration had begun on the Somme when, on a single day, the flower of the British volunteer army had been cut down. Unable to bear the carnage, Gareth had fled the field, to be court-martialled by Chadwick and sentenced to death. Harry had spent the last night with the Welshman and when he had stood by his friend's still-warm body the next morning, he had known his faith was dead too.

He had fought on for another year, now killing men without shame. It had been during his last action with Chadwick – a memory Harry could never face without agonies of remorse – that he had shot down disarmed enemy soldiers who had previously incinerated two of his men with the dreaded *flammerwerfer*. It was a deed that had shocked even Chadwick and made Harry welcome the shell that had sent him into oblivion.

He had recovered from his head wound but in his

shame had refused to return home to Mary and Elizabeth. Learning about his condition, Pierre Levrey, Nicole's wife, had paid him a visit in hospital.

A doctor who had also known military service, Pierre had lost an arm at Verdun. A religious man, he had understood Harry's state of mind and had finally persuaded him to return to his family.

Harry wondered if he would get the chance to see Nicole and Pierre again now that he was back in France. He thought it unlikely, particularly now that the new German offensive was expected. Moreover, he could hardly request leave from Chadwick after asking the officer to pull strings to get him back into uniform.

In God's name why had he done it? It had not only put him in Chadwick's debt, but must also have convinced Chadwick that all his gibes were true and that beneath the skin both of them shared the same blood-thirsty instincts. Nor could he blame Chadwick for believing that when he had so often considered the possibility himself.

Finding the thought infinitely depressing, Harry sought again for his motive. Was it possible, when all other reasons were examined and discarded, that he was simply a man running away from a mother-in-law's malice? He would not be the first man nor the last to find a vindictive woman's tongue more destructive than a rifle bullet. Better that, Harry thought, with a spasm of mordant humour, than to be returning to the war because he enjoyed it.

The sudden jolting of the carriage and the clank of buffers interrupted his thoughts. Turning, he saw the packed crowd of soldiers picking up their rifles and kitbags. A glance through the window showed the train was approaching a siding where half a dozen horse-drawn carts stood waiting. Alongside him the Cockney gave an apprehensive grimace. 'Won't be long now, Sarge.'

Harry nodded. 'Never mind. This year should see it over.'

A flicker of hope, followed by scepticism, crossed the soldier's pinched face. 'You think so? With all them Jerries comin' at us from the East?'

'We'll hold them,' Harry said.

The Cockney eyed him almost pityingly. His reply was lost as the train came to an abrupt halt, throwing cursing men against one another. Then, as an authoritative shout was heard, they began jumping down from the carriage.

Harry followed them. After the fetid carriage, the icy air stung his face. His boots crunched in the snow as he made his way along the siding. Through the shouts and the hissing of steam, a distant familiar noise suddenly swelled in volume. Felt through the ground as well as through the ears, it sounded as if some monstrous beast, insatiable for human flesh, was roaring out its hunger.

A shudder ran through him as he followed the men to the carts. Ahead were the fires of hell. Could any man of sound reason, having suffered them once, choose to return to their torment? Could it be remorse for his killing the disarmed Germans that was urging him back? If it was, it could only mean he was seeking oblivion from a rifle bullet or a shell and that his promises to Mary that he would return were nothing but lies.

Whatever the reason, it could surely only come from a mind that held a deep and compelling sickness. The thought haunted him as the line of carts splashed along the muddy road to the Front.

Chapter 5

The water at the bottom of the sewer was only thinly filmed with ice and quickly filled Harry's boots as he stepped into it. With his tin helmet almost level with the half-demolished cobble road beneath which the sewer ran, he could see the ruins of a French village above him. Apart from a thick brick wall, behind which a British howitzer was sited, the rest was pulverised rubble with only a few truncated pillars and chimney foundations lying at angles like the tombstones of some ancient graveyard.

A flood of obscenity brought his eyes to the front. One of the men preceding him had turned to talk to a companion and caught his shoulder on the fractured end of a beam protruding through the wall of the sewer. A board was nailed to it bearing the inscription *Site of Ste. Marie*.

Harry followed the men from the sewer into a communication trench at its far end. Sounds that had been only a grumble half an hour ago were now becoming distinct and distinguishable. The noise to the left like a giant firecracker was an enemy 77mm whizzbang. The vicious bark to the right was a 5.9, while the roar overhead, like an express train thundering from a tunnel, was one of the heavy German guns hurling a ton shell at some important target to the rear.

At the same time familiar smells were becoming stronger: the acrid stench of lyddite and chloride of lime, the fetid stench of latrines, the reek of stagnant mud. Like the men ahead of him, Harry kept slipping and sliding, the duckboards at the foot of the communication trench were coated with slime and ice.

The January darkness was closing in fast now and conferring nervousness on both friend and foe. The first star shell climbed into the sky, to be followed by the rattle of a machine-gun. As he listened, Harry's mouth turned dry. Hell was very close now.

He passed the first evidence of it five minutes later. In a large dugout on his left, a line of mud-soaked blankets tried in vain to conceal the cold light of acetylene lamps. The dugout was a Field First-Aid Station where doctors worked day and night on bullet-riddled or shell-torn bodies. A man gave a scream of agony as the soldiers filed past. The sound, barely human in its anguish, died into a murmur and then ceased. A man ahead of Harry cursed and lit a cigarette with a lucifer. A moment later a shout 'Make way for stretcher bearers' made all seven men draw to the side of the trench as a stretcher was carried past them, bearing a hardly recognisable creature of mud and mutilation that was moaning for its mother.

Yet as any soldier in the line would have testified, it was a quiet night on the Western Front. Barely two thousand men had died in the last twenty-four hours, far fewer than the daily average of seven thousand since August 1914. The hard frost was the reason. In general the Chiefs of Staff on both sides abandoned their ambitious plans from Christmas until the first green leaves of spring. As a consquence, in spite of the misery of half-frozen limbs, men blessed their respective gods when winter glazed the shell holes and turned their dripping dugouts into ice caverns.

42

Not that this happened often in Flanders and Northern France. Too often, as in England, raw winds and drenching rain was the norm. But this year ice had come and men found relief in it. In summer, shells hurled up dust and pestilence. The unburied dead stared at a man through eyeless sockets and punished him with their stench. The bluebottles and flies, fat from their obscene feasts, settled in myriads on his food and his cracked lips. In autumn and in spring, it was mud that was the hated enemy. Mud that stank, that sucked off a man's boots, that clogged his rifle and billycan, that coated his tongue and his throat. Mud that craved for human flesh so greedily that a man might slip from a duckboard and be drawn down into it before his comrades could save him. To many men on the Western Front, mud was hated more than the enemy.

But for a few blessed days in this new year there was respite. The dead out in No Man's Land deferred their decomposition and even decently covered themselves in white shrouds. The stench of the latrines no longer made a man retch, nor was the odour from his lice-ridden comrades so overpowering.

It was true that the stench of phosgene and mustard still lingered in the icy air and a man still stank when his wet uniform thawed before a charcoal brazier but the infantryman of 1918 was not the sort to look a gift horse in the mouth. Particularly when he had every reason to believe there would be no offensive from either side until the weather changed.

Reaching the end of the communication trench where it ran into the rearmost reserve line, Harry was forced to turn left to find the way to the second reserve trench. Here, in the wasteland between the two trenches, there was a protective belt of barbed wire. As he zig-zagged along the traverses of the reserve trench, he passed tiny dugouts occupied by huddled men in greatcoats and balaclavas. Some were crouched over charcoal or coke braziers, some were brewing tea, some heating tins of maconochie, others were playing cards or writing letters with mittened hands. Few glanced at him or the other six men as they passed by. When darkness fell, communication trenches were filled by an incessant flow of men bringing up water, food, ammunition, shells, barbed wire and all the rest of the paraphernalia required by the insatiable war machine, and already the glow of the braziers was beginning to stain the dusk.

Another detour to the left led him past a trench mortar site and Harry reached the First or Firing Trench. Here, among its traverses, saps ran out into No Man's Land to listening posts and machine-gun nests where half-frozen men waited for sounds that might indicate an enemy attack. Ahead of these posts, just beyond the distance that a powerful man could throw a stick grenade, were the forward barbed wire defences.

There was a subtle difference in the atmosphere of this forward trench. Although men could still be seen playing cards or brewing tea, they talked in lower tones and their weapons and gas masks were always beside them. Frost or no frost, no man could be certain that the Germans would not send over a raiding party to test the strength of the defences or to capture prisoners. If the enemy did, few men trusted the effectiveness of his trench defences to give more than a modicum of warning.

For the British, like the French, had never been inclined to give their infantrymen comfortable or even adequate protection against the weather or the enemy. One reason undoubtedly lay in the position of the two combatant armies. With the Germans occupying so much Belgian and French territory, it was perhaps natural at first that the Allies should plump for a policy of aggression, a head-on collision designed to hurl the enemy back into his Fatherland. Moreover it was a strategy perfectly suited to the British and French generals, most of whom had risen from cavalry regiments whose *raison d'être* was to charge the enemy and shock him into retreat.

Unfortunately such tactics had proved suicidal with the advent of trench warfare and the machine-gun. Yet after four years of immense losses, it seemed only Pétain among the Allied generals had realised that defence in depth can kill far more of the enemy than frontal attack and save a far higher percentage of one's own soldiers. Instead, Foch, the very apostle of offensive action, had by 1918 been given overall command of both the British and French armies, making Pétain's saner military strategy even less likely of acceptance than at any time during the war.

The consequence of this out-dated policy was the assumption that British and French trenches were little more than jumping-off places for the next offensive and so not worthy of more than a minimum of constructive effort.

In fact there was even more to the story than that. Just as they refused their airmen parachutes with the insulting argument that they might then jump to safety if attacked rather than fight, the British and French High Commands argued that if their troops enjoyed comfortable and safe billets, they might be reluctant to go 'over the top' when the order came. So their unfortunate infantrymen suffered cruelly while the Germans, wherever possible, wintered in deep trenches and warm dugouts.

Dusk had turned into darkness before Harry determined the location of his Company HQ although a sliver of moon was hanging in the icy sky. With a low mist forming in No Man's Land, infantrymen on evening standby were eyeing it nervously. With his feet half-frozen in his sodden boots and his back aching from the weight of his equipment, Harry said goodbye to the last of his companions and plodded along the slippery duckboards. As he rounded a traverse, a mortar shell dropped at its far side. Screaming followed the explosion, followed by a cry for stretcher bearers. Half a dozen flares rose immediately from the British firing trench but the mist, silvered by their phosphorescent light, showed no sign of life.

As the minutes passed and listening posts reported no unusual enemy activity other than the nightly mule trains and the chains of men bringing up supplies, the tension began to ease and a partial stand-down was ordered. Men jumped down from the fire-steps and crawled into their dugouts and soon strains of music could be heard. As Harry passed a small brazier he saw a man with a mouth organ. He was playing 'Santa Lucia' and playing it well and in the glow of the brazier Harry saw his eyes were closed. As Harry paused to listen, a deep baritone took up the melody from the trenches opposite. Instead of muffling the voice, the mist seemed to add to its resonance and no one made a sound until the song ended. A moment later cheers and catcalls broke out from both sets of trenches.

Harry could not analyse his feelings as he moved on. Could this be the reason he had come back? Because excessive suffering bares the inner core of men and gives them a rare simplicity? Because here of all places one could see the nobility of man as well as his barbarism and there was hope in the width of the division? Thinking what his fellow soldiers would make of that speculation, Harry smiled but the sense of comradeship warmed him

46

as the strains of the mouth organ followed him down the trench.

He found Chadwick's HQ two minutes later. Like the Company HQ, it was a dugout sited down a small sap at the rear of the Firing Trench, with an entrance riveted by sandbags and sealed by a weighted blanket. Finding no sentry outside to announce him, Harry drew aside the blanket and stepped inside.

An acetylene lamp standing on a small deal table provided the light. As Harry's eyes adjusted to it he saw two men occupied the dugout. One, a young lieutenant whose fair, wispy moustache would have shamed a sixth form schoolboy, was lying on a string bed with a half-filled glass of whisky resting on an ammunition box alongside him. The second man, a major, was seated at the table and busy writing in a notebook. Although he continued writing as the heavy curtain dropped back into place, Harry recognised Chadwick immediately. The black combed hair, the handsome face with its military moustache, the beautifully-tailored uniform and polished cavalry boots. . . . Harry knew no other officer, even under the present favourable conditions, who could look so immaculate in the Line. During his own time in France, men had sworn that if Chadwick had fallen headlong into a shell hole he would have walked out carrying a bottle of champagne.

As always when in the man's presence, Harry felt a flicker of envy and a burn of dislike. Lowering his kit to the ground, he came to attention and saluted. 'Sergeant Miles, sir. Reporting for duty.'

Chadwick laid the pencil on the table, lifted his head, and smiled. 'Hello, Miles. Welcome back.'

Harry made no comment. From the corner of his eye he saw that the young lieutenant had sat up at the sound

47

of his name and was staring at him. As if reading the young man's mind, Chadwick glanced round. 'Here's the chap I've told you about, Dartford. The one who likes war so much he asked me to bring him back from civvy street.'

No remark could have stung Harry more and yet he knew his request had warranted it. He watched the young lieutenant rise and move eagerly towards him, his eyes on the military medal ribbon on Harry's tunic. Before Harry could salute him, the youngster impulsively held out his hand. 'I'm glad to meet you, Sergeant. Welcome back.'

Harry hesitated, then realising to refuse the gesture would humiliate the officer, shook his hand. 'Thank you, sir. Have you been out long?'

'Two months, Sergeant. I came out in the middle of November.'

Aware of Chadwick's amused gaze, Harry nodded and turned back to him. 'I see you've been promoted again, sir. Does that mean your machine-gun section is bigger?'

'Much bigger,' Chadwick told him. 'I've over fifty men now and so far I've managed to keep the Machine-Gun Corps from grabbing them.' Mocking lights entered his eyes. 'In fact I think I could get you a commission now – I've got the necessary establishment. How would you like that?'

Startled for a moment by the offer, Harry shook his head. 'No, thank you. Not for me.'

Chadwick smiled. 'I thought you'd say no. What is it, Miles? Against your Socialistic principles?'

Harry was wishing that was all it was. 'It's not against anything, sir. I'd just prefer to remain in the ranks, that's all.'

'Even though your wife would get a bigger allowance?

48

And you'd be more comfortable when off duty?'

When Harry still did not reply, Chadwick pretended to understand. 'Of course! If you accepted a commission you'd have to go straight back to England to take the course and you don't want that, do you? You've come back to have another crack at the Jerries. Stupid of me!'

Knowing he was being baited and that Chadwick was intrigued about the reason for his return, Harry made no effort to answer. Chadwick eyed him a moment and then waved at an ammunition box standing near the table. 'Forget that for the moment and tell me how things are back home.'

For a moment Harry hesitated. Then, refusing the cigarette Chadwick offered him, he sank down on the box. 'The air raids have stopped – at least they have in the north. But food's getting scarce. Some weeks meat's impossible to get and even vegetables are in short supply.'

Chadwick nodded. 'That's because the ships that normally bring in food have been lent to the Yanks to ferry their men over. Did you see many of them?'

'Not in our area. But I'm told there are plenty of them in the south doing their battle training.'

'That's the problem facing Jerry. He knows he must finish us off before the Yanks tilt the scales against him.'

The young lieutenant, whose bright eyes had been moving from man to man, broke in at this point. 'You don't think they'll replace us with Yanks, do you, sir? Before the spring offensive starts?'

Chadwick laughed. 'Replace us? Three and a half million men? With the ships they've got, the Yanks will be lucky to get half a million across this year.'

The youngster showed relief. 'So our front won't be affected?'

Chadwick winked at Harry. 'No, Dartford. You won't

49

lose your chance to shoot a few Germans. Before you do that, however, I want you to go and find Sergeant Miles a decent billet.' As the youngster hesitated, his voice sharpened. 'I mean now! Off you go.'

Chadwick waited until the blanket over the exit dropped back into place before turning back to Harry. 'All right, Miles. Now you can tell me. What happened?'

The question took Harry by surprise for a moment. 'Happened?'

'Yes. You're the man who was supposed to hate war and all it stands for. Yet you wrote asking me to get you back and you sounded in a hurry about it. Why?'

Although he had known the question must be asked sooner or later, Harry had no idea how to answer it. 'I don't know, sir.'

Chadwick gave him a look. 'Come off it, Miles. You leave a beautiful wife and a cushy billet to return to this squalor. And you tell me you don't know why?'

Feeling embarrassed, Harry laughed uneasily. 'I honestly don't. But does it matter? I don't need to give a reason, do I?'

'Officially, no. But I like to know what motivates my men. Apart from that, I did go to a fair amount of trouble to get you back. Don't you think that gives me some right to ask?'

It was a point Harry had to concede. 'If I knew, I'd probably tell you. But I don't.'

Chadwick eyed him for a moment, then gave an amused laugh. 'You don't want to admit the truth, do you, Miles? All right, I'll answer for you. All that religion and pacifism you used to believe in once bores you now, doesn't it? You've got used to stronger drink out here. You've grown to like and need the excitement of the chase, as I do. Aren't I right?'

50

Harry felt again his old dislike of the man. 'That's my last reason for coming back.'

Chadwick smiled. 'Is it, Miles? I thought you didn't know your reason.'

Harry rose sharply to his feet. 'I don't. But it's not that.'

Chadwick's smile widened. 'How can you be so sure? Something's brought you back and it's not the food or the weather.'

Harry discovered he was sweating. 'Have you finished or can I go now?'

Chadwick's eyes moved to the dugout entrance where the young lieutenant had appeared. 'Have you found a billet for him, Dartford?'

The youngster, whose look of curiosity suggested he had overheard some of their conversation, nodded. 'Yes, sir. He can share with Sergeant Appleton.'

'Good. After he's dropped off his kit you can introduce him to his team.' Picking up a roster list from his makeshift table, Chadwick ran quickly through it. 'Give him Swanson, Dunn and Turnor. They're all reliable men.'

Realising with relief that they were back on a purely military basis, Harry nodded down at the roster list. 'Why am I getting three men instead of two for my gun team?'

Chadwick gave his light, pleasant laugh. 'I managed to snaffle a couple of Vickers during the last beano we had in this sector. After all, why should the Machine-Gun Corps have a monopoly on them? You'll be in charge of one as well as a dozen or so Lewis gunners. You don't mind a Vickers, do you, Sergeant?'

Harry knew the question was purely academic. 'No. We were originally trained on them.'

'That was in my mind. Moreover if Jerry does launch

51

his offensive this spring and it's in this sector, you'll have much more sport mowing him down with a nice heavy Vickers than with those lightweight Lewis guns.'

Harry knew now that his aversion to the man was undiminished. 'May I go now – sir?'

Chadwick smiled and ground his cigarette out in a tin lid. 'It's good to have you back, Miles. Yes, you can run along now.'

Saluting, Harry picked up his kit and elbowed his way out through the gas curtain. Seeing the young lieutenant waiting at the end of the sap, he made towards him. Although the sky above was clear and moonlit, the mist had slid into the firing trench now and was turning soldiers into ghostly apparitions. With both sides aware it was a perfect night for raids, the nervous chatter of machine-guns kept disturbing the eerie silence.

'Did you say it had been quiet in this sector recently?' Harry asked.

Unsure whether to show disapproval at the sergeant's rudeness towards Chadwick or respect for his military medal, Dartford's reply was a clumsy mixture of the two. 'Everyone seems to think so. Apart from Jerry's raiding parties, that is.'

'Has he made many?'

'No more than normal, according to the old sweats.' Disappointment clouded the young officer's expression and made him forget whom he was addressing. 'I can't see Jerry's offensive coming in this sector.'

'Why is that?'

Dartford pointed a finger to the east. 'The Hindenburg Line runs at the rear of Jerry's lines. As it's a defence line, it doesn't make sense he'd attack here, does it? My bet is he'll go for the French in the south. He must have heard about their Army mutiny, so it's only good sense he'll attack them while they're shaky.'

52

Harry was inclined to agree with him. 'Exactly what sector of the Line are we in? As usual the RTO gave us no idea but I noticed a village two miles back called Ste. Marie.'

Forgetting that other ranks were seldom given the luxury of knowing where they were, the young lieutenant looked surprised. 'We're attached to Gough's 5th Army, just south of the Flesquières Salient. About halfway between Péronne and St. Quentin.'

Chapter 6

There was tight security at the Kaiser's Headquarters near Mons that January morning. Armed sentries stood at every entrance and exit and military police, some with dogs, patrolled the spacious grounds. Nor did precautions end outside the gracious chateau. Two MPs guarded the foot of the winding staircase and two others, rifles at the ready, stood outside the door of the well-stocked library.

Three uniformed officers were present inside, all standing in front of a polished table on which a large scale map of France and Belgium was resting. The officer in the centre was the Kaiser himself, a small presentable man with fair, curly hair and a dark moustache. As he gazed down at the map and traced a line on it with a finger, his left arm was folded behind his back, an habitual stance caused by a congenital deformity of that limb.

The officer on his right side was Field Marshall von Hindenburg. A large, stout man, heavily moustached as befitted all military leaders of that time, the elderly Hindenburg was already a legend in his country, for he was the general who had received most of the credit for Germany's decisive victories against Russia. His power was immense: in Germany at that time the Army effectively controlled the Government and Hindenburg was the Army. The Press called him 'The Oak Tree' and although recent strikes and bread riots in Berlin had thrown up a gale that had splintered a few branches, most Germans still believed that the staunch, reliable, and immensely thorough von Hindenburg would lead them to victory.

The younger officer on the Kaiser's left side was General Erich Ludendorff. Another large and stout man, with thinning hair and prone to using a monocle, he was the other half of the formidable Hindenburg-Ludendorff partnership that had led the German Army to victory in the east. With the odd title of First Quartermaster General, Ludendorff had by 1918 a more flexible and imaginative mind than his older partner and more than anyone else in the General Staff realised that the Central Powers must win the war no later than the summer of 1918 or the ever-increasing number of American troops flooding into France would tip the scales. Accordingly, since November he and Hindenburg had been working urgently with their Army commanders and military experts on the best way of achieving that victory. The Kaiser had been kept informed of the broader aspects of the plan but not its details, and after a recent and comprehensive tour of the forthcoming battle line, Ludendorff had requested an audience to give his King-Emperor the full Order of Battle.

After studying the map a moment longer, the Kaiser turned to Hindenburg. 'When is this offensive to begin?'

'On Thursday the 21st of March, Sire.'

The Kaiser glanced again at the map. 'And you are convinced it is right to direct it at the British? Even though their retreat will be across the old battlefields which were laid to waste by our own retreat in 1917?

Surely it will not only give them cover but also slow down the progress of our own troops?'

This time Ludendorff answered him. 'We have taken care of that, Sire. All our troops have had special training. Shall I go into details?'

The Kaiser lifted a hand. 'In a moment, Ludendorff. You do also realise that since the French Army mutinied, it is the British who are the stronger partner? That their infantry is as determined and resilient as ever?'

Ludendorff nodded. 'That is why we must attack them, Sire. If we attacked the French and defeated them, the British and their Empire would continue fighting until the Americans joined them. But if we defeat the British, the French must capitulate and with no foothold in Europe, there would be no point in America continuing the struggle. Public pressure would force her to withdraw her troops and the war would be won, Sire.'

The Kaiser made a grimace of admiration. 'Your logic is impressive, Ludendorff. Very well. What are your specific plans?'

Ludendorff nodded again. 'For months now we have been sifting through our battalions for the fittest and ablest men. These of course include all those transferred from the Eastern Front. We've sent them for special offensive training and formed them into special units called *Sturmabteilung* (Storm-Troops). These men will be armed with light machine-guns, light trench mortars and flame-throwers, and their orders are to keep in constant contact with the enemy.'

The Kaiser frowned. 'Constant contact?'

'Yes, Sire. If they meet pockets of hard resistance, such as machine-gun posts that they cannot neutralise immediately, they are to by-pass them and make for the enemy artillery. Units won't attempt to keep in contact with one another: their task is to infiltrate into the enemy rear positions and to do it as quickly as possible.'

The Kaiser's frown deepened. 'But won't there be a danger of these units being cut off?'

'We think not, Sire. We believe the speed of their attack will so confuse the enemy that he will panic and fall back along the entire sector. To aid this panic, we are reversing the role of artillery and infantry. Instead of the infantry waiting for the artillery to move forward, the infantry will control the artillery support and direct it wherever it is needed.'

'And how will the ground be held after these "Storm-Troops" have gone forward?'

'We're sending special battle units behind them, Sire, consisting of trench mortar teams, field gunners, machine gunners, and engineers. These have been specially trained to take over one another's roles if necessary.'

'What if your men run into tanks, Ludendorff?'

'If they can't be destroyed at once, Sire, they will be allowed a free passage until such time as the back-up teams of artillery can take care of them.'

'And your reserves?'

'They will also be used in a different way. We shall throw them into battle where the attack is being successful, not when it is held up. They will mop up the remaining pockets of resistance and make a solid base behind the Storm-Troops.'

Pondering for a moment, the Kaiser turned to Hindenburg. 'What is your estimate of the divisional strength of the British?'

'Intelligence tell us there are thirty-three divisions, Sire. Twenty-one are in the front line, ten are fifteen miles behind it, and two are twenty-five miles back.'

'And our divisional strength?'

'Much higher, Sire, thanks to the reinforcements from the east. In all we will have one hundred and ninety-two divisions ready to attack. That is around 136,000 officers and 3,500,000 men.'

The Kaiser gave a laugh of disbelief. 'So many? Not for one sector, surely?'

'No, Sire. We shall be using sixty-nine divisions on the forty mile sector of our primary attack. The rest will be spread out along the full length of the British front, from the Channel down to the French at Rheims. They will make their attacks as and when the situation develops. Our hope, however, is that our primary attack will divide the British from their French Allies and roll them back into the sea.'

'How many guns will you have on this primary sector?'

'Over six thousand, Sire.'

The Kaiser gave a start. 'Six thousand!'

Hindenburg glanced at Ludendorff and smiled. 'Yes, Sire. It will be the largest concentration of guns of all time. Moreover they will be used in a new way. At Riga, Colonel Bruchmüller demonstrated that it is preferable to use gas shells instead of high explosives before an infantry attack because gas shells do not churn up the ground and make it difficult for the infantry to advance. So gas shells will be given priority. Also the guns will be fired without registration shoots, which warn the enemy where the shells will fall when the attack begins. One of our artillery captains has found a mathematical way of predicting range and bearing without a preliminary use of the guns. So we are hoping to spring a surprise too.'

'But surely you cannot hope to keep this immense force hidden from the British, Ludendorff?'

'We are doing our very best, Sire – certainly to conceal the site of our primary attack. Every officer with specific

58

knowledge of the offensive is required to take an oath of secrecy. Troop trains, indeed all large scale troop movements, must only be carried out at night. All methods of communication, mail, telephone, radio, dispatch rider, even carrier pigeons, are being watched over by special safety officers. Artillery is being moved up only at night and the gun tracks are obliterated before daylight. Our aircraft are in constant patrol over the concentration area, both to look out for any tell-tale tracks and to keep enemy reconnaissance planes away. Finally, both to rest them and to hide the huge concentration of men, we are keeping the offensive divisions well back of the line until they are needed.'

The Kaiser shook his head admiringly. 'It seems you two gentlemen have thought of everything.' Bending forward he laid a finger on the map. 'Is this then your primary target, the sector marked St. Michael 2?'

Both men bent forward with him, Ludendorff adjusting his monocle. 'Yes, Sire,' the younger man said. 'Our triple attack will be like the stab of a trident. The point will drive in here and the two flanges will follow on either side. As you can see, the southern flank of our attack will be protected by the river Oise at St. Fere. So it will be difficult for the French to provide help, even if they make the attempt which we believe they will not.'

The Kaiser lowered his head further to scrutinise the map. A proud man who disliked using glasses even although his optician advised them, he was having difficulty in reading the print. 'Is this the Siegfried Line?' Turning, he smiled at the Field Marshal alongside him. 'Or what our enemy calls the Hindenburg Line?'

Hindenburg nodded. 'Yes, Sire. Its huge dugouts and deep fortifications will make it an excellent place to mass and conceal our troops before the attack.'

The Kaiser's finger moved across a thick red line on

the map and paused. 'What about the enemy who will face your trident thrust. Which British Army is it and who is its commander?'

'It is the 5th Army, Sire,' Ludendorff told him. 'And its commander is Sir Hubert Gough.'

Chapter 7

The doorbell of No. 57 Ellerby Road rang just before dusk that February evening. Molly, the ingenuous maid Ethel had employed for many years but who was soon to go into war work, answered it and returned to the sitting room in some excitement. 'It's a Captain Watson, ma'am. He's asking to see Mr. Hardcastle.'

Mary, who was sitting on the settee reading to Elizabeth, jumped immediately to her feet, her hand to her throat. Ethel, embroidering in an armchair, lowered the tray cloth to her lap. 'Did he say what he wants?'

'No, ma'am. Just to see Mr. Hardcastle.' Molly could not contain her excitement. 'I think he's an American, ma'am. He speaks funny. You know, the way they do.'

Some of the colour began returning to Mary's cheeks. Ethel rose and went into the hall. 'Yes,' she asked. 'What do you want?'

'Are you Mrs. Hardcastle, ma'am?'

'I am, yes. What can I do for you?'

Taken aback by Ethel's sharpness, the man gave an embarrassed laugh. 'I'm Jack Watson, ma'am. I'm a friend of one of your husband's brothers.'

'Are you an American?'

'Yes, ma'am. I arrived up here three days ago.'

'Then you are making a mistake. My husband had no brothers in America.'

'Your pardon, ma'am, but he has. Arthur's been over in the States for eight years and I've known him most of that time. Doesn't your husband know he went over in 1909?'

'My husband's dead,' Ethel said curtly. 'He died last year.'

At that moment Mary's voice came from the hall doorway. 'What is it, Mother?'

Ethel turned to her. 'It's an American officer who says he's a friend of one of your uncles.'

Mary entered the hall. 'Then shouldn't you invite him in?'

Ethel hestitated, then moved stiffly back. 'You'd better come in, Captain Watson. This is my younger daughter, Mrs Miles.'

The American shook Mary's hand. 'Happy to meet you, ma'am.'

To her surprise, because the newspapers of late had stressed the impressive physical qualities of the American troops, Mary discovered the man seemed to be not only as old as her father had been when he died but also carried some of his excessive weight. Nor could his round face or genial expression be remotely considered warlike. 'Like my mother, I didn't know any of our relations had gone over to America,' she said as Watson released her hand.

'Your Uncle Arthur sure did, ma'am. To Boston in Massachusetts. We've been pals for years.'

'But how did you find us? I'm sure Uncle Arthur can't have our address.'

'I knew your father was a druggist, ma'am, so I made enquiries at the telephone company.'

'You had better take off your coat,' Ethel said as she

led the American into the sitting room. Molly, who was watching the scene with some excitement, helped the American remove it. As he thanked her, Elizabeth suddenly ran forward. 'Are you really an American?'

Watson laughed and bent down. 'Yeah, I'm an American all right. What's your name?'

'Elizabeth,' the girl said solemnly. 'Elizabeth Miles.'

Watson gravely took her hand. 'I'm real pleased to meet you, Elizabeth. If I'd known about you, I'd have brought you some candy.'

'What's candy?' the girl asked.

'Candy? Why candy's a kind of . . .' Watson looked to Mary for help.

'Do you mean chocolate, Captain? Or perhaps sweets?'

The American's face cleared. 'Yeah, sweets. If I come again I'll bring her some.'

The child's bright eyes were moving over his uniform. 'My Daddy's in the Army too. He's in France.'

'Is he? When did you last see him?'

The girl looked up at her mother. 'Six weeks ago,' Mary told him.

'Had he been on leave, ma'am?'

'No. He was badly wounded last year and invalided out. But he volunteered to go back.'

'He must be a brave man, ma'am.'

Mary smiled. 'I think so.' As Watson glanced back at Elizabeth, she asked: 'Have you any children, Captain?'

'No, ma'am. Somehow I've never gotten round to getting married. Too busy with my work, I guess.'

'What is your work, Captain?' Ethel asked as she gestured him to sit down.

Watson sank into an armchair. 'I'm in the food processing business, ma'am. That's how I come to be in the Army. Uncle Sam needs guys who know how to obtain

63

food for the troops and what to do with it afterwards, and asked if I'd help out. As I'd always wanted to see England, I said O.K. So here I am.'

'Does that mean you have your own business in Boston?'

'Yes, ma'am. My Daddy started it up around 1885 and it's grown a bit since then. My brother and I employ around two hundred men, give or take a few.'

There was a more cordial tone in Ethel's voice now. 'If your business is that large, I'm surprised you dared to leave it.'

'My brother's a good manager, ma'am. He'll take care of it.' Forgetting where he was, Watson pulled a cigar case from his tunic pocket, then began hastily pushing it back. Ethel checked him. 'If you want to smoke, Captain, please do so. My husband was a smoker and I like the smell of tobacco.'

'Thank you, ma'am. Then I will have one.'

As he lit a cigar, Ethel noticed the maid still standing in the kitchen doorway. 'Don't stand there like that, Molly! Go and make us some tea. You will have tea, Captain?'

Seeing him hesitate, Mary smiled. 'Americans drink coffee, Mother.'

Ethel frowned at her. 'We haven't had coffee for years, as you well know.'

Watson held up a protesting hand. 'Tea's fine for me, ladies. As long as it's not too much trouble.'

Ethel's glance made Molly vanish into the kitchen. At ease now that he was smoking, Watson gazed round the room with its Steinbeck piano, organ and massive furniture. 'I sure like your place, ma'am. It's just the way my mother said England was.'

'Did your mother come from England?' Ethel asked.

'Yes, ma'am. So did my father, only they were two generations back.'

With this further evidence of pedigree, Ethel's thaw was rapid now. 'How did you come to meet my late husband's brother, Captain?'

'He took a house nearby. So we became neighbours and then friends.'

'What work is he doing over there?'

'He's in real estate. And doing well in it too.'

'Has he any children?'

'Yes, ma'am. Two boys and a girl.'

Although Watson's behaviour gave no hint of it, Mary felt Arthur Hardcastle must have told him about the quarrel her father had had with his family. Whatever its cause, it had been one of such proportions that it had not only isolated William from his parents but from his brothers and sisters too, which had left Ethel and her two daughters ignorant of their whereabouts and fortunes.

Although Mary felt her mother must have the same thoughts, Ethel was the last person in the world to admit to a scandal in her background. At the same time her next question betrayed her curiosity. 'Have you seen any of my husband's other brothers or sisters since you've been in England, Captain? He did come from rather a large family.'

'Yes, ma'am. I've seen one brother and also a sister. They told me the rest have moved out of town.'

'And they are all well and prospering?' Here Ethel clearly felt an explanation was needed. 'I have not done any visiting since my husband died.'

'No, of course not, ma'am. Yes, they're all well.'

When the American ventured no more information, Ethel was left unable to continue her line of questioning. 'Are you stationed here or just paying a visit?'

'Just paying a visit, ma'am. I go back tomorrow.'

Watching her mother, Mary had the odd sensation that she was disappointed. Just as she was dismissing the thought as absurd, Ethel rose. 'Excuse me a moment, Captain.' Walking to the doorway, she glanced back at Mary. 'Do see what that girl's doing in the kitchen, dear, will you? Surely the kettle can't be taking all this time to boil.'

Checking that all was well, Mary returned to the sitting room, to find Watson chatting to Elizabeth. 'I do hope she's not bothering you, Captain?'

'Not a bit, ma'am. She's a fine kid.'

Mary gave him a smile. 'You don't need to call me ma'am. Call me Mary, please.'

Watson looked pleased. 'Is that O.K.?'

'Of course. I'd much prefer it.'

'Then will you call me Jack?' When Mary nodded, Watson indicated the hall door through which Ethel had disappeared. 'Your mother's a fine woman, isn't she?'

Mary hoped her hestitation was not noticed. 'Do you think so?'

Watson nodded. 'Yeah. She's got a lot of style and class.' He paused. 'You don't mind my saying this, do you?'

'Of course not. Why should I?'

'Yeah. She's got the looks I always associate with English women. You have it too, Mary. You know, all cool and composed.'

Mary burst into laughter. 'My Mother and I? Wait until you get to know us better, Jack.'

'I'd sure like to do that.' Watson glanced back at the hall door. 'Do you think I could visit you again before I go over to France?'

'I don't see why not. I'll mention it to mother before you go.'

Watson's thanks were interrupted by Molly tripping in with the tea tray. She glanced pertly at him as she picked up the teapot. 'How do you like your tea, sir?'

The American's ignorance of the tea ritual showed in the vague wave of his hand. 'Any way. Just the way it comes.'

Mary took the teapot from the maid. 'I'll see to it, Molly, thank you. You can go home now if you like. I don't think Mother wants anything else tonight.'

Looking disappointed for once at her dismissal, the maid retreated again into the kitchen. Her place at the tea tray was taken by Elizabeth who, full of a child's curiosity, bombarded Watson with questions about America until her chatter was interrupted by Ethel's return. To Mary's surprise she had changed into a velvet emerald dress that enhanced her complexion and thick brown hair. With a hundred bitter quarrels impairing Mary's image of her mother, it took Watson's look of admiration as he rose to his feet to remind her that Ethel was still a good-looking woman.

Watson's voice made that point very clear. 'If you'll forgive my saying so, ma'am, that's a very attractive dress you're wearing.'

Ethel gave a faint disparaging frown. 'This? Thank you. I was just going to change into it when you arrived. Do sit down. Is your tea all right?'

'Yes, it's fine, thank you, ma'am.'

Knowing it was a lie about the dress, Mary was too astonished to pay much attention to the conversation that followed. Until now, perhaps because children rarely see their parents as objects of sexual attraction or because she knew how deeply Ethel had loved her father, it had never occurred to her that her mother might become interested in another man. Yet tonight it was happening before her eyes.

She could not believe Watson himself was the sole attraction. The social climber in Ethel would be taking full account of the American's healthy financial position.

Yet at that moment the whys and wherefores of Ethel's behaviour did not concern her. Her thoughts were running that if Ethel were to gain another interest in life, it might siphon off the malice she felt towards Harry.

She was encouraged by Ethel's parting words an hour later when the American rose to leave. 'It's a pity you hadn't let us know sooner that you were coming, Captain, or you could have had dinner with us.'

'Thank you, ma'am. I wish I had.' As Watson paused, clearly wondering how he could phrase it, Mary came to his rescue. 'Captain Watson told me he had another few days' leave due to him in March before he goes over to France, Mother. Perhaps he could visit us then.'

As Watson gave her a grateful look, Ethel hid her pleased expression by glancing down at Elizabeth who was standing alongside them. 'I'm sure our little girl would like that: I know she's enjoyed the stories you've told her about America. But you'd hardly want to come up all this way just for a dinner appointment, would you?'

The American was quick with his protest. 'Yes, ma'am. I'd like to come.' Then, using the child as Ethel had done, he bent over her. 'I could bring you that candy then, couldn't I? Sorry – I mean sweets.'

Elizabeth nodded her head vigorously. 'Yes, please.'

The three adults laughed. Handing Watson his coat, Mary said goodbye to him in the sitting room, allowing Ethel to see him to the front door. When she returned, her face was expressionless and her voice casual. 'That was a surprise, wasn't it? All the same it was kind of him to come and tell us about your Uncle Arthur.'

'He seems a very nice man,' Mary said. 'You know he took a fancy to you, don't you?'

Ethel gave a start. 'What on earth does that mean?'

'He was attracted to you. He thought you had style and class, as he put it. He told me so when you were upstairs.'

Something kindled in Ethel's eyes before her cheeks went red. 'How dare he say such things when he knew William was only eighteen months in his grave? Why didn't you tell me?'

'He wasn't being rude, Mother. He just thought you looked very attractive, as I did. What's wrong with that?'

'It's impertinence, that's what's wrong with it,' Ethel snapped. 'If I'd known I'd never have invited him round again.'

Mary was not deceived. 'I'm glad you did. I thought him a very nice man.'

A young voice lisped at them from the settee where Elizabeth had returned to her book. 'I'm glad you did too, Grannie. I liked him ever so much.'

It was the escape Ethel needed. Swinging round, she wagged a finger at the child. 'As for you, young lady, it's time you were upstairs. It's well past your bedtime.'

Chapter 8

The four men, muffled up in muddy scarves and shabby greatcoats, were huddled down on the floor of a machine-gun nest. Although the nest was sited within the ruins of a farmhouse, neither the shell-blasted walls nor the surrounding sandbags offered protection from the icy wind that was scything in from the east. A water-cooled Vickers gun stood on its tripod within the post and a Lewis gun rested on one of the ammunition boxes that littered the floor.

A nudge on his arm made Harry turn his head. 'Cigarette, Sergeant?'

It was a lance corporal who was holding out the packet. Harry nodded and took one. 'Thanks, Swanson.'

Swanson turned and offered the packet to the other two men, one another lance corporal, the other a private. With their hands half frozen in spite of the mittens they were wearing, all four men had difficulty in handling and lighting their cigarettes and it was a full minute before they were able to drop back and suck the warm smoke into their lungs.

Stuffing the packet back in his pocket, Swanson jerked a thumb at the Vickers. He had a pleasant, well-educated voice. 'Do you think we ought to give Bertha

70

another shot of rum, Sergeant? It's freezing harder than ever out there.'

Harry, who during the last month had learned the language and mannerisms of his three-man team, smiled and unscrewed the cap of the water jacket. 'I suppose we had better play safe. Hand me the can, will you, Turnor?'

The second lance corporal moved forward and the two men poured another half pint of anti-freeze into the Vickers jacket. Watching them, the fourth man gave a sceptical grunt. 'You think that stuff works, Sarge?'

Harry shrugged as he handed the can back to Turnor. 'I don't know. They say so.'

The private, by name Dunn, gave a coarse laugh. 'I reckon you'd do better if you pissed in it. That's what they did on the Somme.'

Swanson grinned. 'That was in the summer, old lad, when bladders weren't blocks of ice. If you peed in it now, you'd freeze it up solid.'

Dunn gave a lewd wink at Turnor. 'You mean you haven't enough hose to get into it, don't you, Corp?'

Swanson was seldom at a loss for words. 'Speak for yourself, old lad. We haven't all had it nipped off by those whores in Amiens.'

Swanson was the Lewis gunner in Harry's section. A Londoner by birth, he had been educated at one of the many small private schools that existed at that time. Eight years before the war his father had transferred his jam-making business up north and George had moved to a private school in Hull and then into his father's office. On the outbreak of war, he had wanted to enlist but his father, a martinet, had threatened financial excommunication if he dared take such a foolish step. In the end it had been the Conscription Act of 1916 that had released George from his shackles. He had been called up in 1917

71

and sent to France in the October of the same year. A good-looking man of twenty-four with an impish sense of humour, he was popular with officers and men alike.

As if to illustrate the democratic composition of the British Army in 1918, Charlie Dunn had been a gutter of fish on the Hull docks. With his squat body, large red hands, a flattened nose, blackheads, and teeth that resembled clothes pegs on a line, it could not be said that nature had been kind to Charlie. On the other hand it could not be said that Charlie did much to offset his misfortunes, for he had the foulest tongue Harry had heard since joining the Army. Charlie's every thought seemed centred on the pubic and anal parts of the human body and even old sweats, jaundiced by years of barrack room jokes, would enter a new dimension of depravity when Charlie took the floor.

And if this wasn't enough, Charlie had halitosis. Not mere bad breath but breath guaranteed to halt a man in his tracks as efficiently as a .45 bullet. More than once Swanson had suggested that a far cheaper way of repulsing the enemy would be to scrap the Lewis and Vickers guns and simply put Charlie, armed with a sackful of onions, in their place. The horror of it would spread like wildfire through the German ranks and with Charlie in the lead, the Allies would be able to march straight to Berlin.

In fairness to Charlie he was not a bad soldier. His dislike of the enemy had nothing to do with patriotism, however. Charlie disliked them because they tended to keep him away from his one and only hobby, whoring. Rumour had it that, although he was only twenty-three, he had been married twice (and at the same time) and had ten illegitimate children scattered among the two-bedroomed hovels that stood behind the Hull fish docks. Such scandal-mongering upset Charlie. He insisted he had no more than five bastards, although he privately admitted that his last leave in England might soon raise the score.

The other lance corporal in Harry's Vickers team was an older man, Arthur Turnor. A married man, Turnor had been a rate collector when the war had broken out and had made no attempt to join the Forces until given no choice by the Conscription Act. In appearance he was a tall man with a slight stoop and a somewhat careworn face that made him look older than his thirty-two years. Off duty he seldom mixed with his companions, choosing instead to be alone and to read or write letters. Yet in the few conversations Harry had shared with him, he had found him a thoughtful man clearly anxious to improve his limited education when the war ended. He was not an easy man to know and yet something about him – perhaps a sensitive and introspective nature that was so like his own – had drawn Harry to him and he had made him his Number One on the Vickers gun.

The sound of booted feet in the sap behind them made all four men turn. A moment later Chadwick climbed into the gun post. Although he was wearing battle order, he looked immaculate enough to appear on a church parade. His cultured voice sounded above the keening of the wind. 'Everything's all right, Sergeant?'

Harry nodded. 'Yes, sir. All's quiet.'

Chadwick's eyes rested on him for a moment, then moved to the other men. 'What about you chaps? Have you any complaints?'

Only Charlie Dunn gave vent to his feelings. 'It's bloody cold, sir.'

Chadwick laughed. 'I thought someone would say that.' Reaching into his greatcoat pocket, he pulled out a half-flask of rum and held it out to Harry. 'Share this out when your next brew of tea comes along. It should help to keep the blues away.'

There was a murmur of appreciation from the three men. Harry accepted the bottle without comment and shoved it into a pocket. Chadwick glanced at him again, then sat down on an ammunition box. Pulling out a gold cigarette case, he was about to offer it round when he saw the four men were already smoking. Lighting a cigarette himself, he exhaled smoke, then turned again to Harry. 'By the way, Sergeant, I've just been round your Lewis gun posts. All's well there, so you've no need to inspect them again before you go off duty.'

Harry begrudged his thanks the moment he made them. I don't want his damned favours, he thought. Why does he offer them? Because of shame at what he did to Gareth? Or does he gain some satisfaction from putting me in his debt?'

The wind came again, cutting like a razor over the revetted parapets. As men huddled deeper into their greatcoats, Chadwick rose to his full height and gazed over the sandbags and the barbed wire perimeter beyond. A moment later he gave his pleasant-sounding laugh. 'This is a bit of a treat, isn't it? To be able to stretch one's back and see what's going on.'

Swanson was eyeing him with some concern. 'Better watch out for snipers, Major.'

Chadwick smiled. 'I don't think they're likely to sneak all this way behind our lines, do you?'

Harry spoke without turning his head. 'They sneak in anywhere. You should know that, Major.'

Glancing at him, Chadwick appeared about to make a humorous comment, then changed his mind and gazed again to the east. Except for the detritus of the old battlefield, there was little to see except an occasional bursting shell and a distant line of enemy observation

74

balloons. 'Jerry's certainly got his head down today,' he said. 'Perhaps he doesn't like the cold either.'

When no one answered him, he moved back towards the sap and turned. 'I'm going to send up a brazier for you men. I don't want you or your replacements blocks of ice when Jerry kicks off. You can expect the brazier in half an hour.'

Men stirred in anticipation. Swanson answered him. 'Thanks, Major. Dunn was worried to death about his lady killers.'

'Is that a fact?' Chadwick said. 'Then we'd better take that worry off your mind, Dunn.'

With that he turned and disappeared down the sap. Swanson gave a low whistle. 'An officer that cares about his men? I didn't know the breed existed.'

Harry turned to gaze at him. Noticing his expression, Swanson changed his tone. 'You don't like him, do you, Sergeant? What's the problem?'

Feeling the eyes of the other two men on him, Harry shrugged. 'Perhaps I'm just getting too old to like eager beavers.' To curtail further questions, he pulled the rum flask out of his pocket. 'Why wait for tea?' he said. 'Let's drink our Major's gift now.'

The eager men drew closer, passing the bottle to one another. None of them, not even Harry, bothered to keep watch through the loopholes in the sandbags. To a Front Line veteran unaware of the monumental change of strategy of the Allied forces, it would have appeared an unpardonable offence, for until then British machine gunners had needed to keep on their toes like sprinters in the blocks. Now at long last they shared the luxury their enemy counterparts had enjoyed for so long: to await orders, load their guns, and coolly pick their targets.

The reason lay in the new orders that had issued from

75

Sir Douglas Haig's headquarters the previous December. For the first time since the British Army had entered France and fought alongside its Allies, the emphasis was to be on defence and not attack. The enormous number of German soldiers released from the Russian Front after the Treaty of Brest Litovsk had convinced even the most aggressive of the British commanders that discretion was the better part of valour.

Not that it was realised at first that the full fury of the storm was to break on the British. The French believed they were to face it alone and had been urgently building up their own defences, particularly in the Champagne country where Pétain commanded the French 4th Army. To aid and foster this belief (and also to provide back-up thrusts if they were needed) Hindenburg and Ludendorff had been feeding in reinforcements the entire length of the line, further proof, if proof were needed; of the abundance of troops at their disposal.

However, by the New Year, Allied spies and raiding party captives had convinced the British that the main attack was to be made on their front, although because of the important coal mines around Béthune they believed the offensive would be directed against their 1st Army to the north. Gough's 5th Army was not thought to be under direct threat but nevertheless all contingencies had to be covered and so the British decided an attempt must be made to strengthen the defences of their entire front.

Their problems from the onset were immense. The ground behind their present front lines had been intentionally devastated by the Germans during their 1917 retreat. Every tree, every building, every road or track that might be a help to the British had been flattened or blown up. Apart from the grim debris of war, the land looked like the cratered surface of the moon.

The British intention was to create a Battle Zone some four thousand yards in depth behind their present front line. This would contain two manned lines which it was hoped would slow down and then hold the enemy offensive (for it was accepted their front line troops would be too few to hold it). Behind this cushioning zone there would be a Rear Zone with another manned line. From here reserves would pour forward and counter-attack the halted Germans.

The plan was valid enough. But although by February the forty miles of Gough's front alone was employing 48,000 men – and at that time it was still considered unthreatened – the task was simply too enormous in the few weeks available. Supplies of building materials could only be brought up at night, and with no tracks to guide them through the desolation, carts and lorries either floundered in the mud or toppled into the hundreds of shell holes. Eventually the greater part of the vast army of workmen had to be drawn back into the Rear Zone to begin building roads and rail tracks just to get supplies moving forward.

So it fell on the very soldiers who would have to face the offensive to build their own Battle Zone fieldworks, and the plan called for nearly three hundred miles of trenches with concrete and wire defences. Although men, knowing their lives might depend on their efforts, ruptured themselves in the task, it soon became obvious it was beyond them and the plan was changed. Now isolated strongpoints, each with its barbed wire defences, would be constructed with each one supporting the other with its field of fire. Even these makeshift defences, looked on with scorn by those wedded to the trench system, called for a supreme effort from the weary British soldiers and there were many strongpoints incomplete and many soldiers unfit for combat when

Ludendorff's enormous army checked its weapons for the last time and prepared to attack.

It was because Harry's machine-gun team was sited in such a strongpoint that Chadwick had been able to lift his head over the parapet. Until now the British had used their machine-gun teams either ahead of their front line or in support of it. Now the front line was a thousand yards ahead, manned by soldiers who, with twenty yards of front per man to defend, knew they were expendable.

It could not, however, be said that the machine-gunners and artillerymen who manned the strongpoints felt much better. Every man knew that once the German attack broke through the frail line ahead, they would be cut off from one another and would have to fight on alone until relieved by a counterattack. Outnumbered as the defenders were going to be, the very talk of counter-attacks brought wry and obscene remarks from the British who knew that if the Germans used their new tanks as they had used theirs at Cambrai, strongpoints and their occupants would be blown to pieces or crushed beneath their tracks long before counterattacks could even be considered.

Along with other machine-gun and artillery posts dotted thinly about the Battle Zone, Harry and his crew had been facing this sanguinary prospect for over a fortnight. For although British Intelligence still felt Béthune the more logical objective, captured prisoners, odd aerial reports, and general battlefield rumours had begun to shorten the odds against Peronne and St. Quentin. With Gough's 5th Army realising they might be the ones to face the spearhead of the onslaught, tension was mounting by the day. As the bottle of rum was passed round a second time and Turnor was allowing the last few aromatic drops to linger on his tongue, a series of explosions made every man start and peer over the sandbags. Ahead six ugly blotches of smoke were rising into the icy sky. Men felt their muscles tighten and the blood drain from their cheeks as they waited for the full-scale bombardment they expected would herald the offensive.

A full minute passed before Harry allowed himself to sink back. 'Just a trigger-happy battery commander,' he said, hoping the dryness of his voice did not give him away. 'Or a new crew putting in a bit of range-finding practice."

Release of tension brought a string of obscenities from Dunn. Swanson grinned at Harry. 'Our lad's in good form this morning. Maybe we should send him up to one of those loud-speaker units. The Jerries might think we're orang-outangs and move somewhere else.'

Everyone laughed except the scowling Dunn. Grateful to Swanson, Harry handed round his cigarettes. 'I think we're safe for the rest of the day. Jerry usually launches his attack at dawn or just before.'

No one answered him this time. Men were remembering that their next spell of duty bridged the period from darkness to full dawn and trying to reassure themselves that the attack would not come yet. The mud would surely not be firm enough for an offensive until April at the earliest. And it was, after all, only the 15th of March.

Chapter 9

Jack Watson paid his next visit to No. 57 during the second week in March. In spite of her earlier protestations, Ethel had gone to considerable pains to give him a festive evening. With German submarines taking a heavy toll of British ships, the food shortage was acute by this time and Mary, Molly and even the salesman Willis were all enlisted to see what little luxuries they could find. With meat now qualifying as a luxury, it came as no surprise to Mary that Willis, whom she had always seen as a con-man, came back one day after a trip in the country with a whole leg of lamb. Although he told Ethel it had cost him five pounds – a sum Mary knew was at least a hundred per cent more than the current black market price – Ethel paid it without question, proof to Mary if proof were needed that Jack Watson stood high in her esteem.

In the end all their efforts proved unnecessary because the American arrived with a large parcel full of unobtainable luxuries along with a tin of sweets for the delighted Elizabeth, all of which ensured the family had the best dinner they had enjoyed in two years. As if showing her appreciation (although Mary believed other reasons presided) Ethel ushered Watson into an armchair after his meal, insisted he lit one of his cigars, then went to the cupboard where William used to keep his whisky. 'Would you care for a small glass of spirits, Captain? My husband used to take a glass before he retired at nights and I believe we have half a bottle of whisky left.'

Although Mary was certain the American was dying for a drink, his politeness disguised it well. 'Only if you and Mary will join me, ma'am. But not otherwise.'

Knowing Ethel's prejudice against drink, Mary could hardly believe her reply. 'In that case we might have a small sherry with you, Captain. To toast your safe return from France.'

There were no false heroics about Watson. 'I won't be in any danger, ma'am. They'll probably base me in Paris.'

Ethel handed him a large whisky, then filled two small glasses with sherry for herself and Mary. 'I'm sure you're just being modest.'

'I'm not,' the American insisted. 'I'm just a desk soldier. Heck, you've only to look at me to see that.'

Ethel gave a disbelieving smile and handed a glass to Mary. 'Anyway, here's to your safe return, wherever they send you.'

Watson lifted his glass. 'To you and your family, ma'am. Only won't you call me Jack instead of Captain?'

Ethel's expression told Mary she was wondering if a lady should show such familiarity on such short acquaintance. In the event she submitted with dignity. 'Very well. In that case you must call me Ethel. Is your whisky all right or would you like some water in it?'

'No, thanks, ma'am – I mean Ethel. This is fine.'

Elizabeth, who with great difficulty had obeyed the Edwardian maxim that at mealtimes children should be seen but not heard, now made her presence known by approaching the American's armchair, 'Won't you tell me more stories about 'merica?'

'Please, Captain,' Mary insisted.

'Please, Captain,' the girl repeated.

Grinning, Watson picked the child up and placed her on his knee. 'What kind of story do you want to hear, honey?'

'The kind of stories you told me the last time. About the bears in the forests and the Red Indians.'

Watson glanced at Mary. 'Is it O.K.?'

She smiled back. 'Yes, of course. But only one story. She mustn't be a nuisance and she does normally go to bed at this time.'

Watson's story about a trip he had made in Canada in his youth, interspersed by Elizabeth's eager questions, lasted over fifteen minutes. Seeing Ethel's growing impatience, Mary took the girl from Watson's knee when he finished. 'That's enough now. Captain Watson will be tired out answering your questions. Thank him for his present and then say goodnight.'

The disappointed girl pouted her lip for a moment, then lifted her face to the American. 'Thanks for the sweets and for telling me stories,' she muttered.

Watson laughed, leaned forward, and kissed her forehead. 'Good night, honey. Sleep well.'

With Elizabeth to undress and put into bed, it was ten minutes before Mary returned downstairs. She found Ethel had disappeared and Watson was reading the evening paper. 'Where's Mother?' she asked.

He lowered the paper. 'One of your neighbours came round to the back door and asked if your mother would advise her on something. She told me she'd be back in a few minutes.'

Wondering what could have been so important to take Ethel away, Mary crossed over to the settee. As she sank down on it, Watson's eyes flickered back to the front page of the newspaper. For a man so polite, it was unlike him and she became immediately curious. Since Harry's return to France an anxious examination of the newspaper had been her first priority on coming down to breakfast or returning from work but today Ethel's preparations for the American's arrival had given her no time to see the evening paper.

She leaned forward. 'What is it, Jack? Bad news?'

Hesitating for a moment, he then turned the paper towards her so that she could see the headlines. GERMAN OFFENSIVE ON BRITISH FRONT BELIEVED IMMINENT she read and her heart missed a beat. The American grimaced. 'I suppose it had to happen sooner or later.'

Her mouth felt dry. 'What does it mean, Jack? That we're going to take the brunt of it?'

Watson gave a sympathetic nod. 'That's how it reads. But I wouldn't get too upset about it. They've been wrong before.'

She shook her head. 'No. I've had the feeling all along they'd attack us.' With Ethel absent she asked the question she had wanted to ask since their first meeting. 'Jack, what will the Americans do when this offensive starts? Will they throw in their weight behind us?'

Watson looked uncomfortable. 'They'd sure like to, Mary. Every man jack of them. But it's not that simple.'

She stared at him. 'Not simple? What do you mean?'

The American grimaced again. 'It's Pershing, our Commander-in-Chief. He doesn't want to use our doughboys in bits and pieces to prop up the Allies. His aim is to wait until he has a big enough army to start an offensive on his own. And he has nowhere near that number yet.'

She could feel the blood leaving her cheeks. 'Are you

saying they're not going to help us? Not when the Germans throw in in all those extra divisions from Russia?'

'It's not the fault of the doughboys, Mary. Like me, plenty of 'em have relatives or friends over here. But what can we do when it's Government policy?'

A shudder ran through her. 'My God, it's worse than I thought.'

Watson tried to comfort her but, stunned by his news, she barely heard what he was saying. Nor did she hear her mother's return until Ethel walked into the sitting room. 'I'm sorry about that,' she told Watson. 'Only my neighbour has a touch of bronchitis and his wife wanted me to show her how to use the Nelson inhaler we lent her.' Then she noticed their expressions. 'What's the matter?'

Watson showed her the newspaper headlines. She dismissed them with a tut of impatience. 'Oh, that! They've been talking about nothing else for months. I wouldn't take a scrap of notice of it.'

Mary could not stifle her gasp of protest. 'How can you say such a thing, Mother?'

For a moment Ethel stiffened. Then, as she remembered her role in front of Watson, her voice became full of motherly understanding. 'I know how worried you are, dear. It's only natural. But these newspaper people are such scaremongers: that's how they sell the wretched things. And they have been wrong before, haven't they?'

'That's what I've told her,' Watson said. 'The Germans are clever at laying red herrings. It's probably the French all along they intend to attack.'

To Mary's dismay, she suddenly felt her eyes flooding with tears. Brushing them away, she noticed that Ethel was watching her curiously. Turning towards the American, Mary managed a smile. 'I suppose it's all the waiting. It's been going on for so long now.' When Watson nodded sympathetically, she went on: 'Jack, will you forgive me if I go upstairs now? I don't think Elizabeth's asleep and I've also got a bad headache. Do you mind?'

Watson was on his feet immediately. 'Why, no, of course not. Only I sure hate to see you worried like this. I feel it's my fault.'

She managed another smile. 'Don't be silly. You can't help what General Pershing does. Come and see us again when you're back in England. We'll always be glad to see you.'

Without a word to her mother, she left the room. As she reached the staircase she heard Ethel questioning Watson in low, solicitous tones. Closing her eyes for a moment, she reached Elizabeth's room and stood outside listening. Hearing no sound, she entered her own room and threw herself on to the bed.

Free at last to give vent to her feelings, she cried until there were no more tears left to shed. Then, chilled but too exhausted to undress, she pulled the coverlet over herself. As she huddled beneath it in an effort to get warm, she heard voices in the hall and knew that Watson was leaving.

The voices sounded for a couple of minutes, then the front door closed. A moment later she heard footsteps on the stairs and unaccountably her heart began to race.

The footsteps stopped outside her room and the door creaked open. As she turned her head she saw Ethel standing silhouetted in the doorway.

Her heart was thudding like a piston now. A second later the light was switched on. Nodding grimly, Ethel approached her bedside. 'I thought you wouldn't be asleep!'

Mary raised her tear-stained face from the pillow. 'Has Jack gone?'

'Of course he's gone. He'd little choice, had he? Not after you ruined the evening for him.'

Her voice sounded shaky and distant. 'I'm sorry, Mother. But he upset me by what he said. I thought the Americans would be reinforcing our men. I thought that . . .'

'Who cares what you thought? What right had you to talk about the war tonight? He was our guest, invited here to relax and enjoy himself. And all you did was make him feel uncomfortable over something he can't control.'

'But, Mother, Harry's in France. He's one of those who'll have to face this offensive. How can you expect me not to be worried?'

'And why is Harry in France? Tell me that!'

'I know that he chose to go. But surely that should make you proud of him.'

'Proud? When he's left the business to fall apart?'

A sudden surge of bitterness gave the girl the strength to challenge her mother. 'Who was it made his life so miserable that he had to join up in the first place?'

'That was in 1915, when he had fewer responsibilities. When he was acting like a coward and giving talk to all the neighbours. Things are different now.'

'Why? Because he has a medal you can brag about? Because you know the business can't do without him? Those are the things that are different, aren't they?'

Red spots appeared in Ethel's cheeks. 'Do you think he would have gone back if William had left the two of you the business, as you claimed he had? Not on your life, my girl. He's gone back because the business was left to me and so he doesn't care a hang if it succeeds or fails.'

'That's ridiculous. He cares about the business because Dad built it up and he loved Dad. It had nothing to do with his going back.'

'Then why did he go? Tell me that.'

The girl was only too aware that Ethel was attacking her Achilles' heel. 'I don't know. Perhaps he felt he had to be back with his friends when the offensive began.'

'There couldn't be other reasons, could there?'

Mary gazed up at her. 'What other reasons?'

'He didn't want to come home after he was wounded last year, did he? Did he ever explain why?'

'No,' she confessed. 'But I believe something horrible had happened to him. Something too horrible to talk about. I believe that's what kept him from coming home.'

'You mean something he's ashamed of, don't you?'

Mary's cheeks paled with anger. 'What are you getting at? That he has a girl over there?'

Ethel gave her characteristic sniff of defiance. 'I don't know what he's got. I'm just asking why he was so long coming home and why he went back when millions of men would give their right arms to be out of the war.'

'I've just told you. I think something horrible happened to him the last time he was wounded.'

Ethel's reply dripped sarcasm. 'So horrible he has to go back and experience it again? It makes a lot of sense, doesn't it?'

'Mother, Harry's a sensitive man mixed up in a terrible war. Can't you understand what it might be doing to him?' Hopelessness was suddenly a heavy stone in the girl's mind. 'You could never understand anything like that, could you? Not in a million years!'

Ethel's features tightened. 'There are some things I can understand, my girl. And one is why you're behaving so hysterically and why you were sick yesterday and the day before. Harry's given you another baby, hasn't he? He's given you another and then left you to face all the problems alone. Aren't I right?'

Longing for comfort, Mary's eyes ached with the effort to hold back her tears. 'He didn't know when he left. I didn't know myself until five weeks ago.'

Ethel stared down at her. 'Why didn't you tell me?'

'How could I, knowing that straight away you'd attack Harry.'

Ethel marched to the door and turned. 'You're a fool to love that man. Mark my words, he'll bring you nothing but poverty and unhappiness. I said that to William the day he gave you both permission to marry and I'm saying it to you now. The best thing that could happen to you is that he doesn't come back from France.'

Chapter 10

There was a thaw across the Channel during the third week in March but because the snowfall had been light that winter, it did not leave behind the deep and glutinous mud of previous years. Instead there was only a thin slick of mud over relatively hard ground below, winter conditions that by Western Front standards were almost unbelievably good for an offensive.

The fact did not escape the British troops unfortunate enough to be in the front lines on the night of the 20th, in particular the men in the forward listening posts of the 5th Army. These men, some volunteers, some drawn by lots, needed no warning that a massive attack was imminent. Having heard the muted but tell-tale sounds of supplies and reinforcements pouring into the munition dumps and trenches opposite, they had until a week ago pretended to one another they were only listening to an elaborate enemy strategem. Now they no longer believed in their own self-deception and their only uncertainty was the date the storm would break.

For them it was anything but an academic question. While the battalions in the front line were expendable, there was always the chance some men might survive the initial assault and be able to fall back and join their comrades in the second line. For the men in the listening posts no such possibility existed. After a man had crawled out to reach his post, a barbed wire entanglement called a knife-rest was rolled from a recess in the sap to block his retreat should his nerve fail him at the last. In addition, NCOs sharing the listening posts had orders to shoot any man who attempted to fall back before he had done his duty.

That duty was to fire a green flare from his Very pistol the moment he heard the enemy infantry climbing from their trenches to begin their advance. Such a warning might give his own infantry and artillery a few precious minutes warning. For the man firing the flare, however, it was an act of suicide, for it pin-pointed his position. In minutes, if not seconds, he could expect a bracket of shells to blow him to pieces.

As a consequence, although they knew every night brought the holocaust nearer, men on the 20th could only hope it would end as so many other suspenseful nights had ended, with the morning 'hate' session – the routine early-morning enemy barrage – followed by the stand-down order, and rum and tea.

But old sweats in the listening posts sensed a subtle difference in the air that night. It was true there were the usual flares and the stammer of machine-guns, the occasional enemy shells that gave the impression that all was normal, and yet the flares did not seem so frequent and the shell fire seemed half-hearted. It was as if the giant opposite was tired of tinkering with his prey and was gearing himself up for one massive swipe with his bludgeon. Tense men swung their listening trumpets from side to side but for once could not hear the deep rumble of enemy transports that had been such a feature of previous nights.

Optimists and wishful thinkers blamed the fog. It had been rising from the ground since midnight and by

3.30 a.m. it had reduced visibility to a few yards. In every listening post along twenty miles of front men cursed it or blessed it according to their temperaments. Some saw it as further proof that the devil looks after his own, for it was true that during most of the war the weather conditions had favoured the enemy whether in attack or defence. Others, the innocent recruits, felt it might save them from retaliation and death if they were called on to fire their Very pistols.

To add to everyone's nervousness and discomfort, platoon officers received orders to turn on gas cylinders, proof that Headquarters itself suspected an attack might be imminent. With no wind to waft it forward, the gas turned the mist into an obscene yellow fog and men's curses took on a hollow note inside their claustrophobic gasmasks.

The long minutes crept past. Around four o'clock the British artillery fired a few rounds of shells behind the enemy lines and a few shells came back in return. For once the British infantry welcomed the whizzbangs as if they were evidence the night was normal after all. But all too soon the shelling ceased and an eerie silence fell along the Front. Some men, whose religion had survived the war, crossed themselves. Most men, bitter, cynical, fatalistic or frightened, licked their dry lips, lay their heads on their folded arms, and waited.

The storm broke like the crack of doom at five o'clock, when Ludendorff's six thousand guns opened fire on the forty mile front between the Sensée river and the Oise. To the British soldiers, both in the front line and the Battle Zone, it was as if giants were lifting and slamming down the crimson manholes of hell. Vivid flashes blinded them, massive explosions ruptured their eardrums, torrents of mud and earth heaved up and buried them. Even to those not immediately attacked – and they were few indeed – the shattering noise alone, augmented by two thousand British guns trying in vain to stem the holocaust, was enough to turn blood to water and bones to jelly. Those men left with the ability to think and reason had no doubt that if on the day of their judgement they were condemned to the very depths of hell, they would face no greater terrors than they were facing that morning of the 21st March.

To the defenders, conscious only of their immediate peril, there seemed no pattern to the bombardment: it was simply a hell-sent multi-limbed demon spewing out fire and thunderbolts indiscriminately. In fact Colonel Bruchmüller had registered his guns with Teutonic thoroughness. Only trench mortars, supplied with an abundance of gas shells, were attacking the front trenches. Field guns and howitzers were shelling the Battle Zone and the heavy guns were registered on the Rear Zone.

The result was pure carnage, for nothing was spared. Casualty clearing stations were blown to pieces as indiscriminately as were artillery horse lines and men's billets. Machine-guns and artillery posts, so carefully sited in the Battle Zone, were rendered into smoking shell craters before their occupants knew the Angel of Death was swooping down on them. Wireless installations, junction boxes, buried cables, communication trenches, were all turned into smoking rubble. For forty miles the mist-covered ground spewed up its contents as if it were suffering the collision of a thousand white-hot meteors. For men miraculously surviving the holocaust, senses became numbed and feelings anaesthetized. Friends, blown into bloody fragments before their eyes, were envied. They were the lucky ones. They had died quickly.

The barrage lasted for fifty minutes, then drew back and concentrated on the front line trenches. This bombardment, intended to register the front line, lasted only a few minutes before returning to the Battle Zone where it continued its systematic destruction of control posts and other installations so painfully created during the last three months. It had a further purpose. Many of the shells now falling contained both lachrymary and lethal gases, the former to drive a man to rip off his gasmask, the latter to blind him or destroy his lungs. First-aid posts, themselves under attack, were soon filled by coughing, vomiting, and blinded men.

It was now daylight but the mist was still thick on the ground, giving the shell-shocked Tommies in the forward trenches and listening posts no chance to monitor the enemy infantry attack which they knew must come soon. With the bombardment ravaging the Battle Zone again, there was a momentary respite for the infantry on both sides of the line to prepare themselves: the Germans to steel themselves for the assault, the British to resist them. To some men, trembling from shock, it was not a welcome lull. The massive shelling had numbed fear as it had numbed every other emotion. Now raw nerves were alive again and brave men were afraid their fear would betray them.

For it was now seen that the main weight of the barrage, not just the field guns but the heavier artillery, was slowly but inexorably creeping back from the Battle Zone towards the British front line. The plan was clear. With all possibility of relief destroyed behind them, the forward trenches were to suffer the full weight of all but the very long range enemy guns. Only then would the German infantry attack, and any British survivors would be sandwiched between them and the crushing barrage.

The creeping barrage arrived just before 8.30 and

extended the entire length of the 5th Army front and the southern part of the 3rd Army front. Its effect was devastating and horrific on men who had been given no time to build deep trenches and concrete shelters. They were pulverised, blown to pieces, mutilated, buried alive. Nor did a soldier need a direct hit from the murderous shells to kill him. The size of the shells used meant their very concussion could tear the eyes out of his head or explode the lungs in his body.

As if the barrage were not enough, every trench mortar in the German arsenal added its fire power by 9.30 and charges that sappers had laid beneath the British wire defences were exploded. Ten minutes later green Very lights rose from the listening posts that had survived the onslaught. The German infantry, satisfied the softening up process had been a success, were now climbing out from their trenches and making their attack.

Harry and his team were not in their forward machine-gun post that morning. By one of those orders that can change a man's entire destiny, it had been decided that heavy machine-guns should be drawn back to the first trench of the Battle Zone to provide cover in case a breakthrough should occur and Lewis gun teams should move forward in their place. Although Chadwick's two Vickers guns were not part of the Machine-Gun Corps, at whom the order was aimed, he too had decided not to risk his precious guns and so had ordered Harry back.

It was an order that saved the lives of all four men although, as so often in the scales of war, five others were killed in their place when a heavy shell, whose gun had probably been registered some days earlier by the German barrage balloons, scored a direct hit. Only Harry and Turnor commented on it. Few men believed any longer that their lives rested in a benevolent creator's hands. The majority believed that chance ruled the battlefield and if one man was killed because he took the place of another it was just his bad luck.

As a consequence of this, Harry and his team were not called on immediately to face the onslaught of the German Storm Troops. Superbly trained, the élite of the German Army, there was no walking in formation across No Man's Land for them. They came running forward like sprinters, their weapons being stick grenades, light machine-guns and flame-throwers. Their first line paused for nothing, running round isolated British outposts they could not immediately subdue and leaping across trenches that barred their way. Their task was to create panic and uncertainty among their opponents, leaving the mopping up task to their second and third waves, and in the area of the Oise Valley, where the fog persisted until the late afternoon, their success was spectacular, for in one place they sliced almost through the Battle Zone, leaving behind them bayoneted men, charred bodies and dazed survivors to be rounded up and led back into prison camps.

North of the Oise valley, however, their progress was not so rapid for here the fog had begun to disperse by mid-morning, giving the British machine-gunners a chance to fire on them before they were close enough to use their stick grenades and *flammerwerfers*. For the same reason the front line troops were able to put up a fiercer resistance although the price they paid was fearsome, in some cases entire battalions being wiped out.

As a result the 16th Battalion and Chadwick's machine-gunners were not called into action until the late morning. By that time the last of the mist and the gas had lifted in their sector and they were able to see the peril ahead.

95

Grey-clad soldiers, as numerous as ants, were swarming over the smoking ground, systematically destroying the remaining outposts or killing the British front line infantrymen who were struggling vainly to stop the avalanche as they retreated along the communication trenches. It was crystal clear that only minutes remained before the swarm would turn and hurl itself against the first line of the Battle Zone.

With his men spaced out to give as much protection as possible to the battalion, Chadwick was here, there and everywhere, checking his teams were ready and giving them advice and encouragement. He visited Harry's Vickers team, sited on the right flank of the battalion so as to give maximum enfilading fire, just after 11.30. Although his cheeks were flushed with excitement and exertion, he still looked the immaculate officer hero of a hundred schoolboy magazines. 'Won't be long now, chaps. This is the big one. If we can throw him back this last time, we'll be on our way to Berlin. Any problems, Miles?'

'No, sir. No problems.'

'Good man. I'll be on the other Vickers, so with our Lewis teams strung out between us we ought to be able to hold 'em. Good luck anyway.'

With that he turned and ran back along the trench. Dunn, piling up Lewis gun drums on the firing steps, muttered an obscene oath. Swanson, his Lewis resting on the parapet, gave him a wry grin. 'What's wrong, Charlie? Don't you fancy a trip to Berlin?'

Dunn hid his apprehension under another obscenity. Swanson grinned again. 'You don't need to worry, Charlie. All you have to do is blow on 'em if they get close enough and they'll scream for mercy.'

Turnor, who was crouched alongside Harry and holding the belt of the Vickers gun, attempted a laugh.

His long face was pale and in spite of the cold there were beads of sweat on his forehead. Harry tried to keep his question casual. 'Everything all right, Arthur?'

Turnor nodded jerkily. 'Yes, Harry. I'm ready.'

Harry glanced at him again, then sank down behind the Vickers. With his own heart thudding, his stomach knotted into a hard ball, and his hands clammy and trembling, Turnor would probably be having the same doubts about him. Every man would be equally afraid. Fear, as long as it was not allowed to turn into panic, was paradoxically the emotion that gave a man the desperate strength to fight back. Then, as often happened to Harry in moments of high stress, his thoughts turned whimsical. Was he saying that Chadwick was also feeling sick with fear? It was a conjecture he found hard to believe.

A shrill whistle, a yell of warning from Swanson, and then the rattle of rifle and machine-gun fire interrupted his thoughts. The first wave of Storm-Troops was making for their trench.

They came with awesome élan, running towards the many gaps in the barbed wire that the shellfire had created. Drawing in his breath, Harry squeezed the trigger of the Vickers and hosed a stream of bullets from right to left. Grey-clad figures staggered, toppled over, sank to their knees before dying. Here and there, spared a few extra seconds of life by the revelling gods of war, a man would somehow pass right through the hail of bullets to get within striking distance of the trench.

One such man was coming straight at the machine-gun post just as Harry reached the far quadrant of his enfilading fire. Seeing the danger, Swanson, who had run out of ammunition and was grabbing a new Lewis drum from Dunn, yelled out a warning. Catching sight of the Storm-Trooper, Harry began swinging the Vickers back but the gun was heavy and the German was only twenty yards away. In the second or two it took the Vickers to make its traverse, Harry saw the man clearly, a stockily-built corporal carrying a machine pistol in his left hand and a stick grenade in his right which was already drawn back to make the throw.

In the miraculous way the mind computes vectors in moments of peril, Harry knew the grenade was going to leave the man's hand before the Vickers could line up on him. With peril sharpening his senses, every detail of the German etched itself on his mind; a torn button on his trench coat, a bloody scratch on his hand carrying the machine pistol, his good-looking face contorted by fear, effort, and determination.

As time began to move again, Harry saw the stick grenade begin its parabola a hundredth of a second before the Vickers bullets smashed into the German. At such short range their effect was brutal: the man halted as if he had run into a brick wall. Then, almost cut in half, he toppled forward into the mud.

Harry's own yell of warning was unnecessary: his team had already seen the danger. With no chance to take cover they could only flatten themselves against the icy sandbags and wait for the grenade to explode.

A freak chance saved them. During the earlier bombardment that had hurled the trench defences in all directions, a screw picket with a clump of barbed wire attached to it had fallen like a spear into the mud a few yards to the left of the machine-gun post and the grenade just clipped a top strand of its wire. As it toppled down at the far side of the parapet instead of into the nest, its explosion showered Harry's team with mud and wet sand from the ruptured bags.

There was no time for self-congratulation. The second wave of Storm-Troops was already hurling itself forward. With Turnor guiding the leaping ammunition belt and feeding another into the breech when it was needed, Harry hosed the Vickers gun back and forth, scything men down as a reaper scythes corn. There was no time for horror at the slaughter: that would come later. The issue of life or death was in the balance and even fear had to be suspended until that issue was decided.

No one knew how many waves of Storm-Troops were thrown in. Time lost its meaning as the battle swung to and fro. Here and there, mostly in sections unprotected by automatic fire, enemy soldiers broke through, leapt down into the trenches, and attacked the defenders with bayonets. Frantic platoon officers and NCOs called up reinforcements and vicious hand-to-hand fighting took place in the narrow confines of the trenches. Somehow, however, the invaders were repelled or killed and by the late afternoon the sector was still intact.

This was not the case north or south of it, however, Although Scottish and South African divisions held fast to their Battle Zone on the Quentin Ridge, the Germans, by the extensive use of gas and flame-throwers, were rapidly taking control of the battle area to the north.

The same thing was happening in the south. Aided by the fog, German support divisions were following up their Storm-Troops' success and their artillery was now firing over open sights at British outposts.

The British line, then, resembled a tautening bow, more or less holding in the centre but with its extremes being drawn ever further back in the areas where the persistent river fog had been such an aid to the attackers. By the late afternoon, with nearly all their reserves committed, the British were calling on every man available to them, batmen, cooks, waiters, clerks – any man who had received any basic military training.

Even to men used to four years of slaughter, the

scenes that day were never forgotten. In some ways they were reminiscent of the 1914 days before trenches had taken antagonists underground. Once again, where there was no fog, men could *see* their enemy, and gun batteries were so close to one another they could indulge in personal duels with bloodied scrap metal the price of defeat.

The difference, however, was in the massive increase and quality of weaponry that had taken place since 1914. Flesh against metal had always been the cause of massive casualties in the years that followed but never had flesh been so brutally exposed as on the 21st March 1918. Not only were the British being literally blown out of their trenches and strongpoints but the Germans were equally exposed as they surged forward. By mid afternoon, forty miles of smoking ground was carpeted by khaki and grey-clothed corpses.

Night came at last to the exhausted soldiers on both sides. Yet few if any were allowed to sleep. Frantic orders were coming through to British battalion commanders to fall back here and fall back there to avoid salients being outflanked by the equally fierce attacks the morning was sure to bring. Stretcher bearers were out on both sides trying to cope with the thousands of wounded men lying on the battleground. Nor was the fighting over for even those few short hours. An astonishing number of British soldiers were moving back over the cratered ground in an effort to return to their own lines or to retrieve weaponry lost in the day's battle. Often these forays were to end in bloody hand-to-hand fighting in the darkness. In some cases British artillerymen actually took horses into the battle area and dragged out guns they had been forced to abandon during the day. On both sides there were acts of astonishing heroism that the mist, returning after

100

darkness fell, gave history no opportunity to record.

So the first day of the German 1918 offensive ended. The Kaiser, on hearing about the progress of his armies, was elated enough to award Hindenburg Germany's highest honour, the Iron Cross with Golden Rays. (Why Ludendorff was not given the same honour is something of a mystery). His Chiefs of Staff, while reasonably satisfied, preferred to wait a few days longer before beginning their celebrations. They were only too aware that the territory they had gained that day held certain built-in disadvantages. Their guns, so meticulously registered on British positions that morning, would not have the same advantage on the second day and until the fog cleared they would be firing blind. Moreover the advance they had made could not be continued indefinitely unless supplies could be successfully transported across the shell-torn ground they had won.

Nevertheless these problems were the products of success not failure, and had all been taken into account in the battle plans. The one imponderable factor was the British infantryman. Famed in a hundred battles from Crecy to the Crimea for his dogged persistence, he too had been carefully weighed on the scales and the size of the juggernaut launched against him had been calculated to shatter even his legendary resilience.

That had not yet happened. Although dazed and shocked and forced to retreat, the British had not yet cracked and were already digging out new defensive lines.

However tomorrow was another day and after the success already achieved it is doubtful if Hindenburg, Ludendorff or any of their military specialists, had any difficulty in finding sleep in the few hours left to them before dawn.

Chapter 11

Mary was standing in the hall with the morning newspaper gripped tightly in her hand when Ethel descended the stairs. 'Good morning, dear!' When the girl turned towards her, Ethel saw her expression. 'What on earth's the matter? You look as white as a sheet.'

Mary passed her the newspaper without comment. Ethel gazed at the headlines, then gave a faint shrug. 'So it's come at last! Well, I suppose we were expecting it, weren't we?'

Mary walked past her into the dining room where Elizabeth was having her breakfast. 'Yes,' she said. 'I suppose we were.'

Ethel followed her. 'It'll be their last fling, you know. They'll call for an armistice once it fails.'

Mary bent down and wiped the child's face with her napkin. 'They said that in 1914. And in 1916.'

'I know that, dear, but this time it's different. Everyone thinks so.'

Although Mary knew that in her own way Ethel was trying to make amends for her behaviour after Jack Watson's visit, she was in no mood to meet her halfway. 'Who thinks so? The *Daily Express*? It's been telling us we're winning the war since the first shots were fired.'

A line appeared between Ethel's eyebrows. 'Mr.

Willis believes it. And so does Captain Watson.'

'Willis?' Mary said scornfully. 'What he knows about the war comes from the soldiers' wives he spends his nights with.'

Ethel glanced at Elizabeth, then gave a disapproving frown. 'You shouldn't say such things about Mr. Willis, dear. I've told you that before.'

'Why not? You know it's true.' Then, seeing Elizabeth's eyes moving curiously from one to the other, Mary went on: 'His only interest in the war is whether they'll call him up. Which they will if it lasts much longer.'

'Then what about Captain Watson?' Ethel demanded. 'He must know what he's talking about?'

Although Mary liked Watson, she was in no mood to pander to anyone who was not facing the German offensive. 'Jack's just a civilian in uniform, as he admits himself. He's in Paris, not in the north with our men, and in any case his letter was written a week ago. So what can he know about it?'

With a temper that was always on a short fuse, Ethel was beginning to show impatience. 'Then what do you want me to say? That the Germans are sure to win and they're going to drive our men into the sea?'

Before Mary could answer, Elizabeth piped in anxiously. 'What is it, Grannie? What's happening?'

Mary bent down and kissed her. 'Nothing for you to worry about, darling. Go and fetch your coat. It'll be time to go to school in a minute.'

As the child ran out into the hall, she turned to Ethel. 'I'm sorry, Mother. I know you're trying to help. But I can't stop thinking about Harry over there. I can't help . . .' Feeling her eyes suddenly burn, she turned hastily away.

Ethel's voice was a blend of sympathy and reproach. 'I know how worried you are. That's why I can't under-

103

stand why he chose to go back. Didn't it occur to him how you would feel? Particularly with a child on the way.'

She can't stop it, Mary thought. Even when trying to comfort me, she still has to attack Harry. 'I'm no different to a million other women, Mother. They'll all be just as worried this morning.'

Ethel's face tightened. 'Their men had no choice. Harry had. That's what I can't forgive.'

Sometimes in the darkest hours of the night I find it hard to forgive him myself, Mary thought. Then, dismayed at her treachery, she was about to spring to his defence when Elizabeth returned with her coat. Relieved at the excuse to avoid another quarrel, she helped the child into it. 'I think you can go to school on your own this morning, darling. I've a lot of things to do before I go to work and Grannie hasn't had her breakfast yet.'

Ethel was quick to protest. 'No, I'll take her. I like the walk. It gives me an appetite.'

'But, Mother, it's only four streets away. What harm can she come to? Nearly all the children of her age go on their own.'

Ethel smiled at the child as she crossed the room to fetch her own coat. 'We don't care what the other girls do, do we, darling? We enjoy our little walks, don't we?'

The child's enthusiastic nod did not deceive Mary. The sweets Ethel persisted in buying for her, in spite of Mary's disapproval, more than compensated Elizabeth for any embarrassment she felt at still being taken to school.

Mary watched them both from the front window three minutes later, the girl in her short socks, warm coat, scarf and school hat; Ethel erect in a long tight-fitting coat with a high squirrel collar. The morning was raw and windy, with threatening clouds, and the couple were not halfway to the front gate when Ethel reached out a gloved hand and drew the child against her. Although the gesture could be seen as protective, to Mary it had overtones of possession that once more made her yearn to take the child away to a more wholesome environment.

She went upstairs to tidy Elizabeth's room and by the time she had finished she heard the front door close. Returning downstairs she found Ethel in the hall unbuttoning her coat. She was smiling. 'There, that little job's done. I always feel happier when I know she's arrived safely.'

Mary's reply was short. 'You mollycoddle her, Mother. In the long run she'll suffer for it.'

Never one to take criticism, Ethel frowned. 'I treat her no differently to the way I treated you and Connie. And it hasn't done either of you any harm, has it?'

Mary could not hold back her words. 'You treated us that way? Both of us?'

Ethel stared at her. 'Yes. Are you saying I didn't?'

Yes, I am saying it, Mary thought. Connie, yes. She was always your favourite. But me. . . . Then her mood changed. What was the point in baring old wounds when so many new ones were bleeding? 'Mother, I don't want Elizabeth to grow into a spoilt and pampered child. I want her to be like other children, to learn to take knocks and to take care of herself. Otherwise she's going to find life very hard when she grows up.'

Ethel gave a disapproving nod. 'I suppose this is Harry's philosophy. Let her grow up like the street urchin he used to be. Is that what you want?'

Anger and resentment swept away Mary's self control. 'You always have to blame Harry, don't you? If the sun fell out of the sky it would be his fault!' Her voice rose. 'I won't put up with it, and in any case you're wrong. If Harry had his way he'd spoil her as much as you do. I'm the one who doesn't want her spoiling by a grandmother who hasn't the intelligence to see what she's doing.'

Two red spots appeared in Ethel's cheeks. 'How dare you talk to me like that? Who do you think you are?'

'I'm *your* daughter, that's who I am. So when you hear things from me you don't like, blame yourself. I certainly never got them from Dad.'

'If your father was alive, my girl, you'd never talk to me this way.'

'If Dad was alive, he'd never let you interfere between a mother and her child. And you know it.'

Ethel sneered. 'Interfere? You've a nerve to say that. What would you do without me? How do you think you could live on your husband's Army pay?'

Mary's temper suddenly blazed. 'You dare ask a question like that? You, who destroyed Dad's will leaving the business to Harry and me. If we're poor, you're the reason. And don't try to deny it. Your guilt's written all over your face.'

Ethel gave a gasp of horror. 'How can you say such a thing about your mother? I only hope God doesn't strike you down.'

'Strike *me* down? I don't know how you've the nerve to go to Church. It amazes me you can put flowers on Dad's grave. Aren't you afraid sometimes?'

Ethel gave a sob. 'What a terrible thing to say.'

'What a terrible thing to do! Dad trusted us all. Yet you betrayed his trust as soon as he was dead. I don't know how your conscience lets you sleep. Dad loved Harry but you've done everything possible to harm him. So how can you expect me to have a daughter's feelings for you? Or to want Elizabeth to grow up in such an atmosphere?'

106

Ethel gave another sob. 'How cruel you've become. When I think of the little girl you were, it breaks my heart.'

'If I've changed, Mother, it's because you've changed me. And please don't start crying those crocodile tears. You only cry when you're in the wrong.'

Wiping her eyes, Ethel turned away. 'I'm going upstairs. I'm going to pray that you learn to love and respect your mother again.'

'I'll love and respect you, Mother, when you respect my husband and stop attacking him. If you don't stop it, you know what I'll do.'

Ethel dabbed at her eyes with a cambric handkerchief. 'I suppose it's your condition that makes you act this way.'

'Don't start making excuses for me! I mean every word I say. And don't fetch Elizabeth at lunchtime. If anyone has to go, I'll go myself.'

Without another word, Ethel ran up the stairs. Trembling with reaction, Mary entered the sitting room and sank down on the settee. She was not deceived by Ethel's sudden recourse to tears. Ethel had remembered her threat, made the previous year, that if she persisted in her attacks on Harry, she, Mary, would pack up her things and take Elizabeth away, regardless of what hardships they both might have to face. It was a threat that had worked until Ethel had forgotten herself on Jack Watson's last visit.

Mary was stunned by the intensity of this latest quarrel. From a mere tinder spark, it had burst into a white-hot explosion, proof, if proof were needed, of the bitter resentments smouldering in them both.

Yet as her temper cooled, Mary could not put all the blame on Ethel. Her fears for Harry's safety, heightened by the morning news and her pregnancy, were unquestionably making her less tolerant to aspects of her mother's behaviour that she had managed to live with before.

With no prospect of Ethel changing her ways, she wondered yet again if it would not be better to leave No. 57 and damn the consequences. For herself she would not have hesitated for a moment but as always it was Elizabeth's welfare that made her pause. She could hardly keep her job if she took the child away from Ethel, and with only Harry's Army pay to live on, the effect on Elizabeth would be traumatic. Was it fair to tear her away from her school, her clothes and presents, her very security? Wasn't it wiser to wait until the war ended? If Harry survived, surely they would then have a good chance of a life free of Ethel's meddling.

Aware she was procrastinating again, she roused herself and went over to her office. She was hoping to find forgetfulness in work but business was slack and her thoughts kept slipping to the battle raging in France. She felt that special newspaper editions must be out already but although she kept her ears cocked could not hear the cries of newsboys. Glad now that she had arranged to meet Elizabeth, she slipped out a few minutes before noon and called in a newsagent's shop on her way to school.

To her disappointment there was no more news than that given in the early edition. The offensive was massive, the British Armies were falling back here and there to straighten their lines, but there was no cause for alarm. The offensive had been expected and plans had been drawn up to contain it. Better news could be anticipated soon.

Knowing from Harry what little truth was released to the Press, Mary found small comfort in the note of optimism. Nor it seemed did most of the shoppers she passed on her way to the school. With conscription having now taken men up to the age of forty, there were few women who did not have a father, a husband, a son or a sweetheart at the front. Even the young ones were talking in muted tones and faces everywhere were lined with worry. It seemed that morning that the entire nation was holding its breath as it waited for the outcome of the battle.

Even the children seemed quieter than usual as they began coming out for lunch. Catching sight of Elizabeth, Mary gave her a wave. For a split second she imagined the child's face dropped on seeing it was she and not Ethel. Pushing the thought aside, Mary bent down and kissed her. 'Hello, darling. How was school this morning?'

'All right,' the girl muttered. Then her face brightened. 'We've got a half day today.'

'A half day. What for?'

'I'm not sure but I think it's something to do with the war. Mrs. Saunders said special prayers this morning. We had to pray for our soldiers in France.' The child glanced up at Mary. 'Daddy's one of them, isn't he?'

'Yes. Daddy's in France. What did you say in your prayers?'

'All sorts of things. Like hoping God will take care of them and bring them safely back. And that we'll win the war. It lasted ever so long. And then Mrs. Saunders said we needn't come back this afternoon.'

Which probably meant Mrs. Saunders had a son or husband involved in the battle too, Mary thought. She folded Elizabeth's scarf around her neck and led her up the street. 'What would you like to do this afternoon? I have to go back to work but you can come to the office with me if you like. There are plenty of your books there for you to look at.' She hesitated a moment, then went on: 'Or you can stay at home and keep Grannie company.'

There was no hesitation in the child's reply. 'I'd rather stay at home, Mummy. I still haven't finished that new jigsaw Grannie brought me.'

The afternoon seemed endless to Mary. With no more orders to process until Willis got back from his daily round, she had little to do but think about the battle in France and her quarrel with Ethel. Although anger at Ethel's attacks on Harry had given her the spirit to hold her own today, Mary knew she was basically afraid of her mother. Every time she thought about their next meeting, her heart would begin beating fast and she would feel slightly sick. More and more she wished she had kept her feelings under check that morning. Her fears for Harry's safety were burden enough without the additional weight of Ethel's animosity.

She found herself staring out of the office window. The men who occasionally appeared at the doors of the sheds below were all middle-aged or elderly: a depressing sight with its implications. Moreover, although it was late March there were as yet no signs of spring. The trees that bordered the lane were bare and the back gardens devoid of colour. With dark clouds sweeping over the city, the scene had a melancholy that matched her mood.

Willis arrived back just before five o'clock. Although Mary had often taken him to task for working short days, tonight she was glad to see him. Instead of her usual terse request to see his order book, she motioned at the newspaper that was stuffed into his overcoat pocket. 'What's the latest news of the offensive? Do they give any?'

Willis was breathing hard from his climb up the stairs to the office, a large fleshy man of forty-six years with a

110

fair moustache, long sideburns, and a fruity, self-confident voice. Like her father before her, Mary had never liked him for his bluster, his laziness, and his philandering with customers' wives, but, as William had ruefully confessed, in wartime beggars could not be choosers. There were few men left with both the knowledge of drugs and the ability to drive a car, and even that number was diminishing as conscription widened its net.

It was a combination of circumstances that had made Willis' position secure while Harry was away, a fact that had made him more slothful than ever. On the matter of the bicycle, however, Mary was having her revenge. For although Willis was deep enough into the black market to obtain an extra gallon of petrol here and there, even he could not cadge enough to keep the old Ford running regularly and so for at least three days a week his plump frame was having to suffer the hardship and indignity of cycling. From his comments, a day spent assaulting the German Front Line trenches would have been child's play compared with the privations he suffered.

Today had been one of those days and his sigh was heartfelt as he handed Mary the newspaper. 'What a day, m'dear! That wind must be coming from the North Pole. It was murder cycling up from Hessle Road.'

Mary, anxiously scanning the paper, made no reply. Sinking into a chair Willis pulled off his cycle clips and massaged his calves. When Mary still took no notice of him, he motioned at the newspaper. 'You can't take much notice of that, y' know.'

Hypersensitive to any comment on the offensive, Mary immediately glanced at him. 'What do you mean? Have you heard anything?'

He shrugged his heavy shoulders. 'Most people think it's much worse than the papers are making out. They

111

only tell us what the Government wants us to know. Reading between the lines, it looks as if the Jerries are breaking through everywhere.'

Mary had a sudden spiteful desire to punish him. 'If they do, they'll lift the conscription age to fifty, won't they? I wonder what we'll do about staff then?'

Willis gave an uneasy laugh. 'They'll never do that. What good would we be to them?'

Mary took the cash bag from him and opened the office safe. 'Perhaps that's the way wars should be fought,' she said. 'Use up the old men first and keep the young ones alive. It makes better sense, don't you think?' Locking the money in the safe, she rose. 'I'll take the orders from you in the morning. I want to be home early tonight.'

She saw the chastened Willis outside, then locked up the warehouse. She knew she had been cruel but she had never been able to forgive him for his seduction of an absent soldier's wife.

The wind was bitter as she made her way down the lane and black clouds were piling up in the darkening sky. As she opened the back garden gate of No. 57 her heart began racing again and she had to screw up her courage before entering the house.

Ethel was on her knees when Mary entered the sitting room, offering a piece of the jigsaw to Elizabeth who had the puzzle set out on a tray on the floor. Mary, who had already decided she must try to restore the status quo if life was to be tolerable again, gave them both a smile. 'Hello! How are you both getting on with the jigsaw?'

The glance Ethel gave her seemed to contain a dozen emotions, most of them hostile. Yet among them Mary imagined she saw a coded message: We have to live together, you and I. I because I want Elizabeth near me

112

and you because you need security for her. Therefore we must declare another armistice. Don't think for one moment that any of my opinions about Harry have changed. It simply means we will become actors again, hiding our feelings for the sake of the child.

But will you play your part when I'm not here? Mary thought. Or will you continue to run Harry down in front of Elizabeth, which I'm certain you do in a hundred subtle ways? Feeling they had already declared the doubtful armistice, she moved towards the couple. 'You're getting on well with it, aren't you? Who's found most of the pieces?'

Elizabeth's voice was full of enthusiasm. 'Grannie's found most of them. She's ever so good at jigsaws.'

Ethel smiled as she rose to her feet. 'Nonsense, dear. You've found just as many yourself.' She turned her smile on Mary. 'You must be cold, dear. I'll go and make you some tea.'

They all retired early that night, Ethel under the pretext she had a headache, Mary because she wanted to be alone. She put Elizabeth to bed, read a story to her, then turned out the light and retired to her own room.

Slipping between the icy sheets she tried to read for a while. Finding she could not concentrate she turned out the light, only for her thoughts to fly immediately to France where, sombre and undisciplined, they invented a hundred perils for Harry.

The weather did not help her. The wind was moaning in the eaves and after a sudden flash illuminated the heavy curtains, she heard a far-off reverberation. With her mind obsessed by the war, her first thought was that she was hearing gunfire. Then, as a second flash came, she realised that in spite of the time of the year a storm was approaching.

It came swiftly and fiercely, brilliant flashes of light and ripping peals of thunder that shook the house. As she lay listening she heard a cry from Elizabeth's room. Jumping out of bed she ran into the darkened room, to see the shadowy figure of the girl sitting up in bed. Still half asleep, the child saw her and cried out. 'Grannie, I'm frightened! I don't like those boom-booms.'

Wincing, Mary approached her bed. 'It's Mummy, darling. Don't be frightened. It's only a storm. It won't hurt you.'

The girl began sobbing. 'I hate storms. They're horrible.'

As Mary sat on the edge of the bed and was about to draw the girl into her arms, Ethel's voice sounded from the doorway. 'I'm here, my dear. As your mummy says, it's only a storm.'

The child turned to the silhouetted figure in the lighted doorway. 'I don't like storms, Grannie. Can I come into your bed until it's over?'

Mary broke in before Ethel could reply. 'No, darling. I'll stay here with you.'

The girl began to wail. 'But I want to go with Grannie.'

Mary's voice sharpened in spite of herself. 'No. You'll stay here with me.' She turned to Ethel, still standing in the doorway. 'Thank you, Mother, but we can manage.'

Ethel's reply gave little away and yet there was satisfaction behind every syllable. 'Very well, dear. As you say.' Her tone changed subtly as she addressed Elizabeth. 'Don't be frightened, dear. Grannie's not far away.'

With that she went out and the door closed, leaving only a fringe of light around its edges. Another brilliant flash came a second later, followed almost immediately by a massive peal of thunder. As Elizabeth gave a

114

frightened cry, Mary caught hold of her and hugged her tightly. 'It's all right, darling,' she soothed. 'It can't hurt you.'

The child was trembling and her body felt hot. Mary climbed into bed and put her arms around her. For a minute she would not be comforted. Then her sobs began to cease and her tear-stained face sank into Mary's shoulder. A few seconds later her steady breathing told she had fallen asleep.

The storm spat its venom for another five minutes, then began grumbling away. The chill Mary was feeling as she lay with the child in her arms had little to do with the bitterness of the night. The scene had been a reminder, if a reminder were needed, that it was not only in France that a desperate war for possession was being fought.

Chapter 12

The 16th Battalion was one of the many British units ordered to retreat that night to straighten the front line. For soldiers who had stood their ground all day, it was an incomprehensible order and men swore and cursed as they shouldered their weapons and moved out.

Evidence of the fury of the bombardment in the Battle Zone loomed out of the mist as they trudged wearily along the communication trenches. Disembowelled horses and mules, some still alive, lay in the traces of shattered caissons. Stretcher bearers kept hurrying past with their grisly loads. The concrete roofs and walls of strongpoints stood at drunken angles. First-aid posts lit by paraffin or acetylene lamps, with queues of blinded men still waiting for attention, emerged from the mist like visions of hell. And over and through the screams, sobs, and curses of wounded or exhausted men, there was an all pervading rumble from both east and west: the sound of hundreds of transports bringing up fresh weapons of death for the holocaust on the morrow.

The battalion was halted at an old disused railway embankment. It was a frail enough defensive position but there was flat ground east of it that would give its defenders a clear field of fire if the mist did not favour the enemy again, which by the time the battalion arrived seemed more than likely.

The men were given ten minutes rest and then ordered to dig themselves in on the far side of the embankment. At the same time Chadwick began siting his machine-gun teams. He found a disused artillery post on the left flank of the line and ordered Harry and his team into it. 'This'll do nicely, Miles. I'll leave you to reinforce it while I get the rest of the lads fixed up. Make sure you grab plenty of ammunition. We'll need all we can get tomorrow.'

Hours of feverish work began. As sweating men and horses rushed up ammunition and building material from the Rear Zone, the battalion began dragging sandbags up the embankment and building a barbed wire barricade on its far side. Although the work was killing for soldiers who had fought all day, they knew their survival might depend on their efforts and men slaved on with burning lungs and bleeding hands.

It was gone 3.0 a.m. before Harry felt his post was as strong as the material available could make it and he allowed his crew to rest. Swanson and Dunn were asleep almost before their heads dropped on the sandbags they were using as pillows. Harry, cursed or blessed with nervous energy that could keep him awake for days in a crisis, settled himself down on the floor of the post, put his back against a couple of ammunition boxes, and waited for dawn.

Along the embankment he could hear the clink of entrenching tools as infantrymen dug frantically into the clinker-impregnated ground. Although the mist was rising steadily, it had not yet reached the top of the embankment and the icy stars were still visible. As he reached into his greatcoat pocket for a cigarette he noticed that Turnor, although propped up in the near

117

corner of the gunpost, still had his eyes open. He leaned forward. 'What's the matter, Arthur? Can't you sleep?'

The start Turnor gave suggested his thoughts had been far away. 'What, Sergeant?'

'I was wondering why you weren't sleeping. We've a hard day coming up tomorrow.'

When no reply came, Harry offered him a cigarette. The match he struck lit up Turnor's haggard face with two days' growth of beard. As Turnor sucked in smoke, Harry saw the man's mittened hands were shaking. He blew out the match and sank back, wondering what to say.

Turnor came to his aid. 'I never thought we were going to hold them today, did you?'

'No,' Harry said. 'It was touch and go.'

The darkness could not hide Turnor's shudder. 'God, the way they came at us. As if their lives didn't mean a thing.'

'Training,' Harry said as the man paused. 'Training, courage, and fear. Like us they know they'll be shot if they don't obey orders.'

Turnor drew in smoke again. 'It's madness, isn't it, Harry? Pure bloody madness. We're slaughtering one another like cattle and how many of us know what for?' When Harry did not speak, he went on: 'We're not even merciful when we kill. We mutilate one another, blind one another, choke one another . . .' Turnor drew in a sobbing breath. 'Jesus Christ, I sometimes wish I'd never been born to behave like this.'

Harry was reminded of the self-disgust he had felt himself. 'Don't take it too much to heart, Arthur. It's them or us. That's the way you have to look at it.'

Turnor shook his head and turned away. Christ, Harry thought. I'm talking the way Chadwick would! In the distance the explosion of a heavy shell sent a tremor through the ground. Turnor's cigarette glowed, then faded. His voice, with its flat East Yorkshire accent, sounded again as the reverberation died away. 'Is it true you asked Chadwick to bring you back, Harry?'

Harry felt immediate hostility. 'What if it is?'

Turnor sounded embarrassed now. 'I don't know. It's just that you've got a wife like I have and . . .'

'And what?'

Realising the minefield into which his question was leading him, Turnor beat a hasty retreat. 'Sorry, Harry. It's none of my business.'

'No. Go on! Finish what you wanted to say.'

'It's nothing, Harry. Honestly it isn't.'

Harry leaned forward. 'Don't lie. You think my wife and I must have a hell of a relationship for me to want to come back here. Isn't that right?'

For a moment it seemed Turnor lacked the courage to take up the challenge. Then, picking a shred of tobacco from his cracked lips, he glanced back to Harry. 'I can only put it this way. It took the Conscription Act and the police force to get me away from my wife and into the Army. So like everybody else I've thought you must have had a bad time back home. But, as I just said, it's none of my business.'

'That's right. It is none of your business. Or anyone else's for that matter.'

'I'm sorry, Harry. I didn't mean to pry. Only when we'd all give our right arms to get home, it's hard to understand anybody who wants to come back.' Turnor's laugh was diffident. 'I suppose it makes us feel a bit sorry for him.'

Harry's resentment faded. Glancing at Swanson and Dunn to make certain they were still asleep, he turned back to Turnor. 'It wasn't my home life. That's the last thing it was. What would you say if I told you I didn't know the reason?'

119

Turnor's brows came together. 'You didn't know?'

Harry was wondering if it was the proximity of battle that was dragging the confession from him. 'That's right. Something drew me back but I don't know what it was. Try to make something of that.'

Three shells burst in quick succession. Turnor waited until the din died away. 'Is it the excitement? They say it appeals to some men.'

Harry's dislike returned. 'You mean the killing, don't you? What sort of a savage do you think I am?'

Turnor shook his head in protest. 'No, I only meant the excitement. Some men seem to need it – men like the Major. Only you seem a different kind of person. That's what puzzles me.'

Damn you, Harry thought. Damn you for even coupling his name with mine. He wondered why he was continuing the conversation. Was it because Turnor's accent brought back memories of home? Or was there something about this introverted man that struck a chord in himself? He leaned forward again.

'If you disliked joining up so much, why didn't you become a conscientious objector? Wouldn't that have been the best way out?'

Turnor shook his head. 'Eleanor wouldn't have let me do that. She'd have felt I was disgracing myself.'

For a moment Harry had a vision of a sneering girl and a white feather. 'Why? Was she keen that you should fight?'

'Not in the way you mean. She just felt it was our duty, that's all. She lived in dread of the day I was called up. I could see her losing weight just thinking about it.'

'Don't they all feel that way?'

'Aye. I suppose they do. But Eleanor's got problems some of them don't have.' Turnor searched for the right words and failed to find them. 'I suppose she's a bit highly strung. She's also a very lonely person.'

'Hasn't she any parents to go to?'

'No. They threw her out when she married me. Her father's a company director, you see, and they'd hopes of a good marriage for her until I came along.'

'Don't they have anything to do with her at all?'

Turnor shook his head. 'They told her she was finished if she married me and they've kept their word. She doesn't even get a Christmas card.'

'What about your parents? Can't she visit them?'

'They're both dead. My mother died when I was born and my father died of meningitis in 1909.'

'And neither of you has brothers or sisters?'

'I've one brother but he's over in Ireland.' Turnor paused. 'In some ways it'd be better if she had a kid but the doctor says there's no chance of that. I think that's half the trouble. She's only got me to care about. That's why . . .' He paused and gave an embarrassed laugh. 'It does sometimes make you duck for cover when the whizzbangs come over.'

Harry was no longer puzzled why he felt an affinity with this man. 'You're saying you don't want her to suffer because of her affection for you? You feel you'll be betraying her if you get killed?'

Turnor's startled eyes searched his face. 'You understand that? But how can you when . . .?'

Harry's laugh was harsh. 'How can I understand it when I volunteered to come back? You think I don't feel guilty too? I've never stopped feeling guilty since the day I wrote and asked Chadwick to pull strings for me.' Then, realising what he was saying, he cursed and crushed his cigarette against a wet sandbag. 'Let's shut up now, shall we? We're going to need all our energy to stay alive tomorrow.'

Turnor half-opened his mouth to reply, then nodded

and turned away. Harry propped his gasmask behind his head and closed his eyes. The rumble of the transports was like a distant sea, swelling and fading in waves of sound. A heavy explosion was followed by a great roll of thunder as if an ammunition dump had been hit. We are all in hell, he thought. Where else would a woman's love haunt a man and make death seem a guilty act? Where else would death contain that extra dimension of despair?

The mist crept up and entered the post. Already chilled after his exertions, Harry turned up his collar and buried himself deeper into his greatcoat. He saw the stars were still visible above, however, and wished they were not. Their cold stare suggested a universe devoid of charity or compassion.

Chapter 13

In anticipation of the fierce fighting to come, the battalion's padre held a religious service at 4.30 a.m. Chadwick, carrying an acetylene lamp, entered Harry's post to give notice of it. 'I can only spare two of you. Who would like to attend?'

Fast asleep, Swanson and Dunn did not hear him. When neither of the other two men moved, Chadwick glanced at Harry. 'Don't you want to go, Miles? I'll take your place on the Vickers. It'll only be a short service.'

Certain that he was being baited, Harry shook his head. 'No, thank you, sir.'

Chadwick lifted an eyebrow. 'You surprise me, Sergeant. I always thought you were one of our better types.'

Harry shrugged. 'It seems you were wrong, doesn't it?'

Chadwick gave his light, infectious laugh. 'It does indeed. Oh, well, I suppose the war affects us all sooner or later. But you're welcome to go if you want.'

Knowing what lay behind his words, Harry gazed at him without answering. Chadwick smiled back, then indicated the two sleeping men. 'I shouldn't let them sleep too long or they might stiffen up in this cold. You'll be getting grub, tea, and maybe a tot of rum in about half an hour. Any questions or problems?'

Turnor nodded at the fog-covered ground at the far side of the embankment. 'Does anyone know what's happening out there, sir?'

As always, Chadwick made light of the perils ahead. 'They're moving up, of course, but I don't think we've much to worry about. Our artillery ought to be able to take care of any tanks.'

Turnor gave a start. 'Tanks?'

Chadwick nodded. 'A captured prisoner brought in during the night says there might be a few. So we've had a battery of field guns drawn up on a ridge behind us. They'll soon make scrap metal of the brutes. Any more questions?'

When neither man spoke, Chadwick went to the gunpost exit. 'I'll try to get back before the fun starts but if I can't make it I know you'll do your best.' His smile was directed at Harry, 'Good luck.'

Turnor waited until he disappeared, then turned to Harry. 'Tanks! How the hell can our guns spot them if the mist doesn't lift?'

Harry was having the same thought. Tanks were anathema to the infantryman of the day. Without any kind of anti-tank weapon, they had no way of halting them and their choice was either to run and risk being cut down by the tanks' automatic weapons or hold their position and be crushed under their tracks. Until this year the British, who had invented the weapon, had held a monopoly of the terror, although they had never built enough to exploit the machine's full potential. Now it appeared the Germans had built some and were throwing their weight into an offensive already devastating enough.

Harry sank down on an ammunition box. 'We'll just have to hope for the best. As far as I could tell there aren't any rivers nearby to hold the mist, so we might be lucky.'

With yet another peril to face, men stood by at 5.30 and gazed anxiously into the mist ahead. For all they knew whole arrays of tanks, guns, and Storm-Troops might be massed there and yet they could see nothing but a dark sea that gradually lightened as dawn approached. Men fidgeted, smoked, swallowed to lubricate their throats, and here and there men prayed. Occasionally platoon commanders relieved their tension by firing star shells but they revealed nothing but luminous mist that darkened again as the flares died and sank into it.

By 8 a.m. the tension was such that men began wishing the attack would begin. They were not alone in this wish. German field commanders, although for different reasons, were even more anxious to commence battle. They knew their Storm-Troop losses would be halved or even quartered if they could race forward before the mist dispersed. But they were paying the price of their massive bombardment the previous day. Altough their infantry had had no more difficulty in filtering through the devastated ground than had the British that night, it was a different matter for their guns, supply wagons and even their tanks. Mechanical transports littered the cratered ground and even their horse-drawn guns fared little better. Without artillery cover for their men, field commanders could only curse and pray in turn that the mist would not lift until the situation righted itself and they could once again launch their men forward.

At the same time the morale of the Germans was sky-high after their early successes, and by 9 a.m. they had enough field guns in position to begin a preliminary bombardment of the British lines.

Inevitably it was not as crushing as on the previous day. The guns were not registered, the mist hid the

British lines, and probing patrols had only managed to establish their approximate positions. Moreover the railway embankment was just high enough to give cover to its defenders. Only trench mortars and howitzers could provide the right trajectory: shells from the field guns flew right over it, inflicting little damage on its defenders although they still created carnage among the hastily-erected supply dumps and first-aid posts behind it.

It was a period when the 16th and its fellow battalions could do little else but keep their heads down, pray tanks did not emerge from the mist, and wait for the infantry attack they had expected hours ago.

Providentially for the British the sky was cloudless that morning and optimists forecast the mist would clear once the early spring sun could produce enough warmth. The question was when, however, because 10 a.m. came with no noticeable change in visibility. But the morning sun was warming fast and when, thirty minutes later, the tops of trees could be seen, defenders began to wonder if the enemy was losing his great opportunity. As whistles began blowing the entire length of the German positions, it became clear German field commanders were having similar thoughts. Within seconds the British saw figures in the mist, first ghostlike and then solidifying into menacing creatures carrying weapons of death.

The carnage began. All along the British front machine-guns, rifles and field guns opened fire. The first wave of Storm-Troops did not reach the frail barbed wire defences erected during the night. The second wave reached them but was mown down before it could do significant damage. The third wave poured forward and with wire cutters and explosive charges managed to create gaps for the fourth wave to exploit. These men, hurling stick grenades, came running towards the embankment, only to be mown down in turn by the desperate defenders.

Yet still they came on in seemingly inexhaustible numbers. To Harry, cordite-stained, sweating, firing, re-loading with Turnor's assistance, and firing again, the scene started to become unreal. It was no longer sublime courage he was seeing at the foot of the embankment but the relentless progress of an ant army faced by a fire. There was no thought of retreat or detour. Bodies were thrown in until the fire was extinguished and the survivors could progress. Life was in the corporate body, not in the individual.

In a momentary lull in the firing he heard Swanson cursing alongside him. 'My bloody gun's jammed, Harry! She's damn nearly red hot.'

Dunn was cursing at his elbow. 'Piss on the fucking thing! The bastards'll be back in a minute.'

Harry reached down and tossed a can of water at him. As he straightened he saw Turnor bent over an ammunition box. 'You all right, Arthur?'

The man lifted his sweating face and Harry saw he had been vomiting. He managed a smile. 'Yes, Sarge. I'm all right.'

Harry clapped him on the shoulder, then peered through his loophole in the sandbags. Nodding at Swanson, he fumbled inside his coat for cigarettes and handed them round. 'They're taking a breather, so we'd better do the same.'

No one looked at the embarrassed Turnor as he wiped his mouth with an oily rag: every man knew his turn could be next. Trying to hide the trembling of their hands as they lit their cigarettes, Harry, Swanson and Turnor sank down on ammunition boxes while Dunn kept watch. To hide his own emotion, Swanson kicked at the hundreds of empty cartridge cases that littered the

127

floor. 'We'll be needing more ammo if this keeps up much longer, Harry.'

Relieved at the chance to hide his own battered nerves, Harry turned and counted the full boxes. 'We'll last a while yet but I'll keep an eye on things.'

Dunn's reply was a mixture of scorn and apprehension. 'We'll never keep the fucking bastards out. It's like a bloody football match leavin'. For Christ's sake, were are they findin' 'em all?'

The respite lasted over an hour with only the sullen guns and snipers in action. Occasionally a man would risk his life to glance down the embankment, only to shudder at the sight. Among the corpses piled up on either side of the barbed wire, wounded men, some hideously mutilated, could be seen feebly waving their arms for help.

The second attack came just after two o'clock. Turnor, on watch at the time, gave a violent start. 'Tanks, Harry! Coming out of the wood.'

All four men were at their posts immediately. From a shell-torn wood in the distance, half a dozen grey shapes were emerging. Harry felt his mouth turn dry as he watched them spread out into battle order. His fate, the fate of his team, the very fate of the battalion, was now out of their hands. Unless the field guns behind them could destroy or cripple the oncoming armour, they would all be routed or killed.

Tension tightened like a bowstring as the British field guns opened fire. Geysers of mud began leaping up but for a full thirty seconds no hit was registered. Then, on the far right of the line, a black explosion hid a tank and when the smoke cleared it was seen to be burning fiercely. Cries of triumph broke out from the embankment, only to die away as the rest of the grey mastodons were seen to be still clanking relentlessly forward.

A sudden splatter of bullets on the sandbagged parados behind Harry's gun post told of a new danger: the Germans now had heavy machine-guns registered on the embankment's defences. The reason became apparent when masses of grey-clad figures began assembling around the tanks. The machine guns would give the Storm-Troops some cover while the tanks spearheaded the attack.

With the British infantry helpless, the battle for the moment was a duel between the German tanks and artillery and the British guns on the ridge. As shells screamed over the embankment in both directions, men dug their nails into sweating palms and waited.

Their inactivity was short-lived. Although the German infantry was still out of effective range, it was decided that morale might suffer with the waiting and so orders were given to open fire again. However, with platoon officers and NCOs conscious of the need to conserve ammunition, the rifle fire was only thin and spasmodic.

Shells were bursting all over the cratered ground now as the desperate British gunners increased their rate of fire. A second tank had its port tracks blown off and it circled about like a child's toy before coming to a halt. The remaining four spread out and gave no sign of retreating.

With the Storm-Troops now within range, the defenders were again firing as fast as they could load. As Harry hosed his fire back and forth, he heard Dunn's yell of alarm. 'Watch out, Sarge! There's a bastard comin' straight for us.'

Pivoting his Vickers, Harry saw the rhomboid shape of a tank heading straight at his gunpost with its forward gun firing. Opening fire himself, he held down the trigger only to see sparks flying from the tank's armour.

Realising his heavy machine-gun was useless, he shouted at the three white-faced men alongside him. 'If it reaches us, run when I tell you. Take cover down the embankment.'

Although moving at barely eight miles an hour, the tank was now less than sixty yards away. Knowing it would be protected from the British guns once it reached the lee of the embankment, the machine-gunners held their breath and waited, although Harry continued to fire at the monster's turret.

The tank was less than twenty yards from the barbed wire when a shell burst alongside it. As the smoke cleared it appeared undamaged and hearts sank again. Then Dunn gave a scream of excitement in his best Yorkshire yammer. 'They've skelped the bastard! Look.'

A slick of flame could be seen at the base of the turret. As it grew men could be seen scrambling out and trying to run for safety. None managed more than a few steps as the defenders, relieving their pent-up nerves, poured a withering fire on them.

Relief was visible in Harry's team as they turned their attention back to the German infantry. However the failure of the tanks to effect a penetration appeared to have discouraged their escorts. Under cover of smoke shells and grenades, they began withdrawing, leaving the defenders hardly able to believe their good fortune.

Yet with reports coming in of successes both north and south of the sector, the commander of the German force could not allow this stalemate to continue. After more ammunition was rushed forward and men given a chance to rest, a third attack was launched in the late afternoon.

Once again the tactics were changed. This time the attack was preceded by a hail of smoke shells, a substitute for the mist that had been such an aid to the German Armies to the north and the south. Under the artificial fog, *flammerwerfer* teams were sent forward under the protection of Storm-Troops armed with light machine-guns and grenades.

Although the smoke screens warned company commanders that further mischief was afoot and although men fired at everything that moved in the drifting smoke, it was not until a long tongue of flame leapt through it that the nature of the threat was confirmed. It brought an immediate reaction from the defenders. Many had seen the ghastly effects of flame-throwers and some, like Harry, had seen friends incinerated by them. As a result, although the Allies themselves were now using the weapon, men loathed and feared their operators in equal proportion and a great wave of emotion swept along the front as more oily flames roared out like dragons' tongues, seeking to incinerate any man who stood in their way.

With some *flammerwerchen* reaching the top of the embankment and playing their fiery hoses between the sandbags, the entire picture became confused. Some defenders retreated. Others took protection behind the traverses of the makeshift trench and lobbed grenades back at the flame-throwers. Others had to contend with Storm-Troops who, having lost so many comrades during the day, found themselves at last among their hated enemy and took their revenge. For a full mile, the line convoluted like a piece of string as men shot, bayoneted or incinerated one another in their effort to hold or gain possession.

In their gunpost Harry and his team were suffering their own ordeal. The over-worked Vickers gun had suddenly jammed and at the same moment Swanson had run out of ammunition. The cessation of fire had allowed

131

a *flammerwerfer* team to reach the foot of the embankment and suddenly a great tongue of flame, roaring like a furnace, struck the gunpost. Had either Harry or Swanson been at the loopholes in the sandbags they would have been blinded or incinerated. As it was, the searing flame passed over them, setting fire to the sandbags both before and behind and filling the post with choking fumes.

For a moment all four coughing men were stunned by the narrowness of their escape. Then, realising their peril was not yet over, Swanson clamped a new drum on his Lewis while Harry searched around desperately for a weapon. Seeing Dunn's rifle with bayonet attached standing in one corner, he grabbed it just as a huge German appeared at the top of the parapet, the nozzle of the flame-thrower in his hand. Seeing the four occupants were still alive, he shouted for his team mate to release the pressurized oil again.

Expecting to be incinerated at any moment, Harry acted on pure instinct. Hurling himself forward, he thrust upwards with the bayonet with all his strength. He heard a scream but for an endless second the German stood poised above him, the sinister nozzle still in his hand and pointing downwards. Then, as Harry jerked the bayonet out for another thrust, the man tottered back, still gripping the nozzle. As his comrade gave a shout, Swanson opened fire and shot him. At the same moment the oil fired, jerking the nozzle from the bayoneted German's hands. As it kicked and jerked on the track, hurling out flame like some giant firecracker, the German's legs buckled and he rolled down the far side of the embankment.

No one muttered a word in the smoking gunpost. Sickened by fumes and oil, drained by an excess of emotion, men felt defeat was near if only because of the failure of their life force.

Had they known it, however, their trials were over for that day. The flame-throwers had spent the last of their fuel, a late afternoon breeze was dispelling the smoke, and counterattacks had secured the British line again. The seemingly frail defensive position had proven an insurmountable barrier to the Germans and it had been decided the cost in lives was no longer worth the effort.

The reason lay to the north and south. Here the fog had lasted most of the day, allowing the German offensive to roll on like a juggernaut. With most if not all the British trench defences taken, men were now fighting from ditches, piles of rubble, shell-holes, anything that could give protection to their exhausted bodies. Although no one could say anything with certainly, such was the confusion both in the field and in the British High Command, it was possible that the railway embankment along with the Flesquières Salient had been the only defence positions of the 5th Army to hold out that day.

The irony was that in spite of the resilience and courage shown by their defenders, staff officers with pencils in hand were already debating how far the 16th and its companion battalions should be drawn back to straighten the line. It was perhaps as well for their sanity as well as their morale that the exhausted defenders were as yet unaware of this.

Chapter 14

The shriek of agony, scraping the nerves like a knife across a plate, came again. As it sobbed away, Dunn cursed. 'Why doesn't the sod die and get it over?'

None of the other men in the gunpost answered him. Swanson gave him a warning look and shook his head. Turnor, who had winced at the sound, glanced at Harry who was sitting on an ammunition box at the rear of the gunpost. The starlight hid Harry's expression but although he was sitting motionless, something in his posture hinted at a man nearing the end of his self-control.

The scream came again as it had come for hours, shuddering the unnatural silence that had fallen over the front since darkness fell. It was as though the slaughter of the day had brought a sullen shame to friend and foe. Occasionally a shell would fall, a Very light rise, and a machine-gun give a nervous chatter. But in the main there was a brooding silence that the distant rumble of transports seemed to exaggerate rather than disturb. Death had brought its own silence and when men talked it was in hushed whispers as if they felt the dead were admonishing them for their crimes.

Yet shame had not brought compassion in its wake. British and German stretcher bearers alike who, in the time-honoured way, had gone out at night to search for the wounded, had been fired on and forced to retreat. Perhaps men's very shame, for which both sides believed the other responsible, was the cause, for those who believed themselves damned tend to commit further crimes in defiance of the gods who have condemned them.

Whatever the reason, the wounded had been left out to die and from the silence round the gunpost, it seemed that most had died. Except for one man whose intermittent shrieks of agony could be heard not only by British soldiers half a mile down the line but by the Germans also. They were screams and pleas of such intensity that men wondered how a human being could sustain such agony and remain alive.

The shrieks, the delirious babbling, and the cries for mother had begun before dusk and continued into the night. Hardened soldiers on both sides cursed, winced, or sucked in cigarette smoke. Stretcher bearers pleaded to try again but company commanders remained firm. The enemy had laid down the rules. He must now live or die with them.

To the infantry, however, there was no personal responsibility for the man's pain. He had been one of the many Germans who had stormed their lines that day and anyone's bullet might have wounded him. The situation was very different in Harry's gunpost as Chadwick discovered when he visited them after dusk had fallen. Soiled for once with mud and cordite fumes, he motioned to the four men to remain seated. 'You chaps have put up a fine show today. I'm mentioning all of you in dispatches.' Then he noticed the charred inside of the post and lifted his acetylene lamp to give a closer inspection. 'What the devil happened here?'

Harry made no reply. Seeing Chadwick's frown,

Swanson intervened quickly. 'We had a flame-thrower attack, sir. Thanks to the sergeant, we got away with it.'

Chadwick studied Harry for a moment, then turned back to Swanson. 'Tell me about it, Corporal.'

Swanson obeyed, for Harry's sake describing his bayonet thrust as briefly and clinically as possibly. When he finished Chadwick grimaced and turned to Harry. 'I agree. It does seem you saved your post, Miles. My congratulations.'

When Harry still did not reply, Swanson motioned apologetically at the embankment. 'We think the man that keeps screaming is our man, sir. He rolled down the embankment, so he's probably on the wire.'

Understanding crossed the young officer's handsome face. 'I see.' He glanced back at Harry. 'What's your problem, Miles? You're not feeling remorse, are you? After all, he did try to burn you all alive.'

Harry answered for the first time. 'He was only obeying his orders. Like the rest of us have to. So why don't they bring him in?'

Turnor added his own plea. 'Why don't they, sir? It's hellish sitting here listening to him.'

Chadwick glanced at him. 'We would, Turnor, but they've been firing on stretcher bearers so we've been given orders to leave them where they are. It's a pity but they've asked for it.'

Harry was showing disbelief. 'Are you saying we're going to leave him there until he dies?'

Chadwick shrugged regretfully. 'What choice do we have? We can't risk our men's lives for a dying German.'

Harry rose to his feet. 'That order applies only to stretcher bearers, doesn't it?'

'Yes. Why?' Then as Chadwick noticed Harry's expression, his tone changed. 'Oh, no, Miles. I'm not allowing any false heroics from you. You can put that right out of your mind.'

'But the wire's only a few yards from the embankment. If two of us went, it wouldn't take more than a few minutes to bring him up.'

Turnor added his own appeal. 'He's right, sir. I'd be willing to go with him.'

'Even though the man's on the wire, Turnor?'

'We could take wire cutters, sir.'

Chadwick shook his head. 'Sorry, Turnor. I respect your offer but I can't risk two of my men for a dying enemy. I wouldn't be doing my duty if I did.'

Harry's voice turned gritty with dislike. 'Sorry? Duty? For Christ's sake cut out the hypocrisy. Why not tell the truth and admit that you don't give a damn about the man's pain?'

Chadwick paused, then turned to face him. His voice gave nothing of his emotions away. 'I didn't hear that, Miles: not after all you've done today. When you calm down, you'll realise I've got no option.' Fishing into a pocket, he held out a flask of rum. When Harry ignored it, he offered it to Swanson. 'Here. Share this out! Things won't seem so bad when you've a few tots inside you.'

Turnor's persistence surprised himself as well as the others. 'But he's on the wire, sir! He's being crucified.'

Although Chadwick glanced at Turnor, Harry was only too aware whom he was really addressing. 'It's not the wire that's causing him all this pain, Turnor. It's much more likely that bayonet thrust into his belly.' Without a glance at Harry, who was standing as if turned to stone, he moved to the gunpost exit and turned. 'Put it into perspective. The man did try to incinerate you. If that still leaves any of you with chivalrous ideas about pulling him in, remember this. You're soldiers and heavily-outnumbered soldiers to boot. That means we can't afford to waste one of you on a man who's already as good as dead. That's how the balance sheet of war works out and the way I intend to keep it. Remember it because, as some of you know already, I can be a hard man when my orders are disobeyed.'

With that he turned and disappeared from the gun-post. A full five seconds passed before Swanson released his breath. 'I'll bet he can be hard too. But I suppose what he says makes sense.'

Another scream came at that moment, less piercing this time as if the German was weakening at last or giving up hope. Giving Swanson a look, Harry turned to Dunn. 'Those wire cutters we used earlier. Do we still have them?'

Dunn gave a start. 'You're not goin', Sarge? Not after what the major said?'

'The cutters,' Harry repeated. 'Do we have them?'

Dunn nodded and reached into a corner of the gun-post. As Harry took the cutters from him, Turnor caught his arm. 'You mustn't do it, Harry, Chadwick'll court-martial you.'

Mixed with his urgency, Harry was feeling a strange heady excitement. Pulling away from Turnor he moved to the rear sandbags and blackened his face with the charred fabric. 'None of you are to follow me, you understand? I don't want anyone hurt or getting into trouble with the major. Is that clear?'

Swanson was the first to answer. 'You'll never get him up that embankment on your own. He's a big, heavy man. You'll just get yourself killed trying.'

Harry moved to the exit. 'That's my business. You just remember my order. No one is to leave this post, no matter what happens.'

With that he slipped out. At the top of the

138

embankment he paused to gather his courage. Unlike the two previous nights, there was no mist. Clouds had drifted in during the afternoon and lifted the temperature above freezing point.

Somewhere along the line a nervous machine-gunner opened fire, bringing up in reply a cluster of star shells. Waiting until the alarm died, Harry edged himself on to the track.

The cinders, rustling beneath his body, sounded loud in the silence. As he reached the far side of the track, another star shell plopped in the sky nearby and made a charcoal sketch of the curving embankment. Dropping his head in his arms, he lay as motionless as his thudding heart would allow.

The flare sank down and darkness returned. Crawling forward again on his elbows, he turned his body round and went feet first down the embankment.

Although relatively high, the slope was not steep and he had no difficulty keeping his feet although bushes rustled and cold twigs scratched his face. For the moment the German's screams had ceased but Harry could hear his delirious voice coming from his right side and he worked his way in that direction.

He encountered his first dead body when halfway down, a mound that gave gruesomely under his feet. As he shifted to the right his feet struck a large metal canister and he knew the body belonged to the second *flammerwerfer* operator whom Swanson had shot.

Held precariously by a bush, the canister shifted beneath his feet and gave a metallic rattle. With more flares immediately soaring upwards, he had to freeze although he was lying awkwardly with his back against the embankment.

This time, however, he kept his eyes open and in the brilliant light he could see the glinting barbed wire of the barricade which had been erected at the far side of a ditch that ran along the foot of the embankment. Huddled bodies lay on both sides of it, the majority on its far side but many in or around the ditch: the remains of those who had penetrated the barricade only to die as they stormed the firing line itself.

The darkness returned, allowing Harry to slip to the foot of the slope. The uneasy silence had returned but he could hear no further cries from the German. Fearing the man might have died and knowing he had no chance of locating him in the darkness, he was compelled to wait.

A minute passed before he heard a single scream, followed by delirious mutterings. They came from the barricade and told Harry that Turnor was right: the wounded German had somehow crossed the ditch and reached the wire before he collapsed.

The ditch was wide and full of water. Unable to leap it because of the darkness and the noise he would make, Harry was compelled to lower himself into it, the icy water reaching up to his waist. Drawing himself up its muddy bank, he began his crawl towards the wire.

Forced to stop at intervals as star shells burst, it was another five minutes before he found the German. To his horror he discovered the man was literally impaled on the wire. Crazy with pain and despair, he must have thrown himself forward in an effort to break through and the barbs had sunk deep into his face, hands and legs. Without the reason left to extract the barbs, he had threshed about in his agony and driven them even deeper.

If Harry had felt before he must try to save the man, it became an obsession with him now. No matter that he must rise to his feet to do it, no matter that German night parties might be patrolling the far side of the wire, planting explosive charges or searching for ways through it, the thing had to be done or he felt he would never rest again.

He knew the darkness and the man's writhing would make it impossible for him to extract the barbs from his flesh. The best he could do would be to snip off the wire close to the wounds and leave the rest to the medics. With the decision made, he drew the wire cutters from his pocket, took a deep breath, and rose to his feet.

His presence seemed to excite the German's delirium and his wild threshing made the wire difficult to grip. It also dragged it across Harry's own face and hands. As he painfully snipped strand after strand he imagined the jangling sounds must be carrying to friend and foe alike. Nevertheless he believed he had cut the German free when a sudden line of star shells rose from the German trenches. Heart in his mouth, he did the only thing left to him and threw himself on the barbed wire alongside the German.

The barbs sank into his scalp, his face, into his arms and thighs but he knew he must not move. Trapped like an insect in a spider's web, waiting for a machine-gun or a sniper to maim or kill him, his mind took him back to his religious teaching at chapel when he was a child. To his young mind a crown of thorns had not seemed that cruel. Now, as the barbs raked him and blood ran down his face, he understood the true agony of that crucifixion.

With both men spreadeagled on the wire, the alarm this time seemed to last for minutes. More flares rose, machine-guns chattered spitefully at one another, and a few shells exploded before both sides decided no attack was forthcoming. Painfully withdrawing the barbs and wiping the blood from his eyes, Harry lowered the German as gently as possible to the ground.

The ordeal that followed was too intense to be

remembered in its entirety although certain details etched themselves on his mind for ever. There was the blood he felt on the German's coat, still oozing from the ghastly wound his bayonet had inflicted and which he could not staunch. There was the sight of the man's ashen face, the cruel barbs of wire protruding from his cheeks as if he were some creature put together in a mad scientist's laboratory. There was the icy, heart-bursting struggle to cross the ditch and haul the man's dead weight up its muddy bank. Most of all, he was to remember the screams that came from the tortured body as he tugged and heaved it forward.

To cross the gap between the ditch and the embankment he drew the man's arms over his shoulders and carried him bodily. He no longer took notice of star shells. To die would be a massive relief from the pain of bursting lungs and over-taxed muscles. As the wire still attached to the German's arms dragged across an eyebrow and almost blinded him, he felt a sudden hatred for the man and wanted nothing more but to fling him down and escape. Instead he tightened his grip and stumbled forward until the embankment rose before him.

It was then he felt defeat. Although the shallow declivity fell no more than twenty feet, no Himalayan mountain could have looked higher at that moment. With sweat dripping down his face, his lungs sobbing for air, and every muscle in his body trembling with fatigue, he knew he could never haul the heavy German to the top.

Yet the impulse that had driven him from the moment he had heard about the order to the stretcher bearers would not be defeated now. Sinking alongside the German, who had lost consciousness again, he took deep, sobbing breaths for the ordeal ahead. Then, whispering delirious words of encouragement to the inert man, he picked him up bodily and dug his feet into the soft earth.

He had climbed no more than six steps before he slipped and he and his burden rolled back down the slope. Thanking God the man was unconscious, he took his arms this time and, walking backwards, tried to drag the German after him. This time he managed eight steps before his legs buckled and both men tumbled down once more.

Seizing the man's arms, he dug his heels into the bank and tried again. Heaving, sobbing, cursing, he moved up inch by agonised inch. He no longer cared if flares were going up and he was caught in their light. The stars bursting behind his eyes were far bigger and brighter. His stomach retched with the strain and vomit poured from his mouth but still he hung on to his burden. The demon that had taken such a vice-like grip on his mind was merciless. The German must be rescued or he must die trying to save him.

By now he had lost all sense of time and place. He knew only the promptings of an agonised body that screamed for the mercy of oblivion. Yet he did not release his grip of the German even when urgent rescuers, scrambling down the bank, tried to take his burden from him. Somewhere on the fringe of his consciousness he heard a slap like a stick hitting a sandbag and a gasp of pain, but none of it made any sense to him. It was not until he was lying on the floor of the gunpost that the demon in his mind released its grip and allowed him to sink at last into oblivion.

Chapter 15

The rising dawn wind was penetrating the shrunken planks and sending icy draughts round the old hut. It flickered the flame of the paraffin lamp and made the shadows of Chadwick and Harry dance grotesquely on the bare walls. The officer was seated on a shell case. Harry, whose scalp and hands were heavily bandaged, was standing to attention. 'You wanted to see me, sir?'

Chadwick sounded dangerously calm. 'Yes. You can stand at ease, Sergeant.'

'Thank you, sir.'

Chadwick lit a cigarette. His eyes were held by Harry's face. Although ravaged by exhaustion, with deep cuts and scratches down both cheeks, it was not the face of a man concerned about an act of insubordination. Instead it suggested a man relieved of an intolerable burden.

Chadwick exhaled smoke. 'You look pleased with yourself, Miles. Are you?'

'No, sir. Not pleased. Only relieved.'

Chadwick's brows came together. 'Relieved? What the hell does that mean?'

'I've found something out, sir. I know now why I had to come back to France.'

Chadwick's frown deepened. 'What are you talking about, Miles?'

Harry's eyes lowered to his face. 'Haven't you guessed?'

Chadwick gave a sudden start. Then a small vein appeared above one temple of his handsome face. 'Are you saying to me that your rescuing that German proves something?'

'It does to me. Doesn't it to you?'

The officer's eyes reflected an unfamiliar emotion. Then, under tight control again, he leaned forward. 'It proves only one thing, Miles. That in spite of everything else, you're still an undisciplined soldier. You not only disobeyed my orders tonight, you also lost one of your men. Do you know about that?'

'Yes, I've heard. A sniper got Turnor in the leg. But they say it's only a blighty wound.'

'It's one man fewer to hold back the Jerries, damn you.'

'That's true. He shouldn't have tried to help me.' Harry paused a second and then went on: 'At the same time I think he was right to do it. I think they all were.'

The officer's look of dislike intensified. 'You think it was right to risk four lives over an enemy who is almost certain to die?'

'Yes, I do. We've been fighting and killing one another for four years and by this time I don't think any of us know why. They're in grey and we're in khaki and that's supposed to be enough. But tonight it was just another fellow human being who needed help and I think all my men felt it.'

Chadwick lifted an eyebrow. 'So you were making a point against war? A religious one, perhaps? I thought you'd got over that claptrap long ago.'

'I wasn't conscious I was making any point. I doubt if the others were either.'

145

The mocking voice became malicious. 'Then perhaps it was to make amends for those two German flame-throwers you shot in cold blood last year. Have you considered that?'

Harry winced. 'Perhaps it was. Who can say?'

Chadwick's expression suddenly hardened. 'By God, Miles, if you think you can play out your acts of repentance under my command, you'd better think again. You do realise I can have you shot for disobeying my order tonight?'

'I know that,' Harry said. 'Just as you had Gareth Evans shot.'

Chadwick's gaze moved over him. 'You've never forgiven me for that, have you?'

'No, and I never will. He was a scared kid and you killed him for it.'

'He showed cowardice in the face of the enemy, Miles. Any officer would have done what I did. Otherwise our Army would disintegrate.'

'Only you and I knew what happened. You could have covered for him if you'd wanted to.' For a moment Harry's dislike of the man spilled over. 'But not you. Not the perfect soldier who always does his duty.'

Chadwick laughed. 'You hate me for that, don't you. Miles? You're still the Socialist who wants to tear society to bits and create God knows what kind of shambles from the pieces.'

'You don't know anything about Socialism, sir. So if I were you I wouldn't make a fool of myself.'

His contempt made Chadwick flush with anger. 'I know how bloody ridiculous your Brotherhood of Man philosophy is. Men don't fight for equality, Miles, at least not after they've climbed up the ladder themselves. They fight for land, for money, for power, for women, for anything but the other man's welfare. They enjoy

146

their aggression and their rivalries just as they enjoy the thrill of the hunt. Why can't you accept the inevitable and live with it?'

It was all coming out now, Harry thought. The admissions, the accusations, the baring of souls. '*You* don't just accept it, Chadwick. You revel in it.'

Chadwick laughed again. 'What if I do? It's good for my country. It makes me a better leader in peacetime and a better officer in war. So who's the loser?'

'That man on the wire was a loser. So is every kid with T.B. and every miner with lung damage. It's never occured to you that a man's strength should be used to pick people up from the mud, not ram them back into it, has it?'

Chadwick's expression showed he believed he had won back the initiative. 'Don't try to fool me, Miles. When you first came under my command I thought I was getting a conscientious objector who hadn't the courage to be one. But not after our first engagement. I saw then that you were one of us. You found combat the most exciting experience of your life. You came alive over here. Don't look like that and pretend you fought and killed out of necessity. It wasn't necessary to kill those two Jerry flame-throwers. But you killed them just the same, something even I wouldn't have done.'

Harry nodded. 'You're right. I did believe I was one of you. That's why I didn't want to go home. And when I got home, it was the reason I wanted to come back. I didn't know it then but I had to find out the truth about myself.'

At that moment there was a knock on the ramshackle door and a mud-stained private appeared. Giving Chadwick a salute, he handed him a slip of paper. 'From Colonel Wilson, sir. He says it came from Brigade and it's urgent.'

147

As the soldier saluted and withdrew, Chadwick opened the paper. Giving a sardonic laugh, he glanced back at Harry. 'Believe it or not, they're moving us back again.'

Harry shrugged. 'Why not? It's a mad war.'

Chadwick studied him as he slipped the paper into a pocket of his greatcoat. 'We've still a minute left, Miles. You were saying you had to find out the truth about yourself. Are you telling me you found out that truth tonight?'

'Yes, I did.'

'And that was why you disobeyed my order?'

'I don't know that. It wasn't in my mind at the time. But now it's done, you can't believe the weight that's fallen from my back.'

'You're making this up, aren't you? It's too preposterous otherwise.'

'It might be preposterous to you, Chadwick, but not to me. I've disliked your kind all my life. You're supposed to be well educated but you're the least enlightened men I know. You judge men by the ties and suits they wear, not by their words and their beliefs. You've lost the one thing that makes men fit to rule this world – compassion. You're physically brave but you're moral cowards. And your standards disgust me. My father called you anti-life men, killing for sport and working men to death in your enterprises. No man has ever been more right.'

There was a pallor now behind Chadwick's bronzed cheeks. 'You hate me because you know how alike we are, Miles. The only difference between us is that I was born with wealth and you weren't, which has made you Bolshevik-minded. But temperamentally we could be brothers.'

Harry shook his head. 'Once that would have worried me, Chadwick, but not any longer. I'm free of you now.

But I'm grateful for one thing. You brought me back so that I could find out the difference. So I thank you for that.'

A shell went over the hut like an express train, to burst in a heavy rumble that sent the paraffin flame dancing. When silence returned Chadwick had regained his composure although his voice was hoarse as his eyes fixed on Harry again. 'You're not free of me, Miles. Don't think that for a moment. I can have you punished whenever it suits me but at the moment we need every man we've got. So you'll be under open arrest until things quieten down and I decide what to do with you. Now rejoin your men and prepare to move back.'

Harry nodded and came to attention. Returning his salute, Chadwick watched him until he disappeared from the hut, then cursed and reached into a pocket for his cigarettes. As he lifted one to his lips he noticed his hands were shaking and cursed again.

Chapter 16

The Front was still quiet when Harry arrived back at this post. He shook his head at Swanson's anxious question. 'No I'm to carry on for the moment. Under open arrest, of course.'

Swanson gave a whistle of surprise. 'I thought you were for the big drop. Particularly after Turnor was hit.'

Harry's face tightened. 'I ordered you all not to help me.'

Swanson glanced at Dunn. 'You'd never have made it on your own. You were all in when we reached you.' When Harry made no reply, he went on: 'Anyway, Turnor's happy enough. He was grinning all over his face when they carried him away. It's only a blighty wound, so he'll be able to spend a few weeks with his wife again. You couldn't have done him a bigger favour.'

'What about the German?' Harry asked.

Swanson grimaced. 'Christ, he was in a mess, wasn't he? I don't know how he'd lasted so long.'

'Did the stretcher bearers give him a chance?'

'Not from their faces.' Then, noticing Harry's expression, Swanson went on quickly: 'But you can't say, can you? Some men can survive anything. If he does live, I hope he invites you over for a holiday after the war. You did a hell of a job getting him out.'

Harry turned away. 'Talking about getting out, we're on our way again. The orders reached Chadwick just before I left.'

Dunn's string of obscenities brought a yell for silence from somewhere down the firing line. Swanson's voice turned hoarse. 'They're going to pull us back? After we held out all day? For Christ's sake why?'

'Jerry must have broken through north or south of here. They can't leave us or we'd be exposed.'

Dunn's obscenities, only a decibel lower, came again. Harry motioned him to be quiet. 'It's no use belly-aching. I want you both ready to leave as soon as Chadwick gives the word.'

Dunn's disgust was not confined to the gunpost. All along the line tempers flared as men who had fought all day to keep their defences intact were ordered to quit them without another shot being fired. A few were kept back to make the enemy believe the line was still manned, the rest were formed into groups and with the strictest orders to keep noise down to the minimum began another weary march westward. Harry's team, made up to full strength again by a brawny youngster named Apps who carried the Vicker's 35 pound tripod as if it were a paperweight, was among those ordered back, and even Dunn's obscenities were silenced as they slithered and slipped in the darkness. Until the order had arrived the battalion's morale had been high, for had they not held out against everything Jerry could throw at them? Now, retreating for no reason apparent to them, morale plummeted and men either cursed their officers or trudged on in silence, an even worse sign of dejection.

Had they known it, the situation was even more serious than the orders suggested. To the north the ferocity of the offensive had eaten deeply into the Battle Zone of the British 3rd Army but had at least been halted by

151

that Army's reserve battalions on the last line of that zone, a situation critical enough in all consequence. To the south, however, the situation was much worse. Forced to withdraw behind the Crozat Canal during the night, the British 5th Army had found its front extended by five miles and because of the heavy casualties it had suffered, in particular its losses of heavy and light machine-guns, the line had been too thinly held for the ferocious attacks the Germans had made on it that second day. By nightfall the situation was desperate with the entire Southern Battle Zone of the 5th Army lost and breeches already punched into the makeshift line that had been formed behind it, breeches ready to be exploited by the enemy when he renewed his offensive the following day.

There was no rest for the British even though most of the men had not slept for forty-eight hours. Unwashed, filthy with mud and dried sweat, with feet half-frozen in soaked boots, they spent most of the night digging trenches and piling up sandbags to give themselves a modicum of protection. When allowed to rest at last, soldiers sank down where they had stood and in the darkness it was impossible to tell which of the dark mounds were men and which were upturned earth.

But men were not allowed long to escape in dreams. The grey impatient hordes were only waiting for the dawn and the horizon had barely lightened before another massive bombardment rained down on the defenders. Flesh cringing, weary men stood by, knowing the Storm-Troops must soon be launched at them again. But before they came, just as the red sun had cleared the horizon, enemy aircraft came swooping down to attack them. To men unused to air attack, it was an ordeal as unnerving as anything they had experienced, and they had barely recovered from the shock when the Storm-

Troops came running at them again with stick grenades, light machine-guns, and flame-throwers. Full of élan in spite of their earlier losses, the Germans drove straight at the holes punched through the British lines the previous day and the outnumbered defenders could do little to stop them. Reeling back from their makeshift trenches, they took cover in shell holes, ruins, anything above or below ground that could offer a man a chance to continue his defiance.

The scene then on the third day of the offensive resembled a sandbar being eaten away by the incoming tide, although the progress of the tide was not uniform along the entire front. Some sectors, in particular the Flesquières Salient – which was the pivot on which the British retreat was swinging – held out all day. Many smaller posts also held out, although at appalling cost to their defenders. Battalions were cut down to companies, companies down to platoons. In many cases entire British battalions ceased to exist.

A further casualty was the British communications system. With the runnels of the tide eating everywhere, officers had no way of learning what was happening north and south of their positions, whether they should retreat or hold fast. In the absence of orders, many chose to hold their ground, only for their hearts to sink when they saw the contact flares of the Storm-Troops arching into the sky behind them.

Fortunately for their morale, the 16th and its companion battalions had no knowledge of the carnage and confusion north and south of them. Their withdrawal told them the divisions on both their flanks must have been forced back but after their own dogged resistance the previous day it seemed reasonable to assume the rest of the 5th Army was conducting a retreat as orderly as their own.

The true seriousness of the British position only became clear after another day of bloody fighting when messages reached the 16th HQ. Isolated by the German successes on both of their flanks, the six battalions of the Royal Naval division who had defended the Flesquières Salient so valiantly had been forced to evacuate at last. Up to today the Germans had bent back to breaking point the two ends of the British bow but the handgrip had remained fast. Now their immense pressure had succeeded in prying away that tenacious hand and the entire bow was recoiling. If they could maintain their offensive now, they could surely drive the British armies into the sea.

The two-seater biplane with RFC roundels came diving down over the ruined village. As it levelled off less than a hundred feet above ground, a man waved a gloved hand from its rear cockpit and dropped a weighted bag. British soldiers waved back and one of them, crouching low against snipers, ran out to retrieve it.

The plane circled until the message was picked up, then began to climb. It was still within sight of the troops below when two German scout planes dropped on it like hawks out of the sun. There was a rattle of machine gun fire and a thread of smoke began to trail from the two-seater's engines. As the two German aircraft went in for the kill, a cheer rose from the watching infantrymen as three French planes appeared and forced the Germans to break off their attack.

For half a minute, while the two-seater made its escape, the five scout planes wheeled and circled over the village. Then, in the way a pub brawl sucks in spectators, the sky became full of aircraft as more Allied and German fighters piled into the fight: the clash of titans in the spring of 1918 was by no means confined to the ground forces. The two-seater, the original cause of the conflict, sank down out of sight of the infantry.

The weighted bag had fallen on the eastern outskirts of the village, close to the ruins of a mill that Chadwick had chosen for one of his Vickers gunposts. His second post, sited in the ruins of a cottage, could be seen a hundred and fifty yards to the right. Manned by Harry and his team, it stood alongside a shell-torn road that led up a shallow hill.

Seeing the soldier pick up the bag, Chadwick nudged the young lieutenant alongside him. 'Go and get that message! Quickly!'

Dartford, whose haggard young face betrayed his disillusionment with war, hesitated. 'Shouldn't it go to the Battalion Commander, sir?'

'Which one?' Chadwick said sarcastically. 'They've hardly a company between the lot of them. Go and get it for me! Only watch out for snipers.'

Dartford climbed gingerly over a shattered wall, bent double, and ran towards the soldier. Chadwick saw the soldier hesitate, then hand the bag over. As Dartford began sprinting back and passed a wall, Chadwick saw a splash of brick dust as a sniper's bullet just missed the young lieutenant.

Panting hard, Dartford handed over the bag. His voice was curious as Chadwick pulled out its contents and read them. 'What does it say, sir?'

Chadwick pushed the message back into the bag and handed it to him. 'Take it to the HQ dugout. I'll be back in a few minutes.' Before Dartford could reply, he vaulted over the wall and began running through the rubble towards the second gunpost. As a sniper's bullet zipped past him, he jumped down into one of the sewers that the survivors of the 16th and its companion battalions were manning. Pushing past weary, unshaven men,

155

he worked his way towards Harry's outpost. Reaching the end of the sewer system, he had to climb out into the open and sprint the last thirty yards. Motioning to the machine-gun crew to stay at their posts, he sank down on an ammunition box.

'You all saw that observation plane of ours just now?' When the men nodded, he went on: 'It dropped a report saying a large concentration of troops along with a few tanks is moving towards us. So we can probably expect an attack some time today. You all know what your orders are?'

The unshaven faces of the four men betrayed their feelings although all of them jerked their heads again. The Order of the Day, straight from the British Commander-in-Chief himself, Douglas Haig, had been read out to all men that morning. *Every position must be held to the last man. There must be no retirement. With our backs to the wall and believing in the justice of our cause, each one must fight on to the end. The safety of our homes and the freedom of mankind alike depend upon the conduct of each one of us at this critical moment.*

The stirring words had been seized on avidly by the British Press and public spirit had soared both at home and in base areas in France. However, the ones called on to do the standing and the dying, the poor bloody infantry, were considerably less enthusiastic. More than one junior officer had blushed with shame when reading out the exhortation and for once even Chadwick had made no effort to quell the obscene and bitter comments from his men.

Nevertheless the situation was as serious as the words suggested. Not only had Gough's 5th Army almost ceased to exist but the 3rd Army had been driven back almost to Albert, nearly twenty-five miles behind the front line that had existed on 21st March. In three weeks the German offensive had gained more territory on the Western Front than the Allies had won in three years of fighting.

But the weariness of the troops on both sides was immense. The British and the few French divisions who had been sent up from the south to assist them had taken a terrible mauling. Some men, driven out of their minds by the horror of it all, had been seen to pull off their gasmasks when lethal shells were bursting around them to end their misery. Others, tottering about like drunken men, had been impossible to awaken once they collapsed. The rest, by some miracle of the human spirit, had fought, retreated, turned and fought again while their friends had perished in a dozen ghastly ways around them. Some of these survivors no longer felt fear. To be afraid a man has to be alive and many men looked and felt like automatons.

However, they were not alone in their weariness. The Germans had been making massive efforts since the offensive began and the strain was telling on them too. Their logistics were another increasing problem, for their systematic destruction of the land the previous year had included wellheads and streams and they were now paying a heavy price for their scorched earth policy.

Nevertheless, since the 21st March they had been the victors almost everywhere and so it was easy for their officers to convince them that if they made one last effort the British would crack, the naval blockade would be lifted, and the privations of their families back in the Fatherland would be over.

The situation, then, along the entire northern front rested on a knife edge. Could the exhausted Allied infantry, ordered to stand or die, hold back the onslaught at last, or could the Germans, also weary and growing short of supplies, make the final breakthrough that would bring the British defences from the Channel to the Oise collapsing like a house of cards? History was in the making that day.

Chadwick appeared to have no doubts as he chatted to the four men. Although now as muddy as they were, he was still the schoolboy idol in his behaviour. 'We'll stop them this time, chaps. Intelligence says they're running out of steam: in fact, they were seen looting in some villages up north. We'll push them back and then we'll keep that date in Berlin.'

Swanson took an apprehensive look at the shallow hillside ahead that hid all signs of enemy preparations. 'Have you any idea how many tanks they'll be throwing at us, sir?'

'No, I haven't,' Chadwick told him. 'But the message said only a few, so we'll have to take it at face value. I wouldn't think more than half a dozen. That's the way they seem to be using them at the moment.'

Before Swanson could reply, Chadwick indicated the *pavé* road, then turned to Harry. 'I've sited us near the roads because if they come in a rush again, they'll probably use them. Otherwise the shell holes will slow them down. If I'm correct, we'll both have a clear field of fire. All right?'

When no one replied, Chadwick moved to the back of the post and prepared to make his dash for cover. Harry, moving to his side, checked him. 'I'd like a private word with you, sir.'

Chadwick glanced back at the watching men. 'Private?'

Harry led him behind a second broken wall of the one-time cottage. 'We're safe from snipers here.'

Chadwick nodded and eyed him curiously. 'What do you want?'

Harry jerked a thumb at the men back in the gunpost.

158

'I want to ask a favour. I'd like my men taken out and given cover back in the village.' He went on before Chadwick could interrupt: 'I can handle the Vickers on my own.'

Chadwick looked amused. 'You can't be serious.'

Harry pointed at the *pavé* road ahead. 'You said yourself they'll probably come down that road. If they come in sufficient numbers, we'll never throw them back. Whereas back in the village the men will have a chance.'

'We did draw lots who should have this post,' Chadwick reminded him.

'I know that and I'm not complaining. But I don't see why my men should be exposed like this.'

'They're soldiers, Miles, and are expected to play their part. Have you forgotten the Order of the Day?'

'Sod the Order of the Day, Chadwick! We've all given as much as we can, so why do we need an insult like that? How many thousands of men have those stupid bastards to kill before they learn from their mistakes?'

There was an element in Chadwick's smile that Harry could not place for a moment. Then, as the officer answered him, he realised it was triumph. 'What's brought about this self-sacrificial gesture, Miles? Have you heard about Turnor too?'

Harry gave a start. 'What about Turnor?'

'I got the news this morning. It seems he died on his way to the field hospital. The sniper's bullet must have nicked an artery. Anyway, it burst and he was dead before they could stem the flow of blood.'

Harry felt as if he had been struck in the stomach. It was a full five seconds before he could speak. 'What about the German?'

Chadwick shrugged. 'No one knows about him, although he probably died too. You see now what your insubordination did, Miles. It cost Turnor his life and leaves his wife a lonely widow.' As Harry's cheeks paled further, Chadwick nodded. 'Yes, I know about Turnor's problem with her. You forget I have to censor your letters.'

Pulling himself together, Harry made his last appeal. 'Then leave Swanson with me and let Dunn and Apps go back into the village. Even if you have to make a stand there, they'll have a better chance than in this gunpost. It won't weaken us here, I promise you.'

Chadwick smiled again. 'You're not going to wash away your sins that easily, Miles. This gunpost's a key point and it'll remain fully manned. Sorry, but that's how things are.'

'You never change, do you?' Harry said. 'In the middle of this slaughterhouse you can't find room for a little compassion.'

Chadwick pushed himself away from the protecting wall, moved to the rear of the post, then turned. 'You know, Miles, on reflection I think there is a difference between us but it isn't one that worries me. Sentimentality isn't a strength. It's a weakness that can harm others as you've just found out to your cost. The world belongs to the strong, Miles. It always has and it always will.'

'And that's the world you want?' Harry asked bitterly.

Chadwick gave a laugh as he prepared to leap over the rear wall and run for the cover of the sewers. 'It's the world we've got, Miles. And I don't know of another, do you?'

The attack began forty minutes later, from a source no one expected. Suddenly the air was filled with German aircraft flying at zero height and strafing everything in their path. In an effort to keep the Allies in the dark about his armies' movements, Ludendorff had drafted in as many of his *jastas* as could be spared and they were being used that morning to soften up the defenders before the main attack was launched. In terms of firepower, their efforts were puny beside the massive war machines available to their ground forces but because they could fire downwards into the trenches and sewers, their harassment value was considerable. For five minutes the air seethed with bullets as the aircraft flew up and down firing their machine-guns while cursing infantry fired back with rifles and Lewis guns.

Harry's gunpost was a target singled out and plane after plane came diving on it. But with Harry and Swanson standing their ground and firing back, most of them veered off and only one burst of bullets entered the post and ricocheted with wild screams off the broken walls. As the aircraft, running low on ammunition, responded to a Very light from their leader and followed him eastwards, Dunn, whose phlegm had been disturbed by the unusual form of attack, found obscenities to hurl after them that even on his terms were excessive.

Shrill whistles a moment later explained the reason for the attack. Under its cover German troops had surmounted the hill and now began pouring down towards the village. As the defenders opened fire, shrapnel, mortar and smoke shells began falling among them.

The slaughter began again. Grey-clad figures came swirling out of the smoke, to be cut down by rifle and machine-gun fire. Men shouted orders, yelled to give themselves courage, screamed as they were hit. A few, succumbing to that terrifying battlefield phenomenon known as battle ecstasy, hurled themselves at the murderous guns as sexually-aroused men will clutch a desirable woman.

Harry, swinging the heavy Vickers backwards and

161

forth, found his thoughts turning feverish as the slaughter went on. How many men had he killed this far in the war? A hundred? Five hundred? A thousand? What had been the question he had sobbed out to Nicole after his first engagement? Would the men he had killed be waiting for him when his time came to die? If he had been afraid then, how much more should he be afraid now? The dead in their hundreds, waiting for their revenge. . . . In that moment of delirium he found the thought terrifying.

A cry from Swanson drew his attention to the hilltop where the sinister shapes of tanks were rising. Certain they would not be repulsed again and that his end was near, he turned his cordite-stained face and shouted at the three men crouched alongside him. 'If one breaks through, get out of here! Never mind that order. Just go!'

Although the tanks could only move at a walking pace, their very slowness added to their menace. A further threat was the protection they offered to the Storm-Troops who were advancing behind them. Once again Harry's thoughts turned feverish as he saw his bullets sparking off the tanks' armour. Was Chadwick right after all? There was little pity in nature. The weak chick was soon hurled from its nest. The jackal sought the newly-born. The lion did not run past the lamb. Did not this war prove the same pitiless rules applied to men? Those advancing monsters, made by man himself, knew nothing of compassion or courage. Their steel tracks would crush into the rubbish tip of memory every self-sacrificial act and valiant deed done in their path.

Was he, then, being punished for breaking the natural order of things? There was no denying that his act of disobedience had caused the death of a comrade and left a lonely woman broken-hearted.

The leading tank was seventy yards from Harry's post now, its tracks splintering the *pavé* stones. Watching it, brave men felt their blood run cold. Tanks did not kill with shells and bullets. They ground their tracks into shelters and burst open men's bodies.

Shells were now exploding round the tanks as the British field artillery sought their range. In the gunpost to Harry's left, Chadwick, unthreatened by the armour, had ordered his crews to pour flanking fire on the troops advancing behind them. But the smoke made sighting difficult and more Storm-Troops were advancing behind the armoured screen.

As the vectors remorselessly decreased, Harry knew his premonition was right. Even if the guns succeeded in stopping the tanks, there were now enough Storm-Troops forward to swamp the gunpost. He felt no fear, only intense regret. For a while he had found peace of mind after rescuing the German from the barbed wire. Now, after the news of Turnor's death, that peace had gone. His only achievement in returning to France had been to provide the gloating Moloch and Mars with yet more sacrificial pawns when the gods were already sated by the offerings showered on them. In addition to that he had condemned Mary and Elizabeth to the mercy of Ethel.

The memory of his wife and daughter brought a pain so sharp he thought for a moment he was wounded. He would never see them again, nor would he see his unborn child that Mary had told him about in a recent letter. In the remaining few seconds left, he realised the true extent of his loss. Had his religious faith remained intact, he could have believed only time would separate them and their reunion. Now, with his faith destroyed, that time would be all eternity. A sob broke from him and in the darkness of his despair he fired and fired again at the advancing grey-clad figures, every bullet an act of bitterness against those who would soon destroy his future and his salvation.

The foremost tank received a direct hit from an eighteen pounder and burst into flames. But its destruction came too late to save the gunpost. Storm-Troops were near enough and plentiful enough to silence its cursed guns. As they ran towards it they began fixing their bayonets. Machine-gunners were hated by both sides and mercy was seldom shown to them.

Harry was shouting for his men to withdraw as he hosed the Vickers back and forth. He never knew if they would have obeyed him because as bullets sliced into the sandbags and stick grenades sailed over the shattered walls, Dunn sagged down with a bullet through his head and Apps began to die from a severed arm. Apart from Harry, only Swanson was still in action and his Lewis ceased firing when a shell from the second tank hurled a shower of bricks over him. As he lay half-buried beneath the rubble, a stick grenade exploded in front of the Vickers gun, blasting in the protecting wall and hurling Harry to the ground. As he lay there half-stunned, a huge German leapt over the rubble. Maddened by fear and the death of friends, the man glared round the post and saw that Harry was still alive. Shouting an oath in German, he drew back his bayonet and ran forward.

The fall of Harry's gunpost was witnessed from Chadwick's position which at that moment was not under attack. Seeing Germans swarming towards it, Chadwick had taken command of the Vickers himself and done his best to ease the pressure. But there was no stopping the enemy onslaught and as Chadwick's ammunition belt ran out he saw enemy infantrymen, some of them with fixed bayonets, about to leap into the gunpost. Yelling for his Number One to re-load, Chadwick turned back, only to find that drifting smoke hid the scene from him.

Alongside him Dartford was showing distress. 'It's over, sir. They've taken the post.'

Chadwick cursed. 'Shut up, you fool, and keep up your covering fire.'

Dartford, who had never seen Chadwick disturbed before, turned to his Lewis gunner but the man shook his head. Smoke had totally hidden the other gunpost now and friend was indistinguishable from foe. Dartford glanced at Chadwick again. 'They held their ground, sir. Right to the end.'

Chadwick cursed again. 'What did you expect? Whatever else he might have been, Miles was a brave man.'

'What will happen about his charge, Major? Will it still go on his records?'

At that moment the Vickers Number One slammed down the breech cover of the gun and slapped the officer's arm. Chadwick's reply as he sank down again behind the Vickers was a mixture of regret and irritation. 'No, of course it won't. If he's dead, his account's closed. Now get back to your duties or we'll be the next to go.'

The battle raged all day the full length of the British line. In places the line bulged but nowhere did it break. The massive tide had run its course and from that day, although a few waves still washed against the seawalls, Ludendorff knew that his great offensive had failed.

There were a number of reasons. One was the law of diminishing returns that had bedevilled both sides throughout the war. With every advance made over shell-cratered ground that left roads and supply lines behind, logistic problems had grown in inverse proportion to the attacker's success while the reverse became true of the defenders who were driven nearer to their supplies and reserves. Another factor not taken into account by the German High Command had been the poverty of its infantry. Not a poverty of numbers or courage, for the grey-clad soldiers had fought with immense élan. But as the British naval blockade had tightened its grip, German soldiers and civilians alike had been denied luxuries of every kind and during their advance soldiers had encountered houses and farms stocked with food, wine, and items that to many were only a memory. As a consequence some men had broken off their duties to loot and drink and in some sectors this had affected their combat efficiency.

But this was a relatively unimportant factor beside the one Ludendorff had feared the most: the stubbornness in adversity of the British infantryman. Through their long history British troops had grumbled about their lot with an enthusiasm that had often made their Allies fear for their dependability. But as always when the call had come, some deep-rooted, almost atavistic instinct of defiance had astonished both friend and foe. It had happened at Crecy, at Agincourt, at Waterloo and now it had happened here. Outnumbered and outgunned, they had dug in their heels and fought doggedly for every inch of Allied soil until their resistance had finally exhausted their enemy. The irresistible had finally given ground to the immovable and although exhausted soldiers, who knew there were many battles to be fought yet, dared not voice the thought, a feeling began to creep into numbed minds that perhaps the mighty German war machine had reached its high watermark at last.

But the cost had still to be counted and during that week and those that followed, the dreaded brown envelopes began arriving at thousands of homes. Women turned pale, broke down, or walked away in numbed

166

silence. Others, facing a future of loneliness and impoverishment, either cursed the politicians who had sent their men to war or decided in silent grief that their lives had lost all shape and meaning for ever.

One of the latter was Turnor's wife, a pretty young woman who looked as if her own life had been snatched away as she gazed down at the telegram.

Others, like Mary, behaved differently. As if she had been expecting the news all along, she stood gazing at the piece of paper and into the future from which all love and happiness seemed to have been stolen. In the silence that falls on a mind numbed with grief, she heard Ethel calling from upstairs to ask if any mail had come for her. Rousing herself as the woman called again, Mary moved towards the staircase and prepared to give her mother the news.

Part 2

Chapter 17

The tea-room was almost empty when Mary entered it. Choosing a table near the window, she shook her head at the young waitress who approached her. 'I'll order later, thank you. I'm expecting someone.'

As the girl nodded and withdrew, Mary gazed through the window. Across the road a queue was forming outside a bread shop. Although it was a bright spring morning, there was little conversation among the women as they shuffled forward. The war had taken its toll of human spirit on the Home Front as well as on the battlefields, and although the German offensive had been held, few women could see an end to the years of misery and heartbreak.

The sunlight dipped for a moment and Mary saw herself mirrored in the glass, an elegant figure wearing a wide-brimmed hat and a calf-length black coat trimmed with Persian lamb. The expensive coat, which would eventually serve to hide her pregnancy as well as a garment of mourning if the need arose, was a present from Ethel. Although she had given the impression it was a gift of sympathy, at times Mary had wondered how much rejoicing lay behind it. The days of her daughter's attachment to a Socialist and a man below her station might well be over. Freed from his seditious influence

Mary might, in spite of the encumbrances of children, still find a husband whom Ethel could introduce with pride to her friends.

The sunlight returned and Mary saw the eyes of the women opposite turning on a young Army officer who had just stepped out of a taxi. Tall and handsome, wearing an immaculate uniform complete with ribbons for gallantry, leather cavalry boots and carrying a blackthorn cane, he was enough to draw the eyes of any woman. To complete the picture of the perfect war hero, he had a pronounced limp which he was clearly doing his best to disguise. As he passed the whispering women, one of the younger ones said something that made him smile. Lifting his cane in acknowledgement, he turned and crossed the road.

Mary's heart was beating hard as she waited. Feeling now that the tea-room meeting had the undertones of an assignation, she found herself wishing that she had invited Chadwick to No. 57. Yet with Ethel fully acquainted with his aristocratic background, it had seemed unlikely she would have given Mary much opportunity for a private talk with him there.

The doorbell rang as Chadwick entered. As he paused to glance round, women at the tables ceased their chattering to look at him. Catching sight of Mary, he limped towards her. 'Mrs. Miles?'

When she nodded, he lifted his cane in a salute. 'Good morning! How good of you to come. May I sit down?'

Her heart was hammering so hard now she felt breathless. 'Yes, of course.'

He lowered himself into the chair opposite her, leaving his right leg stretched out alongside the small table. He gave her a humorous grimace. 'Sorry about that. But it doesn't bend too well yet.'

As she had feared, words were difficult to find. 'Does it hurt you?'

172

He smiled at her question. 'No, not now. I'll be as right as rain in a few more weeks.'

At that moment the waitress returned to the table. No older than sixteen, too young for military service, she looked full of hero worship. 'What can I get you, sir?'

Chadwick glanced at Mary. 'Tea and scones? Or muffins?'

'Only tea, thank you.'

'We'll have scones too,' he told the girl. 'Have you any cream?'

The girl hesitated. 'Not really, sir. But. . . .'

'But what?' he smiled.

She lowered her voice conspiratorially. 'I think we might find you a little, sir. I'll speak to the manager if you like.'

'You will? That's very kind. Try to scape up a little jam for us too, will you?'

The girl smiled back. 'Yes, sir. I'll do me best.'

As she tripped away, as dazzled as if she had spoken to the King himself, Chadwick turned back to Mary. 'I'd have come to see you earlier if it hadn't been for this confounded leg. But they only allowed me out of hospital last weekend.'

She nodded jerkily. 'Yes. I gathered that from your letter. It's really very good of you to come so soon.'

'Nonsense. Your husband was one of my men. It's the least I can do.'

She winced at his use of the past tense. Although one part of her needed to know what had happened to Harry in case she could find hope in it, another part was terrified in case the truth left her in despair.

His eyes were moving over her. Although he had remembered from their one encounter that she was attractive, he had forgotten the details of her appearance. Now, with maturity adding character to her face,

173

he saw she was a beautiful woman with soft skin, full lips and long golden hair. Her grief was still apparent but seemed to heighten rather than diminish the appeal of her expressive eyes. He slid a hand into his tunic pocket and drew out a gold cigarette case. 'Would you think me rude if I asked permission to smoke?'

For the first time she realised that he too was feeling embarrassed. 'No, of course not. Please do.' She shook her head when he held out the case. 'No. I don't smoke myself.'

He clicked a lighter and drew in smoke. 'It's one of those nasty habits one acquires in the Army. I know I'm going to have trouble breaking it when the war's over.'

She could not decide whether she was impatient or glad that he was postponing the purpose of their meeting. 'Will you bother to try?'

He smiled. 'Probably not. Except that they say it's bad for you if you're keen on sport.'

She felt as if they were two wary animals, circling and sniffing one another in case a fight was forthcoming. 'Are you keen on sport, Major?'

His eyes met her own. 'Certain sports, Mrs. Miles. Like horse-riding and fox-hunting.'

Was he challenging her, she wondered. Or was there an element of apology in his remark? Aware she was still procrastinating, she pretended to remember. 'Oh, yes, of course. We saw you at Burton Stather, didn't we? Before the war.'

His reply surprised her. 'Yes. I behaved abominably that day. I really don't know why. It was quite unpardonable. You must remember?'

How could she forget? she thought. She and Harry had been staying at his grandparents' cottage at Burton Stather, a place they had both loved to visit. With their wedding only three weeks away, the weekend in the country had been pure magic for them until on the Sunday, when they were out walking, Chadwick and a friend had seen them and ridden over. After mocking and teasing them, Chadwick had suddenly snatched off Mary's hat and thrown it into a tree, at the same time remarking to his friend 'what a pretty filly' she was. When Harry had reacted, Chadwick had ridden his horse at him and then, while Harry was recovering, had galloped away. Although the couple had later spent their honeymoon at the cottage, the knowledge that Chadwick's father was the landowner and that his son might appear at any time had shadowed the honeymoon for Mary although she had never admitted it to Harry.

Remembering the incident hardened Mary's resolve. Why should she spare him, she thought, after the things he had done to Harry during the war? 'Of course I remember,' she said. 'I couldn't understand why you behaved that way to us. We weren't doing you any harm.'

He exhaled smoke but not before she noticed his expression. Surely it could not be admiration for her frankness? And yet his words suggested it. 'You're quite right. I've no excuse. Except that I was much younger and the young often do cruel and stupid things.'

It was an apology she had not expected and she was glad the arrival of the waitress saved her making a reply. As the girl laid a dish of cream alongside a plate of scones, Chadwick gave his light, pleasant laugh. 'So you found some? Aren't you a clever girl?' As the girl blushed, he pressed a coin into her hand. 'Buy yourself something nice. You deserve it.'

The startled girl stared down at the half sovereign in her hand. 'You're givin' me all this, sir?'

'Yes, why not? It isn't often we get served with cream these days. Spend it and enjoy yourself.'

175

Looking stunned by her good fortune, the girl threw a backward glance at the officer as she made for the kitchen.

Crushing out his cigarette, Chadwick gave Mary a smile. 'Who'll be mother?'

Pulling herself together, she poured the tea. As she lowered the teapot, Chadwick held out the plate of scones. She shook her head. 'No, thank you. I only want tea.'

The quirk of his mouth was a mixture of humour and regret. 'After all the trouble that poor girl has gone to? You can't disappoint her. Have one! Just to show willing.'

She bit her lip, then nodded. 'All right. Just one.'

He handed her the dish of cream after she had taken a scone. 'After all, you haven't any worries about your figure, have you? Not a girl as slim as you.'

She felt herself blush, then had a rush of anger. She had come to hear what had happened to Harry and he was talking almost as if he were courting her. Although terrified at what she might hear, she braced herself. 'Please tell me about Harry now, Major. Don't hold anything back. It's better that I know everything.'

As she held her breath, she saw him wince and wondered if she had misjudged him and his intention had been only to help her relax. For a moment he sat very still. Then he nodded and raised his eyes. 'You do understand that I didn't see everything? His gunpost was nearly two hundred yards from mine and there was a great deal of smoke about.'

Her throat was tight, forcing her to swallow. 'I understand. Please go on.'

'I think his second gunner had been knocked out. He was on a Lewis gun. Your husband was manning a heavier machine-gun and he went on firing to the end.'

Below the table her hands were gripping the straps of her handbag. 'The end?'

He nodded. 'A party of enemy infantry attacked his post. I saw one or two of them leap into it but not what happened afterwards. A smoke shell burst nearby and hid everything from sight.'

'But his gun stopped firing?'

'Yes, it must have done.' When she did not speak, he went on: 'He couldn't have got away, and in any case we'd all been ordered to stand our ground to the end. But what exactly happened to him, I'm unable to say.'

She felt as if a heavy door in her mind had swung closed. 'You're really saying he was killed, aren't you?'

He showed a rare discomfort as he shifted in his chair. 'I think you should face the possibility, Mrs. Miles. I'm not saying he might not have been wounded and then captured. In spite of what our newspapers say, the Germans aren't barbarians and they take prisoners whenever possible. But the circumstances here weren't propitious.'

Beneath the table her hands were clenched, an unconscious act of self-control. 'Then why didn't the telegram say he'd been killed? Why did they say missing?'

'That would be because his body wasn't found. It's the usual wording when they can't be specific.'

She seized on that like a drowning man clutching a lifeline. 'Isn't that odd? Surely if he'd been killed his body would have stayed in the gunpost?'

His eyes searched her face as if weighing up how much more she could take. To help him she said quietly: 'Tell me everything, please. It's much kinder, really it is.'

His terse nod was for her courage. 'There were a large number of shells falling at that time. It's possible one might have exploded in his gunpost. If one did . . .' Frowning, he broke off and reached for his cigarette case again.

There was a crash of plates in the kitchen, followed by

a scolding voice. When the noises ceased, she had regained her self-control. 'I understand. Then you didn't see into his gunpost yourself after the attack was repulsed?'

'No.' His voice had a more confident ring now that he was talking about his own misfortunes. 'I was knocked unconscious some time later and copped a shell splinter in my leg. Before I could say Jack Robinson, they'd shipped me back to Blighty.'

The realist in her was affirming that Harry was dead and the door closed for ever but the love in her would not accept it. 'But if a shell didn't fall into the post, then surely there must be a chance he's a prisoner?'

Unable to tell her about the carnage of the battlefield, of men so mutilated or dismembered that their mothers would not recognise them, he began to show restlessness at the pressure she was putting on him. 'There's always a chance, Mrs. Miles. But I don't think you should put too much faith in it.'

For the first time that morning her voice faltered. 'I must have faith, Major Chadwick. So don't discourage me, please.'

He frowned and shook his head. 'He should never have gone back. Why did you let him?'

'Let him? How could I stop him? He was driven to it.'

His brows drew together. 'Driven? I don't follow you.'

For the first time she knew he was not being honest with her. 'His conscience wouldn't let him rest, Major. And I think you know why.'

'You mean he felt guilty at not being with us at the Front? There wasn't any need for that. He'd done his bit.'

'Yes,' she said quietly. 'He had. More than his bit.'

Seeing her expression, he frowned again. 'I suppose

178

you blame me for helping him to get back. It was a mistake, I see it now. Only he was a damn fine soldier.'

Certain of his deceit now, she had a sudden urge to punish him. 'There was only one reason he had to go back, Major. And that reason was you.'

He gave a start. 'Me? I don't understand.'

'I think you do. He felt he'd grown too much like you and had to find out the truth once and for all. He felt you liked the war and were a man who enjoyed killing for its own sake.'

His handsome face showed resentment but not the anger she had half expected. 'How can you avoid killing in a war? It's your duty to kill the enemy.'

'It's how you feel when you kill them that worried Harry. He was afraid he might have become like you. And he couldn't live with that belief.'

He gave a harsh laugh. 'The war must have affected him more than I thought. Do I look like a man who enjoys killing his fellow men?'

'No, Major, you don't. But that doesn't prove anything, does it?'

'A soldier has to kill, Mrs. Miles. Harry found that out like we all did. Once he got over that religious rubbish, he became a first-class soldier. In fact, in the end he shocked even me.'

She nodded. 'You mean the two Germans he shot after they'd been disarmed, don't you?'

Chadwick stared at her. 'He told you about that?'

'Yes. He told me everything.'

'Surely not before he went back?'

'No. In a letter he wrote me from France.' The catch in her voice was barely noticeable. 'It came a week before the telegram arrived.'

'But I censor all my men's mail. I never saw such a letter from him.'

'You wouldn't. It came in one of those green envelopes that escape censorship.'

Chadwick took a cigarette from his case at last. As he raised a lighter to it, she saw with satisfaction that his hand held a faint tremor. 'What else did he say in this letter?'

'He told me about the wounded German he'd brought in. And about the talk he'd had with you later. When I'd read it I understood why he'd had to go back.'

There was a brief silence while Chadwick returned the case to his pocket. Then he shook his head. 'He was like me, Mrs. Miles. More than he ever knew. That was the reason he disliked me. And why he acted as he did.'

She stiffened. 'Like you? Never in a million years! I told him that but he had to prove it himself. And he did.'

'Did he?' Chadwick said.

'Yes. His letter said so. Going back might have killed him but at least his mind was put at peace.'

He opened his mouth to deny it, saw her eyes were brimming with tears, and changed his mind. 'Whatever there was between us, I respected him for his courage. I'd like you to believe that.'

She blinked back her tears. 'I do believe it. And I appreciate your coming into town today to see me. It wasn't something you had to do.'

He studied her pale, beautiful face, and felt his throat tighten. 'I don't want us to be enemies, Mrs. Miles. Let me help you if I can. My father has got quite a lot of pull upstairs or I'd never have been able to get Harry back. Let's use him again to help us. If he gives the Red Cross or somebody a push, they might find out something. Would you like me to do that?'

There was no way she could refuse. 'You know I would,' she said quietly.

'Then leave it to me. I'll start things moving as soon as

I get home and we'll see what happens. Is it all right if I ring you at home or come round to see you when I get more information?'

'Yes, of course. I'm nearly always at home or in the office.'

'Then that's settled.' He grimaced at the plate of scones and the cream. 'Are you sure you won't have another?'

'No, thank you.'

'But you have a little girl, haven't you?' When she nodded he turned and waved the young waitress over. 'I'll get the girl to wrap them up and you can take them home for her.'

She did not attempt to argue and ten minutes later found herself in a taxi on her way to No. 57. Outside the house he helped her out, insisted she took the parcel for Elizabeth, and then took her hand. 'I'll be in touch,' he told her. 'In the meantime, try not to worry too much.'

Glancing at the house she saw a lace curtain twitching and knew that Ethel was watching them. Feeling he was holding her hand too long, she drew it away. 'Thank you for your help,' she said. 'I do appreciate it.'

With that she turned and hurried up the front path to the house, uncomfortably aware he was standing on the pavement watching her. It was only after she had closed the front door that she heard the taxi start up and drive away.

Chapter 18

The guard unlocked the door and threw it open. '*Eintreten! Schnell!*'

A push sent Harry stumbling inside. The bright sunlight dimmed as the door was closed and locked behind him. For a moment the fetid air made him gag. Pausing while his eyes adjusted, he saw the wooden floor of the hut was covered with straw palliasses. Most were occupied by soldiers but few turned their heads to glance at him. The atmosphere was one of exhaustion and despair.

Wondering which empty mattress to take, Harry started forward. As he passed by a fly-speckled window, a sudden excited shout made him halt. 'Harry! It's you, isn't it? Harry Miles?'

Turning, Harry saw an unkempt uniformed figure rising to his feet. He recognised the man's voice before his pale gaunt face. 'Swanson?'

A thin hand gripped his own. 'Harry! I thought the bastards had finished you off. When did you get in?'

Harry was thinking that in the circumstances there was no man he would sooner have encountered. 'This morning. How long have you been here?'

'A week after the Jerries over-ran us. I was only bruised and concussed. But I thought you were a goner.'

Heads were rising curiously to survey the newcomer as Harry gave a rueful laugh. 'I thought so too when a big sod came at me with a bayonet. He got me in the shoulder at his first pass and was aiming at my stomach when an officer pulled him back. That's about all I remember until I woke up in a field hospital.'

Clearly delighted at the reunion, Swanson turned to the men around them. 'It's my old sergeant, Harry Miles. I thought he was dead.'

A cynical Australian voice answered. 'Good on you, mate. What do you want us to do? Throw him a party?'

Never at a loss for words, Swanson grinned. 'Why not? How about one of those cigarettes you scrounge from Fritz?'

'Cigarettes. Your mind's goin', Swanson.'

'Come on. I know you have some.'

Grunting something, the Australian was about to lie back when there were cries of assent from the prisoners around him. Swearing, the Australian reached inside his palliasse and threw a cigarette up at Swanson. 'I hope it poisons yer, mate.'

Swanson grinned at Harry. 'It probably will.' Striking a lucifer, he lit the cigarette, took in a long appreciative drag, then passed it to Harry. 'They're a bit strong. So take it steady at first.'

Harry drew on the cigarette, then burst into a paroxysm of coughing. As laughter sounded round the hut, the Australian grinned. 'Takes a man to smoke 'em, Sarge. What were you in? The Girl Guides?'

Wiping his eyes, Harry turned to Swanson. 'What the hell are they made of?'

Swanson grinned. 'Haven't you had a Jerry cigarette before?' When Harry shook his head, he went on: 'They use dried leaves, bark, and God knows what else.'

'C'mon, Swanson, you know better than that.' It was

183

the Australian again. 'They use the corpses, mate. Boil 'em down and use the fat for margarine, the bones for soup, and the hair for fags. Waste not, want not. That's Jerry's philosophy.'

Grinning, Swanson led Harry to a vacant palliasse and drew him down. Around them, as if the moment of excitement had exhausted them, men sank back again and closed their eyes. Harry glanced at the far door. 'Why do they lock you in?'

Swanson shrugged. 'God knows. Maybe they're afraid we'll break out and storm the cookhouse.'

'The food's bad, is it?'

'Bad? It depends what you call thin cabbage soup and a hunk of rye bread.' Swanson pointed at a row of buckets at the other end of the hut. 'That's where the stink comes from. It can be murder when some poor bastard gets dysentery.'

'What about Red Cross parcels?' Harry asked.

Swanson took the cigarette, dragged hard on it, then passed it back. 'The old sweats say they used to get them once. But that was before our blockade began to bite and Jerry's transport system was still working properly. They say it's months since the last batch got through. Maybe they're being pinched but more likely the system's broken down. We aren't sure but it's a matter of life or death here.' He pointed at two empty palliasses alongside them. 'On average we lose a man every fortnight. They're supposed to go into hospital but we know there's a special hut where they're taken to die.'

Harry was frowning. 'You're not saying it's a deliberate policy to starve prisoners to death?'

'Oh, Christ, no. They give us all they can, I'm sure of that. It's our blockade that's strangling Jerry. One of our guards, Fritz, says they're killing cats and dogs back

184

home for food. It's all going to the troops, They'll be the last ones Hindenburg allows to starve.'

'What about mail?' Harry asked.

Swanson grimaced. 'That's a joke. No one's had a letter for months and they don't even give us paper to write on any more. Mail's just a memory here.' Then, seeing Harry's expression: 'What are you worried about? Your wife?'

Harry nodded. 'She's going to think the worst if she doesn't hear from me.'

'At least she'll know you're a prisoner. The Jerries send off the details from your dog tag.'

'That's what's worrying me,' Harry said. 'My tag wasn't on me when I woke up in hospital. I gave my details to a little fat corporal who came round but he hardly looked the reliable type. Have you complained about the mail?'

'What do you think? All they do is shrug their shoulders. Mind you, when food isn't getting through either I suppose you can understand it's not their top priority.' Swanson reached for the cigarette again. 'Did you hear anything in hospital about what's happening on the Front?'

'No. There was a security blanket over everything. The only news we got was from an old Army doctor who strutted up the wards every night telling us the British Army was being driven into the sea. No one, not even the German orderlies, believed him.'

Swanson grimaced. 'Why not? They were going through us like a dose of salts when we copped it. And the further they advanced into France, the more food they'd capture.'

'I'm not so sure,' Harry said. 'I had the feeling Jerry was running out of steam too.'

'Let's hope you're right,' Swanson said, motioning

again at the empty palliasses. 'If you aren't, there mightn't be many of us left to tell the tale.' Then, with his natural resilience, his tone changed. 'Mind you, there could be another interpretation to those palliasses. When I first came new prisoners were filling 'em as fast as men were taken away. But lately the intake's dropped right down.'

Harry was quick to grasp his point. 'You think that could mean Jerry's on the retreat again?'

'It could mean that, couldn't it? Unless Jerry's decided he can't afford the grub any longer and has stopped taking prisoners.'

'You're getting to sound like Charlie Dunn,' Harry said. 'Cheerful to the end.'

Swanson emitted a foul-smelling puff of smoke. 'Poor bastard! He copped it early, didn't he?' Then, with the mordant humour of the combat soldier, he grinned. 'Mind you, it could be a godsend for Hull's virgins if there're any left. And it isn't as if there won't be any little Dunns in the future to keep us safe from invasion. Think of a dozen of 'em lined up on the cliffs and blowing for all they're worth. There isn't any army in the world could take that. I tell you, Blighty's safe for at least fifty years.'

As Harry laughed, a whistle was heard outside. 'Roll call,' Swanson told him. 'One hut at a time.'

'Why is that?' Harry asked.

Swanson grinned. 'Can't you guess? If they only check one hut at a time, the other's can't see how we're all thinning out. Who says the Jerries are stupid?'

Chapter 19

Ethel peered through the lace curtain of the front window, saw who was standing in the porch, and gave a start. Running back into the living room, she took an urgent look in a mirror. Seeing a few hairs were out of place, she carefully adjusted her twin combs, then straightened the collar of her high-necked dress before hurrying to the door. Her voice when she opened it betrayed nothing of her intense interest in the visitor. When the need was pressing enough, Ethel could be an excellent actress. 'Yes, Major. What can I do for you?'

Chadwick lifted his cane to his service cap. 'Are you Mrs. Hardcastle?'

'Yes, I am.'

'My name is Chadwick, Mrs. Hardcastle. I wonder if I might see your daughter, Mrs. Miles.'

Ethel allowed her expression to relax. 'Oh, yes, Major Chadwick. Mary has mentioned your name. I understand you offered to try to get information about her husband.'

'That's right. May I see her?'

Ethel stood aside. 'She's over in the office at the moment but I can call her on the telephone. Please come in, Major.'

She led the tall young officer into the sitting room.

'I'm afraid you'll have to forgive us if things are a little untidy this morning. But Elizabeth – that's Mary's daughter – has only just returned to school and children do leave things in a state, don't they?'

Chadwick, who had barely glanced at the well-appointed room, ignored her apology. 'Did you say Mrs. Miles is in your warehouse?'

Ethel knew this was one of those times when praise for Mary was not only needed but should be unstinted. 'Yes. She manages my late husband's business, 'She's such a clever girl. I don't know what I'd do without her.' She motioned at an armchair. 'Do sit down, Major. May I make you a cup of tea before I call Mary over?'

Chadwick sank into the chair with some difficulty. 'No, thank you. But I would like a word with you first if I may.'

Ethel gave a tut of sympathy as he eased his wounded leg forward. 'Mary said you'd been wounded. Does it hurt very much?'

Chadwick's reply was curt. 'No. Tell me, Mrs. Hardcastle, how did your daughter react after our meeting a week ago?'

Ethel sank decorously down on the settee. 'She seemed heartened after you promised to find out all you could about her husband. Because his body wasn't found, she won't accept that he might be dead.'

Chadwick frowned. 'I tried to tell her not to make too much of that. It really proves very little.'

Ethel, agog with curiosity at the purpose of his visit, leaned forward anxiously. 'You haven't brought bad news about Harry, have you, Major?'

Chadwick, who knew a great deal about Ethel from censoring Harry's letters, was not deceived. 'I'm afraid I haven't brought any news about him at all, Mrs. Hardcastle. My father has been trying hard but so far

188

without any result. He and I will go on trying, of course, but frankly things don't look good.'

Ethel's voice sank into a whisper. 'Are you saying that Harry is dead?'

Certain of her deceit, Chadwick felt no need to mince his words. 'I've thought it all along, Mrs. Hardcastle. Infantrymen hate machine-gunners and I couldn't see the Germans who broke into his gunpost letting him live. The only mystery to me is what happened to his body.'

Ethel shuddered. 'The poor boy. How dreadful.' With a muted sob she drew a lace handkerchief from her sleeve and dabbed at her eyes. It was an act that hid her growing excitement. If Chadwick had no further news to give Mary, why had he not telephoned her instead of paying a visit? There could be only one reason for that, Ethel decided. Taking a shuddering breath, she bravely dried her eyes. 'Is this what you are going to tell Mary, Major?'

Chadwick was thinking again what a deceitful bitch she was. 'I've already said as much to her. I can't say that he's definitely dead because there's the slimmest of chances he might have been taken prisoner. But it's not a chance that anyone should build their hopes on.'

For a moment Ethel almost betrayed herself. 'Are you sure of that?'

'As sure as anyone can be in the circumstances. The best advice I can give you is to get her used to the idea that he's dead. As her mother you can do that better than anyone.'

Ethel dabbed at her eyes again. 'I've already told her she shouldn't cling to false hopes. But she won't listen to me.'

Chadwick shrugged. 'That's natural enough. It's going to take time. But in the meantime, without raising her hopes, I'll go on trying to find out what happened.'

'You're very kind,' Ethel said. 'We'll never be able to thank you enough. 'Do you think. . . .' She hesitated as if unwilling to ask the favour.

Chadwick raised an eyebrow. 'Think what, Mrs. Hardcastle?'

'I know it's asking a great deal from someone as busy as you, but is it possible for you to see her now and then? Perhaps because you served with Harry, I had the feeling she drew comfort from the few words you had.'

Chadwick almost betrayed himself by smiling. So that was her game. With Harry out of the way, an ambitious mother was going to make all the mileage she could out of the situation. At the same time nothing could have suited his plans more.

He gave a thoughtful nod. 'Of course I'll see her, if you think it will help. Although, of course, that will depend on her.'

Ethel was only too aware this was the problem. 'She might be a little hesitant at first because of the circumstances. But if you impress on her that Harry is the reason for your visits, I'm sure she'll be glad to see you.' When Chadwick made no comment, she rose to her feet. 'What would you like me to do, Major? Shall I telephone for her to come over?'

Chadwick rose himself. 'No. She might not like to leave the office empty. We'll go over and talk to her there.'

Mary gazed at Ethel angrily. 'You'd no right to encourage him, Mother. He could ring me if he had anything to say.'

Ethel's gaze was innocence itself. 'I thought it would brighten you up to talk to him about Harry.'

'Brighten me up? The only thing that'll brighten me is to hear Harry is safe. Just talking to Michael Chadwick isn't going to help me.'

'Then why didn't you tell him so when he asked if he could come round again?'

'How could I when you interfered and said how nice it would be? After all, he is doing me a great favour trying to trace Harry. I daren't do anything to discourage him. You must have known that.'

Ethel turned haughty. 'I'm only too aware he's doing you a favour. A man in his position must have a thousand things to do. I don't think you realise how lucky you are, my girl. When he suggested coming round, I could hardly believe my ears.'

Mary's eyes were full of suspicion. 'Did he suggest it, Mother? Or did you?'

Ethel stiffened. 'I? Why on earth should I suggest it?'

'Come off it, Mother. You've never stopped talking about him since that morning he brought me home. The son of Sir Henry Chadwick of The Grange. . . . You'd give your right arm to get him interested in me.'

Ethel was tempted to tell her that Chadwick was already interested but bit back the comment in time. Instead she conquered her temper and gave a distressed sniff. 'How can you think such things of me when we still don't know what's happened to Harry? I was thinking of your welfare, that was all. But no matter what I do, you always think the worst of me, don't you.'

Although her suspicions were strong, Mary had to admit there might be justice in Ethel's case and her tone changed. 'All right, Mother, let's put it this way. I don't like Michael Chadwick but because of the way he's treated Harry in the past I'm prepared to use him all I can. If that means I have to see him now and then, then I suppose I'll have to put up with it. Fortunately it won't be for long. He'll be going back to France once his leg heals.'

Ethel looked disappointed. 'Do you think that's likely?'

'Of course, it is. Chadwick won't pull any strings. He enjoys war too much.'

Ethel gave another sniff. 'That's a funny way of putting it. Most people would say he's a very brave man.'

Mary could not help the comment: 'You didn't say that when Harry volunteered to go back.'

Ethel opened her mouth to argue, then decided against it. 'Anyway, I still think it's very kind of him to be so concerned about you and Harry. It shows what a good officer he is.'

'Perhaps. But remember, Mother, I don't want you encouraging him the next time he pays us a visit. Leave me to handle him. Are you listening?'

Tempted to make a sharp reply, Ethel checked herself. After all, she thought, what more could she have expected at this point in time? The thing that mattered was that her daughter and Chadwick were going to meet reasonably often, something that was beyond her wildest dreams twenty-four hours ago. It was a situation that must have possibilities and she, Ethel, must exploit them to the full. Satisfied with her day, she donned her most conciliatory manner. 'Of course I won't interfere, dear. Like you, I only want to find out what has happened to Harry, and it does seem Major Chadwick is our best bet. So let's leave things as they are and not quarrel any more about him.'

Chadwick visited Mary five times in the next four weeks. Although he assured her his father was still making enquiries about Harry, he was forced to admit that no further news was forthcoming. 'The Red Cross say things are in a bad way in Germany now and it's getting more and more difficult to find out details about prisoners. To be fair, it's not the Germans' fault. It's their communication system that's breaking down.

News still comes from their larger prison camps but it's the smaller, isolated ones that are causing problems.'

His words had acted like oil on the smouldering embers of her hopes. 'Then that could be the answer! Harry's in one of those small camps whose records have either got lost or haven't reached the Red Cross.'

There was no dousing her hopes, and although Chadwick secretly believed Harry was dead, he did not attempt to do so. On the one hand it seemed pointless until proof was forthcoming and on the other hand it would lose him all excuse to see her again, and that was something Chadwick was finding more and more difficult to accept. From the first sight of her at Burton Stather he had been struck by her beauty but had known nothing of the woman within. Since censoring Harry's wartime letters to her, however, and secretly reading some of her replies, he had discovered a depth in her that matched her appearance.

Nevertheless, until his meeting with her in the tea-room he had decided his interest in her was due only to her being Harry Miles' wife for, ridiculous though he found it, he had never been able to see Miles as a mere NCO under his command. Instead, although they were officer and sergeant fighting a war against a common enemy, Miles had always seemed a dangerous antagonist in a dimension beyond it. Time and again Chadwick had laughed at his imaginings but always they returned. For a man not given to metaphysical speculation, his preoccupation with Miles both irritated and disturbed him.

Whatever had triggered off his interest in Mary at the beginning, he had felt a strong physical desire for her during their tea-room meeting. It had grown during the weeks that followed until it was now a heat that was burning him.

It was not a sensation Chadwick welcomed for he was a man who believed it was enfeebling to need anyone, and particularly a woman. Need spelt weakness in Chadwick's dictionary, and while women were there to be enjoyed, only weaklings allowed them to dominate their minds or their bodies.

As a consequence there was resentment mixed with his desire and it was growing apace with it. Why did he want this woman so much? Already her belly was beginning to swell with the child of a man who had disliked him so much he had died to prove himself different. And however Mary was trying to hide it now, her dislike of him had been manifest in the letters she had written to Harry.

Then what was the impulse that drove him to see her? She was beautiful, yes, but with his looks, his wealth and his position he could have beautiful women at the click of his fingers. Yet he continued to humiliate himself – he could think of no other word – with a woman who had told him he could never match up to her husband in a million years. The anger and aggression the memory evoked made him think of his emotions when engaging the enemy in France.

Lying on his bed with his thoughts, Chadwick saw her again in his mind's eye, her long golden hair, her lovely expressive face, and her full shapely breasts, and felt his loins tighten with desire and some other impulse he could not fathom. At that moment Chadwick knew he would never rest until he had had sex with this woman and exorcised the ghost that was haunting him.

Chapter 20

The phone rang as Mary was searching in one of the wooden filing cabinets for a customer's address. Crossing to her desk, she picked up the receiver. 'Hello.'

'Mary!' It was Ethel. 'The Major is here. He wants to know if he can come over?'

The girl frowned. 'Has he any news?'

'I don't know, dear. But he'll tell you when he sees you.'

Don't lie, Mother, she thought. You would have started pumping him for news the moment he put a foot inside the door. She hesitated, then realised she had no option. 'All right, Mother. But let him know that I'm busy this morning, will you?'

Ethel's voice dropped. 'Don't let him think he's not welcome, dear. He is doing you a big favour after all.'

About to reply tartly, the girl bit her lip instead. 'Just send him over, Mother. Leave the rest to me.'

She watched the tall, lean figure of Chadwick crossing the sunlit warehouse yard five minutes later. With his wound having healed almost fully during the last few weeks, his limp was barely noticeable now. He disappeared from sight for a moment, then she heard his footsteps on the stairs. 'Come in,' she called as a tap on the door followed.

Smiling, he advanced towards her, his hand out-stretched. 'Hello, Mary. I hope this isn't inconvenient.'

She indicated a chair alongside the desk. 'I am rather busy this morning as it happens but things can wait for a little while. Have you any news?'

He shook his head wryly as he dropped into the chair. 'Not much, I'm afraid. Father's been in touch with London again but he's still drawn a blank.' He went on before she could comment: 'I'm keeping on at the old boy, of course, but I have to be a little careful because of his health.'

'Is he ill?' she asked.

He grimaced. 'Yes. It seems his heart's not too good. Mother got the news last week. It's all his drinking and smoking, I expect. He's been told to cut down and he doesn't like it one bit.'

'I'm sorry,' she said. 'Harry always says what a fair-minded man he is.'

Seeing Chadwick's lips quirk, she suddenly realised it was a remark that touched old scars but he made no comment. Instead he smiled. 'It's brought him up with a jolt, I think. He called me in the other day and gave me a lecture on how to run the estate when he's gone. He's afraid I might put money into other things than land and buildings.'

'Why is that?' she asked.

'I once said he ought to diversify and invest in commerce and industry. He didn't take to the idea at all.'

'Is that what you would do?'

He shrugged. 'I might. But that's looking a long way ahead, I hope.'

'I hope so too. He's not an actual invalid, is he?'

He laughed. 'Good heavens, no. He's still chasing the young maids around the house and he never misses his Sunday hunt.'

She felt relief. 'Then we're not imposing on him in asking for his help?'

'Not at all. It's just that I can't put too much pressure on him. Even so, I'm sure he's doing all he can.'

She knew she had to be satisfied with that. 'Would you like a cup of tea or coffee?'

'No, thanks. Your mother gave me tea before I came over.' He paused. 'Are you sure I'm not being a nuisance this morning?'

She hoped that her slight hesitation did not show. 'No, of course not. It's just that I do the weekly accounts on Fridays and try to get them off in the post the same day. But I'm all right for a few more minutes.'

'Good,' he said, giving her his attractive smile. 'In any case, I shan't be a nuisance again. I have to report back for duty on Tuesday. In a way I'm not sorry. I've felt a bit of a fraud these last two weeks with my leg almost better.'

Almost at once her relief turned to dismay as she wondered if it meant his efforts to get news of Harry would cease. 'I'm sorry,' she said. 'You've done so much that I'd have thought they'd have let you stay in England. After all, the war can't go on much longer, can it?'

He shrugged. 'I wouldn't like to say that. From all I hear Jerry is fighting harder than ever. I don't think he can win now but defeating him is a different matter. We must keep the pressure on him or he'll demand unacceptable terms when the end does come.'

She shuddered. 'It seems awful that men have to go on dying when everyone knows there must be an armistice sooner or later.' She hesitated, then could hold back her question no longer. 'What about Harry, Michael? Will you still be able to let me know if your father hears anything?'

'Of course. Don't worry about it. I'll tell Father to contact you the moment any news comes through.' As she sank back in relief, he smiled. 'Now I've a little favour to ask you. Don't say no until you've heard me out.'

Apprehensive at what might be coming, she nodded. Before speaking, he drew his chair a few inches nearer her desk. 'I've wanted to ask you before,' he said, 'but I never felt it was the right time. But now I'm leaving for France you might feel differently. I want to take you out to dinner on Monday night. I know a place in Swanland that's very discreet and does marvellous food.' As she opened her mouth to protest, he smiled and put a finger to his lips. 'You promised to hear me out, remember?'

She nodded and waited as he went on: 'Don't say no, Mary. I'll be on the train the next morning. I'll look after you like a queen and I'll see you're home promptly at midnight. Do me this one favour.'

Conscious of her debt to him, she first used an excuse that could not offend. 'I can't leave my daughter with Mother, Michael. Not after she's had her all day.'

He smiled. 'Yes, you can. It's all been taken care of. Your mother's already told me she'll be only too happy to look after Elizabeth. She thinks as I do, that you need a change.'

The knowledge he had brought Ethel into his invitation made her mood less conciliatory. 'Michael, Harry's missing. He might even be dead. What kind of woman would I be to go out and enjoy myself at such a time?'

He nodded. 'I appreciate that but it's nearly three months since you got the telegram. And I'm only asking you to have dinner with me. As I said, I probably wouldn't have asked you so soon if this order hadn't come through. But war doesn't give one time to obey the social conventions, does it?'

198

His move towards her had put him fully into the summer sunlight that was streaming through the window. Handsome and tanned, with his beautifully tailored uniform enhancing his lean, hard body, he was a man to turn any girl's head. As his eyes met her own and she saw the expression in them, she felt her skin prickle. Disgust at herself made her rebuke stronger than she had intended. 'Aren't you forgetting that I'm pregnant? What decent woman goes out at a time like this with a man who's not her husband? I'm surprised that you could ask me.'

He showed contempt at her excuse. 'It hardly shows on you yet. Wear a loose fitting dress if you want to but in any case no one will know.'

'I'll know,' she said. 'I'm sorry, Michael, but I can't do it. Please don't ask me again.'

His expression began to harden. 'You don't give much away, do you?'

She felt instant apprehension. 'What does that mean?'

'It means you don't give much back in return. All I've asked is for you to have a harmless dinner with me. Two hours or so sitting at a table talking to one another. Is that so much to ask at a time like this?'

His words confused her. 'Try to understand, Michael. I can't stop thinking about Harry. I wouldn't enjoy myself and neither would you.'

'Let me worry about that. Are you telling me that Harry would begrudge you having one night out after all the work you're doing here for him?'

'It's not that Harry would begrudge anything. It's how I would feel. *I* don't think it's fair on him, that's why I'm saying no.'

His lips curled. 'Is that all you are then? A conventional housewife afraid of what equally conventional housewives might think of you? My God, I had a better opinion of you than that.'

199

She saw for herself now that Harry was right: he was capable of cruelty. For that very reason she knew she must be very careful. 'I know Monday's your last night, Michael, and it's very flattering you should ask me to spend it with you. But although I understand I still. . . .'

Interrupting her, he rose to his feet. 'Although you understand, you still can't make the gesture. That's what you're saying, isn't it?' He went to the door and turned. 'Don't think any more about it. I'm sorry I asked. I won't get a chance to see you again before I leave but I'll try to ring you when I get back from France, whenever that will be.'

Without his saying a word about Harry, she was certain it was an ultimatum. She gazed at his sullen, handsome face for a full five seconds before she nodded her head. 'All right, Michael,' she said quietly. 'If Mother will look after Elizabeth I will have dinner with you. Make the arrangements and in the meantime I'll ask Mother what time she'd like us home.'

Harry awoke with a start. At first, weakened by hunger, he could not identify the sound. Then he saw that McLean, the Australian, was hammering on the locked door of the hut. 'C'mon, you bastards! Get a stretcher in here!'

For a moment the hut swung round dizzily as Harry sat up, making him grip the side of his palliasse. 'What's the problem, McLean?'

The Australian glanced round and swore. 'It's Webb. The poor sod's choking.' Turning back, he took a savage kick at the door. 'C'mon, you lousy Krauts. Open the door and get some medical attention in here!'

Knowing Webb was a friend of the Australian, Harry rose with an effort and crossed the floor. Webb, grey-faced, was fighting for breath and saliva was trickling from his mouth. As Harry turned him on his side to prevent him choking, he heard a rattle in his throat. Glancing at Swanson who had followed him, he drew him aside. 'Mac's right. He's in a bad way. I think he's dying.'

Another prisoner, a waif-like Cockney called Cooper, was now bending over the choking man. He gave a bitter laugh as he turned to the Australian. 'You're wastin' your time, Mac. He'll be happier dyin' in here than in the death box.'

Swearing at him, McLean took another kick at the door. This time a bolt was withdrawn and two armed guards appeared in the doorway. One of them shouted something and hit the Australian in the chest with his rifle butt. The other, a lance corporal, looked embarrassed and restrained his colleague as he was about to strike McLean again. Swanson let out his breath in relief. 'Fritz is back. Thank God for that.'

Fritz Brunner, a man of the land, had been a fine physical specimen until a severe chest wound had downgraded him to prison camp duties. A simple, religious man, he was liked by the prisoners and when he had disappeared from duty a week ago, men feared he had been posted. Instead he had been given compassionate leave, to attend the funeral of his mother. In normal times a few days home leave was expected to restore a soldier but the gaunt weariness of Brunner as he bent over the dying British prisoner gave witness to the privations of German civilians.

Emaciated prisoners gathered round him as he called to the other guard to bring a stretcher. With death stalking them all, few of their questions concerned the dying Webb.

'Can't you get us more food, Fritz? We're so weak we can hardly stand.'

'How's the war going, Fritz? Do you know who's winning?'

'What's it like at home? Haven't they had enough yet?'

Brunner was careful to check the doorway was empty before replying in his halting English. 'Things are very bad now. People are growing angry with the Government.'

There was a stir among the prisoners. 'How angry, Fritz?' someone shouted.

'Some are very angry. Some throw stones at soldiers, and loot food shops in the cities.'

Harry pushed forward. 'Do you think it could be revolution, Fritz?'

The German's stolid face stared at him. 'Revolution?'

'Yes. People turning against the Kaiser and Hindenburg.'

Brunner shook his head. '*Nein*. Not yet. Hindenburg is too strong.'

'You mean the Army is still in control?'

'*Ja*. They shoot people who loot and go on strike.'

'But do you think you're losing the war?' Swanson asked.

'*Ja*, I think that. But we will not stop fighting yet.'

'Why not?'

The German shrugged. 'Men are too afraid. They are shot if they disobey.'

There was a groan from the ring of emaciated men. A Welsh voice sounded above it. 'What about our mail, Fritz? Why don't we get any?'

Brunner shrugged again. 'It is the Army. They have taken all the vans and all the trains. There is nothing left for. . . .' His voice changed tone as his fellow guard and two orderlies with a stretcher entered the hut. '*Achtung!* Stand back! All of you.'

McLean bent over Webb as the dying man was lifted on to the stretcher. 'S'long, cobber. Don't worry. They'll take care of you.'

The man's bloodshot eyes moved to him. He tried to speak but the rattle returned to his throat. Prisoners watched until he disappeared and the door was closed and re-locked. As men trooped back to their palliasses, the Cockney voice was heard again. 'We ain't going to see that poor sod again. He'll go straight to the death box.'

McLean turned savagely. 'Shut your mouth, you Pommy bastard! Do y' hear me? Shut it or I'll fill you in.'

Cooper, whose thin cheeks were disfigured with ulcers, gave a shrug. 'You're not saying' you still believe in miracles, are you, cobber?'

The Australian glared at him, then sank down exhausted on his palliasse. Swanson, who had lost at least fifteen pounds since Harry's arrival, grimaced at him as the two men returned to their beds. 'What do you make of all that? Do you think Jerry's cracking at last?'

Harry could feel his weakened legs trembling as he lowered himself down. 'I suppose it depends how long their Army can keep them quiet. Or how quickly we and the Yanks can make them sue for an armistice.'

Swanson managed a wry grin. 'Unless Fritz is giving us the big kiddo and it's us who're taking the stick.'

Harry shook his head. 'No, I can't see that. By this time the Yanks must be making a difference.'

Swanson, whose shirt sleeves were rolled back, was eyeing one of his emaciated arms in distaste. 'Let's hope someone forces 'em back soon, or Jerry might get the idea of using us as scarecrows.'

There was no reply from Harry. Exhausted by the incident, as were the rest of the prisoners, he was now sinking into a brown sea of sleep in which the pangs of memory and the pain of hunger could momentarily be forgotten.

Anxious though Allied prisoners of war were to learn details of the war, they would have found precious little to comfort them during that high summer. It was true that the unprecedented German offensive to capture the Channel ports had been held (although at fearful cost) and for a brief while the Allied Press had hinted that the massive German storm might have blown itself out at last. This suggestion, however, was more a political expedient than a forecast, born of the need to restore public morale after the appalling casualty figures that had filled British newspapers during April and May.

The truth was that Ludendorff was far from defeated. If the British armies in the north had held him, then they must be weakened. He would launch a feint attack in the Champagne country, in the vicinity of Chemin des Dames. If this feint was launched on a scale large enough to seem like an offensive in its own right, then the British would be compelled to reinforce the French, just as the French had reinforced them earlier in the year, and a way through the Somme and the Flanders Plain to the Channel might then be created.

The feint was launched in May and ironically was too effective. With Ludendorff's crushing superiority in manpower and the brilliance of his staff officers, the French were hurled right back to the Marne. On this river, less than fifty miles from Paris, the Germans were able to bombard the city with their long range artillery. Ludendorff was now nearer to Paris than von Moltke had been in 1914 and so could hardly be blamed for his subsequent action. Abandoning his plan for the Channel ports, he decided to make the capture of Paris his chief objective, with the shattering effect on Allied morale that loss would bring.

It proved a disastrous mistake. The threat to Paris finally convinced Pershing the time had come to commit his young and fresh American troops and with their enthusiastic and courageous help the Allies were able to bite into the flanks of the German salient and seal it off. The result was Ludendorff had neither taken Paris nor defeated the British and captured the Channel ports. He had become a victim of his own success.

In hindsight it proved to be a German defeat of great significance but this time the Allied celebrations were more muted. To civilians and soldiers alike, the German war machine was begining to resemble a military phoenix. No sooner was it thrust back in one sector than it rose more formidably in another.

Nor could the Allies, and in particular the British, draw comfort from the talk of acute food shortages in Germany. Forced to lend precious ships to the Americans to get their troops into France as quickly as possible, and with submarines menacing their remaining ships, the British did not find their food ration invested them with a feeling of superiority over their German mirror images. Instead, as the rationing tightened, their fears grew for their menfolk who were prisoners of war.

To many, like Mary, who still clung to the hope that Harry was among them, it seemed that only a quick end to the war could save their lives and yet as the summer months passed by she could see no sign that the war would end that year or even in the next.

Chapter 21

Chadwick slowed down the car and glanced at her. 'Do you mind if I stop and have a cigarette?'

Mary hesitated. 'No, not if you want to.'

He drove off the road on to a wide grassy verge and switched off the engine. From the hilltop the river Humber could be seen, its broad expanse shimmering in the moonlight. As Chadwick opened his window, she heard the cry of a night bird. Below the hill a line of tiny sparks betrayed the passing of a train. The far off clatter of its wheels came, then a silence so deep she could hear the hot metal of the engine cooling.

The flare of his lighter momentarily lit his face. For a full thirty seconds he did not speak. Then he turned to her. 'Did you enjoy the dinner?'

She nodded. 'Yes, thank you. Very much.'

He studied her for a moment, then drew on his cigarette again. 'You weren't very talkative. So I wondered.'

He had taken her to a restaurant that had clearly never heard there was a food shortage and whose prices had ensured it was patronised only by the rich. They had been served by soft-spoken waiters, eaten off plates of the finest porcelain and drunk champagne from crystal glasses. Feeling her dress totally inadequate for the occasion, she had been embarrassed and had told him so. 'I didn't know we were coming to a place like this, Michael. You should have warned me.'

He had looked amused. 'What on earth are you worried about? The reason people are looking at you is because you're the best-looking woman here. Don't blush like that. It's true.'

His reassurance and confidence had carried her through the evening although it was a lie to say that she enjoyed it. His pleasant and often amusing conversation had made her laugh at times, but her pleasure had been tainted by the thought that she was being wined and dined by the very man who had put Harry through such mental and physical distress. The feeling of being a traitor to her husband had inhibited her conversation.

To make things worse there had been moments when she had felt flattered to be his companion. From the behaviour of the waiters and the admiring glances and whispers of the fashionably dressed women, it was abundantly clear that he was a celebrity in these circles. To disturb her further, his tanned face had seemed to grow more handsome as he had kept on filling her glass.

Another cry of the night bird brought her back to the present. 'I'm sorry if you found me quiet,' she said. 'But you must understand that I'm not used to that kind of restaurant.'

He exhaled smoke. 'Then you ought to be. A woman with your looks should be taken out everywhere, not kept at home in purdah.'

She laughed. 'You make me sound like some pretty doll. I'm a flesh and blood woman, Michael, not a thing to be put on display.'

'You're a beautiful woman,' he said. 'And beauty deserves attention.'

There was a thickness in his voice that told her she

must change the conversation. 'What's the time?'

He frowned, then glanced at his watch. '11.45.'

'Then don't you think we should go when you've finished your cigarette? I don't want to keep Mother up too late!'

He flicked ash through his open window. 'Don't worry about your mother. She told me it didn't matter what time we came home.'

The knowledge Ethel was pulling strings again made her bite her lip. 'Even so, I don't want to be late myself. Remember I have to work tomorrow.'

He frowned again. 'I haven't forgotten. In fact it's something I want to talk to you about.' He turned to her. 'Tell me about the business. It's not going well, is it?'

Realising he had been talking to her mother in some depth, she knew it was pointless to deny it. 'No, but that's because of the war and because we can't afford a good salesman. Once Harry comes home we'll get our old business back.'

'*If* Harry comes home.' he said. As she winced he went on: 'Face it, Mary. You can't run a business, you can't even run your own life, on a twenty-to-one chance. You've a child already and another on the way. You must think about them.'

She felt herself sobering fast. 'Is that what you think Harry's chances are?'

'If you want the truth I think they're less than that. None of us were taking prisoners in March and April, Mary. It was that kind of a battle.'

She felt tears burning her eyes. 'Why are you saying this tonight? Is it necessary?'

'Yes,' he said. 'It's necessary because I'm not going to get another chance before I go back to France. I want you to make me a promise. That's the real reason I brought you out.'

She stared at him. 'What kind of promise?'

He began to speak, then paused as a car went past them, illuminating with its headlights the trees that flanked the quiet road. Its tail-lights disappeared round a bend before he spoke again. 'If it turns out that Harry is dead, I want you to wait for me. Do you understand what I mean?'

In the darkness her eyes were wide with surprise. 'Wait for you?'

'Yes. Don't get involved with any other man. If you'll promise that I'll put money into your business right away. Then you can employ a decent manager and get another salesman. If the business is as basically healthy as you say, that should put it on its feet again.'

She could hardly believe what she was hearing. To give herself time to recover, she laughed. 'You've had too much champagne tonight, Michael. Put your cigarette out and let's go home.'

Irritation entered his voice. 'This isn't a joke. I'm deadly serious.'

She saw it was true. 'Then I don't understand. What exactly do you mean by "wait for me"?'

'Stay free. Don't get attached to any other man. Surely that's clear enough.'

'If anything happened to Harry, I'd hardly go looking for another man. What sort of woman do you think I am?'

'Then that's all right then.'

'No, it isn't all right. I want to know what you mean by offering me money. Are you suggesting we get engaged?'

He shifted restlessly. 'Something like that, I suppose.'

'You suppose? I'm getting more out of my depth by the minute. If you offer me money, you must have something in mind. Were you thinking of marriage?'

He shifted again, resentfully this time. 'Perhaps. I hadn't thought that far. But yes, I suppose it's possible.'

The suggestion was so preposterous she could not be angry with him. 'Michael, I really think we should be starting back.'

His handsome face was showing resentment now. 'Don't you think you should give more thought to your situation? In four months or so you're going to have two children to look after. If you do as I ask, they would go to the best schools in England. And what about your mother? You want to get away from her, don't you?'

She gave a start. 'How do you know that?'

'It's not difficult to see when the two of you are together. But I knew it before I met her. Don't forget I used to censor Harry's letters.'

She remembered he had told her that in the tea-room. It had not seemed to affect her then but now she felt as if he had seen them both without their clothes. 'So you know everything about us?'

He frowned. 'Of course I don't know everything. But I know the kind of woman your mother is and how you're worried about her influence on Elizabeth. If you did as I ask, you could both get away from her.'

'You're asking me to become your mistress, aren't you?' she said. 'To be given a love nest where you could visit me two or three times a week?'

'I never said that. I asked you to wait for me.'

'You never said it because you were afraid how I'd react. But that's what you mean, isn't it?'

His voice turned sullen again. 'I told you I found you a beautiful woman. So is it surprising I want to see more of you? It's just damned unfortunate they're calling me back again at this time.'

It was the thought he was returning to France that kept her temper in check. 'You do realise you're insul-

ting me, don't you? And there is something more. You
haven't once asked me how I feel about you. Or don't
you consider that important?'

'Of course it's important,' he muttered. 'Or why
should I be asking you?'

'You haven't asked me that. You've told me how good
it will be for my business and my children. You've made
it sound like a business proposition.'

He made no attempt to hide his irritation. 'You want
to keep the business going, don't you? And you are
worried about Elizabeth. So what's wrong with my mentioning them?'

She wished her mind was clear. A shiver ran through
her. 'Take me home now, Michael. I'm feeling tired.'

He ignored her. 'I'll be back in France in a few days.
That doesn't leave me much time to get money through
to you, so I must have your answer tonight.' Before she
could speak, he went on: 'You needn't worry about
paying me back if Harry does turn out to be a prisoner.
That'll just be my bad luck.'

For a moment his offer mollified her. 'I can't take
money from you, Michael. It's out of the question.'

His voice suddenly turned harsh. 'Why not? You
might be only too glad of it when you find out the truth
about Harry.'

Nothing more was needed to bring her resentment to
the surface. 'You won't allow me any hope, will you?
And you ignored what I said a moment ago. So now I'll
tell you. I don't love you, Michael. I don't even know if I
like you. Harry is the only man in the world for me and
no two men could be more different. I'm sorry but after
all you've said it's better you know the truth.'

His reaction both surprised and alarmed her. She
heard him suck in his breath and saw his face darken with
an emotion she could not understand. Cursing, he threw

211

open the car door and jumped out. Breathing hard, he stood there a moment as if struggling to regain his self-control. Then, cursing again, he slammed the door shut and crossed to the far side of the road where he stood staring down at the river.

She sat watching him, a tall uniformed figure silhouetted against the moonlit sky. As the seconds ticked past she began to relax. She was allowing her imagination to run away with her. If his reaction had been intense, it could only be because his feelings for her were equally strong. She never knew whether it was sympathy or self-interest that made her climb from the car and walk over to his side.

'I'm sorry, Michael, but you can't be that surprised. If you've read our letters you must know what Harry and I mean to one another. And you can't say that I've ever led you on.'

He neither moved nor spoke. Wondering why she was feeling afraid, she tried again. 'It's all been a bad mistake, hasn't it? I shouldn't have come out with you tonight. Only you made me feel you wouldn't bother any more about Harry if I didn't.'

His face was black in the moonlight as he turned to her. 'Harry,' he said. 'It's always Harry, isn't it?'

She was close to tears now. 'What else do you expect? He's my husband, the father of my children. He's the only man I've ever loved.' Hardly knowing what she was doing, she laid a hand on his arm. 'Take me home, Michael. Please.'

A sudden movement above the hedge had caught his attention. A large white owl was swooping down from the moonlit sky. As their eyes followed it, it hovered over the road, its huge wings beating noiselessly. A second later it pounced into the long grass on the verge, to rise almost immediately with a small, dark creature in its talons. As Mary heard a faint, terrified squeal, a shudder ran through her. 'That was a vole, wasn't it?'

He made no reply. His eyes were following the bird as it carried its victim away. It was only when it vanished that he turned to her. 'You lied to me just now,' he said. 'You've wanted me too. I saw it in the office last week and I saw it in the restaurant tonight.'

She had the sudden feeling she was talking to a different man to the one she had dined with. Even his voice seemed to have developed a predatory ring. 'You're imagining things, Michael. I'm going home now. It's getting very late.'

As she turned for the car, he caught her arm and swung her round. 'What's the hurry? Your mother doesn't mind. And it's a beautiful night.'

She tried to pull away but instead he swung her round to face him. Before she could protest, he jerked her against him and clamped his mouth on her own. She tried to push him away but his grip round her waist only tightened. As she struggled, one of his hands rose and gripped her breast. As he bent her body backwards, she felt the hardness of him pressing into her groin. Panic-stricken, she managed to free her mouth. 'For God's sake, Michael! Have you gone mad? Let me go!'

His laughter was hoarse and mocking. 'You've got to fight me a little, I know that. I don't mind. We'll both enjoy it all the more.'

His mouth clamped on hers again. She tried to kick but he was too close to her. Lifting a hand she tried to claw at his face but he grabbed it and twisted it behind her. As she gave a muffled cry of pain he swung her off her feet and carried her to the verge behind the car. There he lowered her down on the grass and dropped on top of her. As their lips parted for a moment, she gave a frantic cry. 'I'm pregnant, Michael. Have you forgotten?'

213

He laughed in reply and tried to undo the back buttons of her dress. When they proved difficult he seized the front neckline and ripped the dress open, exposing her neck and bodice. He was breathing heavily now and she felt his lips burn her exposed skin. She made another desperate attempt to free herself but his weight and strength easily pinned her down. Although his handsome face, less than six inches from her own, was dark with desire, it contained another elemental emotion that terrified her. His laughter came again. 'Go on, you silly little bitch. Fight as hard as you can.'

Realing that her resistance was only exciting him, she tried to go limp but he was too sexually aroused now for it to make any difference. Gripping the neck of her bodice he ripped it apart to expose her breasts. Seizing them in his hands so that the nipples protruded, he took one and then the other in his mouth, squeezing, sucking, and biting them in turn. She screamed and screamed again but the only response on the quiet road was the rustle of an alarmed animal in the nearby hedge.

His knees were now prising open her legs and she felt his hand fumbling in her groin. Sobbing with fear she tried to claw his face again, but he buried it between her breasts so that she could only reach his thick, dark hair. As she tore at that, he forced her free arm down to the grass again. Then, shifting his weight, he reached down and unbuttoned himself.

Although almost exhausted she struggled again as he tried to remove her lower garments. Finding difficulty because of her ample petticoats, he was forced to turn and use both hands. Grasping her opportunity she pushed herself up and clawed again at his face. This time she was successful but as her nails tore down his cheek, he cursed and struck out at her. As she fell back half-stunned, she felt one of his hands reach her bare thigh

214

and run greedily up it. As it reached her groin, panic gave her new strength and she threw herself sidewards and kicked with her upper leg.

The move was successful in that it drove him back for a moment and repulsed his groping hand. But as she struggled to rise, he seized her legs again and dropped back on top of her. As she struck at him, the erotic movement of her naked breasts seemed to divert his desire for a moment and once more he began to manipulate them. He took her nipples in his mouth and she felt his hardness pressing and pressing again against her groin. As she fought for breath his body suddenly went into spasm, pumping and jerking against her. Realising what had happened but not daring to move, she waited until his spasms had died away, then she wriggled from beneath him, ran round the other side of the car and tried to cover herself with her torn clothing.

A full minute passed before he walked round the car and her heart began thumping in fear again. Instead, he sounded embarrassed. 'I'm sorry about that. I suppose I wanted you too badly.'

She thought at first that he was apologising for trying to rape her. 'You're sorry! My God, and to think I trusted you.'

He seemed not to hear her. 'I've never known it happen before. I suppose it was because you put up such a fight and it made me over-excited.'

It was then she realised what he was apologising for. 'It's all that saved you,' she panted. 'If you'd raped me, I'd have gone straight to the police. As it is, I still ought to go to them.'

He gave a scornful laugh. 'What, and become a laughing stock when I deny everything? No, you won't. You'll keep your mouth shut or you'll get into serious trouble.'

She was trembling with shock and outrage. 'And

you're supposed to be a brave man! Attacking a pregnant woman! At least I know Harry was right about you. You're vicious and you're cruel. In fact, you're nothing but a sexual deviant.'

His face darkened again. 'Watch your tongue! Who the hell do you think you are?'

'I'm the woman you've just tried to rape. A pregnant women whose soldier husband might be dead. What will happen if I lose my baby?' The thought suddenly terrified her. 'I'll kill you if I lose it! I will! As God is my witness I will.'

She began to run hysterically down the road. Cursing he ran after her and seized her arm. 'Where do you think you're going?'

She fought to break free. 'Anywhere to get away from you.'

He dragged her back to the car and pushed her inside. As she tried to escape through the opposite door, he pulled her back. 'Sit down or I'll hit you. I mean it, so don't move.'

She spoke to him only once on the journey back to Ellerby Road, her voice bitter. 'I suppose all that talk about finding out what has happened to Harry has just been an excuse to see me?'

He replied without looking at her. 'No, I don't break promises where my men are concerned. I've done everything I said I would do.'

Cold and still trembling, she felt unable to raise the matter again. Outside No. 57 he caught her arm. 'If you and your mother know what's good for you, you'll keep quiet about this. It would be your word against mine and you know what that would mean.'

She gave a bitter nod. 'I know. I'm only the wife of a sergeant. But there's something we know that they don't, isn't there? That the sergeant is a hundred times a better man than his commanding officer. Isn't that right, Major Chadwick?'

Once more she heard his sharp intake of breath. Before he could speak the answer blazed like an explosion in her mind. 'Of course! All this is because of Harry, isn't it?'

His dark, handsome face stared at her. 'What are you talking about?'

She laughed at his expression. 'You're jealous of Harry, aren't you? You know he's a better man and because you could never defeat him, you tried tonight to harm him through me. You, the great war hero!'

For a moment he sat as if turned to stone. Then, without warning, he struck her violently across the mouth. 'You bitch,' he said hoarsely. 'You stupid ignorant bitch.'

She felt blood running down her lower lip. Stumbling out of the car, she supported herself against its door for a moment. Then, with outrage giving her strength, she turned back to face him. 'You can never defeat Harry, Michael. Not through me or anybody else. You're not fit to clean his boots and you never will be.'

'Harry's dead,' he said brutally. 'Rotting in the mud like thousands of other corpses out there.'

She steadied herself again. 'Dead or alive, he'll always be a better man than you. And all your life you'll know it.'

With that she turned and ran towards the house. Cursing, he revved up the car engine and drove away.

Chapter 22

Although the hall was lit when Mary entered the house, it was empty, giving her hope that Ethel had retired to bed and she might reach her room unseen. The hope was killed stone dead a moment later when she heard sudden, hurried footsteps in the sitting room. Bracing herself, Mary turned to face her mother.

Ethel's first words betrayed her eagerness. 'Well, how has it gone, dear? Did you enjoy your. . . .' Her voice changed almost comically. 'What on earth's happened?'

Outrage made Mary strike out at her as she pushed past. 'Your wonderful Major Chadwick tried to rape me. That's what's happened.'

Ethel put a hand to her throat. 'What on earth are you saying?'

Mary threw back her coat to show her torn dress. 'You see this? He assaulted me on our way back from the restaurant. The man you said was a such a gentleman.'

Ethel was looking incredulous. 'Major Chadwick? You can't be serious.'

Mary indicated her torn dress. 'Do you think I did this? Or this.' Pulling up her hemline she showed a stain on her white petticoat. 'Do you know what that is, Mother?'

Ethel looked afraid to ask. 'You're not saying. . . . Oh, no, I can't believe it.'

'You can believe it all right, Mother. It's all that saved me from being raped.' Suddenly the girl's self-control broke down. Dropping on the settee she began sobbing hysterically.

Looking uncertain and bewildered, Ethel sank down beside her. Before she could speak, Mary turned and flung her arms around her. 'Oh, Mother, it was horrible. He was like an animal. He laughed when I fought him.'

For a moment Ethel's maternal instincts came to the surface and her arms tightened around the girl. 'There, there, dear. You mustn't be so upset. Are you sure he didn't manage to. . . .' Ethel wanted to say 'rape you' but the conventions of the day defeated her.

Mary's tears were soaking through Ethel's dress. 'No. . . but that was because I struggled. He enjoyed that . . . that's what made it happen too quickly. But, oh Mother, it was awful. I wanted to die.'

Ethel patted her shoulder solicitously. 'Where did this happen, dear?'

'On the top of Swanland Hill. He said he was stopping to have a cigarette.'

Ethel hesitated. 'Did you let him kiss you, dear?'

Mary shook her head again. 'No.'

'Are you quite sure? Did you have wine or champagne at the restaurant?'

'We had champagne, yes. I didn't want any but he kept on filling my glass.'

Almost imperceptibly Ethel's tone changed. 'Then couldn't that be the answer, dear? You're not used to drink and it went to your head. It does happen to young women, you know.'

Unused to her mother's solicitude and drawing comfort from it, Mary was at first unwilling to believe what she was hearing. Then she drew back her tear-stained face. 'What are you saying? That I encouraged him?'

'Of course I'm not, dear. But you know what men are. It only requires a woman to change her manner in the slightest way for them to mistake it for willingness. And the Major is returning to the Front tomorrow.'

Mary drew back. 'You're finding excuses for him, aren't you?'

'Of course I'm not. I'm just saying that without realising it you might have given him the wrong impression. And you must remember that men like Major Chadwick have been under terrible strain for years.'

'So have millions of other men but they don't go around raping women. Why should he be any different?' Disappointment at her mother's reaction turned the girl's voice bitter. 'But he is Sir Henry Chadwick's son, isn't he?'

Ethel stiffened. 'You know that's not the reason.'

'Do I, Mother? Haven't you been trying to push me into his arms ever since he came round that first time?'

Ethel was beginning to bristle. 'I've hardly noticed you discouraging him, my girl, if we're throwing accusations about. And you didn't have to go out with him this evening if it comes to that.'

'You know well enough why I've kept on seeing him. No one else can help me find out about Harry. But he's only been using that as an excuse to see me. Surely you can see how contemptible that is.'

Ethel almost shrugged but stopped herself in time. 'At least it does show how strongly he feels about you.'

'How he feels about me? Trying to rape me when I'm pregnant? For God's sake, whose side are you on, Mother?'

Ethel's frown deepened. 'I'm not excusing him. I'm saying that probably you both had too much to drink. It's one reason I've always been against it. People do all kinds of things they regret when under the influence.'

'Drink had nothing to do with it unless it brought out the animal in him. Didn't you listen to what I said? He enjoyed hurting me. What sort of man likes doing that to a woman?'

'That was the drink,' Ethel said. 'He'll telephone you tomorrow to apologise. See if he doesn't.'

Mary's swollen lips set. 'He'd better not. By God, he'd better not.'

Ethel rose to her feet. 'Sit there and I'll make you a cup of tea. It'll make you feel better.'

Mary rose with her. 'I'm going upstairs. I won't feel clean until I've washed away the feel of his hands on me.'

'I'll bring a cup up to your room,' Ethel said. As Mary moved towards the door, she went on: 'Try not to be too upset, dear. After all, things didn't go too far, did they?'

Mary halted abruptly, then swung round. 'There was only one reason for that. He got his satisfaction too soon. That was all that saved me.'

Ethel winced. 'I still think it was the drink. After all, he did bring you home afterwards, didn't he?'

'Only because he didn't want me to go to the police.'

'You can't be certain of that, dear. He was probably already regretting what he'd done. How were things between you when you arrived home?'

'How do you think they were? I told him why he'd done it, and that was when he hit me.'

Ethel shook her head. 'I don't understand.'

'Don't you see, Mother? He's jealous of Harry but could never defeat him. So tonight he tried to get back at him through me. I didn't think he'd realised it until I told him. Then he went half crazy.'

Ethel looked genuinely puzzled. 'But why on earth should he be jealous of Harry?'

221

Mary stiffened. 'You wouldn't understand that, would you, Mother? Harry cares about life, about people's feelings, about their pain. He's everything Chadwick isn't and Chadwick knows it.' For a moment satisfaction overcame the girl's distress. 'He hated it when I told him that.'

Ethel hesitated, then frowned. 'Do you think that was wise?'

Mary stared at her. 'Wise? I don't follow.'

There was a calculating look in Ethel's eyes that had not been there before. 'Think about it for a moment. Neither the Major nor his family will want a scandal and yet as I'm a witness to the state you were in when arriving home, we are in a position to cause one, aren't we?'

'What are you getting at?'

Ethel moved towards the girl. 'Whatever you say, the Major must be attracted to you or I'm sure he'd never have behaved that way. So if you play your cards right, it shouldn't be difficult to come to some arrangement.'

Mary gave a start. 'Arrangement? You surely don't mean asking them for money?'

'Of course not. I'm thinking of something much more permanent for you.'

The girl gave a gasp of disbelief. 'You're talking about marriage, aren't you?'

'Why not,' Ethel said defiantly. 'As I say, the man must want you badly or he'd never have lost control of himself like that. And although I know how you must feel tonight, things will seem quite different in a day or two. You must remember you've lived a sheltered life and don't know much about men. It's not unusual for them to behave this way, you know. Not men who're as active and virile as the Major.'

Mary could not believe what she was hearing. 'You're defending him now, aren't you? You, who made Dad's life a misery if Connie or I even looked at a man, never mind one who'd act this way. What's happened to all that prudery of yours?'

Ethel's face set. 'I'm only trying to give you some sensible advice. Remember that half the women in the country would throw themselves into the Major's arms if they got the chance. And here you are with the opportunity to have him and all that you do is call him names.'

'Mother, the man tried to rape me. Or is rape different when a member of the aristocracy does it? Do they have some privileged dispensation? Surely you can't be such a snob as to think that?'

Red spots of anger and guilt stained Ethel's cheeks. 'I'll tell you what I do think, my girl. That sooner or later you're going to have to face facts. Everyone but you believes Harry is dead and where does that leave you? You've got a daughter already and another child on the way. The business is losing money hand over fist and things will get worse when your baby arrives and you can't get to the office. Yet you're prepared to throw over the chance to marry a man who would not only take care of your unborn child but would also put money into the business. So why is it so shocking to try to make you see sense?'

Remembering what Chadwick had said, Mary felt a chill running down her spine. 'How do you know about the money? You've discussed it with him, haven't you? Behind my back.'

For a moment Ethel seemed about to deny the charge. Then she drew herself to her full height. 'What if I did? Father left me the business, didn't he? And you're my daughter in spite of the way Harry tried to take you away. The Major promised to take care of us all and I believe him.'

Mary was trembling with anger and shock. 'You're

disgusting, Mother! You're a whoremonger, prepared to sell me to the highest bidder! Chadwick never wanted to marry me. He wanted me to be his mistress. My God, what would Dad say if he heard this? He'd pick you up and throw you out of the house.'

Guilt tore away the wraps from Ethel's self-control. 'Don't bring your father into it! Take a look at your own foolish pride instead. One day you'll learn how expensive pride is, my girl. I won't be here for ever to look after you and what'll happen then? Your wonderful Harry hasn't exactly left you with a fortune, has he?'

They were deadly enemies now, throwing every weapon to hand at one another. '*You* look after *me*,' Mary repeated. 'When I run Dad's business for you and provide you with your income? My God, Mother, I sometimes wonder if you're sane.'

'Never mind about my sanity,' Ethel sneered. 'Worry about your own. What sane woman would go on believing her husband was still alive after all the things she's been told?'

Mary stared at her with disbelieving eyes. Then, with a cry of despair, she ran upstairs to her room. For a moment she stared at herself in the mirror, her long golden hair dishevelled and mud-stained, her mouth swollen, her dress half torn from her shoulders. With another cry she threw herself on her bed and cried as if her heart would break.

Chapter 23

For Mary the weeks that followed were the darkest of her life. Until her clash with Chadwick she had been sustained by the hope that Harry was still alive and that sooner or later news of his whereabouts would reach her, either from Chadwick's father or from the War Office itself. Although secretly the hope had never been a strong one, it had nevertheless shown remarkable resilience in face of the chill winds of doubt, and at times had burned brightly enough to drive back the darkness that was always ready to invade her mind.

After her quarrel with Chadwick and her mother, however, she could no longer rely on its constancy. It was true that at times it would burn with an almost febrile light but now she suspected it was only an act of defiance against the forces that tried to extinguish it. More often it would flicker feebly or die altogether, leaving her in a grey limbo in which she went through the business of living without finding a meaning for it.

She would censure herself at such times. Possessing one child already and with a second growing in her womb, she had ample reasons to face the future, if not with joy then at least with purpose. All around her women were losing husbands or sweethearts without such precious mementoes of their passing.

But such thoughts were of little use at nights when she lay alone and sleepless in the double bed and the only light came from a fitful moon outside. Then the gnarling ache in her heart would turn into pain and overwhelming sorrow. Memories would parade through her mind to torture her. The golden day before their marriage when she and Harry had walked along the riverbank near his grandparents' cottage: the day that to Mary Miles had always seemed perfection. The drowsy hum of summer, the gently-flowing river, the love in her that had threatened to burst her heart. The gentle way Harry had drawn her down among the clump of trees, the words of love he had spoken, the sunbursts that had glowed in the trees above them. On that day time had paused for them and all the glory that was young love had lifted them up on its soaring wings.

At other times she would remember their honeymoon at his grandparents' cottage. The crisp autumn days and the brown leaves that their love had turned into gold. The warm glow of oil lamps, the billowing white clouds of the feather bed that had carried the congress of their bodies up to the stars. And always the memory of Harry's gentleness.

Her yearning would come back to her like a burning thirst and she would turn to the empty pillow alongside her and pound it in her agony. How could he be dead when he was so alive in her heart? How could a world of such sunlit promises turn so suddenly into a wasteland of ashes?

Bitterness would flood her at such moments. Why did life offer such happiness and then snatch it away? For the rest of her life was she to feel sorrow every time she saw a river, an old-world cottage, or white clouds sailing before a laughing breeze?

Nor could she lessen her grief by thinking of the

millions of women here and abroad who were sharing the same grief. A great sea of woe was engulfing the world and she found no comfort that others were drowning in it also.

During this time her relationship with her mother had returned to the armistice conditions that had existed before Chadwick had entered their lives. Mary sometimes thought of them as the last two survivors in a storm-tossed boat: enemies and yet each needing the other to bring the vessel safely into port.

In one aspect of that journey, however, Ethel would not play her full part. With the price of drugs soaring, with business debts mounting as hard-pressed shopkeepers could not meet their bills, and with Willis bringing in fewer and fewer orders, Mary was forced to make a request to Ethel at the beginning of August. 'Mother, we can't leave these debts any longer.' Suppliers are patient with us because of Dad and Harry, but it can't go on indefinitely. We're also going to need a new salesman if Willis is called up. This time we must get a good man and that might mean paying him more money.'

Ethel had baulked immediately. 'I'm not putting more money in. If the business can't stand on its own two feet, then it'll have to go.'

Her reply reminded Mary of her father's complaint that Ethel was totally devoid of business sense. 'Mother, you get an income from the business and so does Connie. If it goes under, you'll lose that. And selling it won't help you because you'll get next to nothing for a bankrupt business. So either way you'd lose.'

Ethel's lips had tightened. 'I notice you don't mention the income you get.'

'I didn't mention it, Mother, because I haven't been drawing it out for the last three months. I've only been taking my wages. I only need a couple of hundred pounds to keep our creditors happy for a few more months. By then the war might be over and things could improve all round.'

'I don't believe in throwing good money after bad,' Ethel complained. 'In any case, how are you going to manage after your baby's born? Who'll manage the business then?'

'I'll manage, Mother. I'll only be away a few days. After that I'll take the baby with me to the office.'

Ethel had given her little sniff. 'Don't think I don't know why you're making all these sacrifices. You want to keep the business going in the hope Harry comes back, aren't you?'

She had not denied it. 'It's one reason, but don't forget I have to earn a living myself. And there's Dad too. He created the business out of nothing and I can't forget how proud he was of it. Surely we both want to keep it going for his sake?'

In the end Ethel had compromised. She would put in a hundred pounds and relinquish her monthly income until the business recovered. But she would not stop or reduce the income Connie received. It was not a satisfactory solution but Mary felt that it might enable her to keep the business running for a few more months.

September came and Mary could stand the lack of news no longer. The thought came to her that if Sir Henry had received word of Harry and had passed it on to Michael in France, he might have felt his task was done. Alternatively Michael might not have given him her address, in which case the Squire might have difficulty in contacting her, if indeed he went to the trouble. Although she admitted to herself the possibilities were faint, nevertheless she felt her heart beating faster when she plucked up the courage to phone The Grange.

A woman with an impatient, cultured voice answered her. 'This is Lucinda Chadwick. Who is calling?'

Mary's mouth felt dry. 'My name is Mary Miles. Mrs. Miles. I wonder if I might speak to Sir Henry.'

'Sir Henry? What do you want with my husband?'

She explained as well as she could. 'I'm sorry to bother you but with the Major back in France I've no way of getting any news that might have come through.'

She wondered if it was her imagination or whether a note of caution entered the woman's voice. Although Michael would have made no mention of his behaviour before he left for France, his mother might have known about his earlier frequent visits to No. 57 and feared that he was developing a permanent relationship with her. 'I'm sure Sir Henry would have let you know before his illness if he had heard anything, Mrs. Miles. Unfortunately I don't know what has happened subsequently.'

'I'm sorry. I didn't know Sir Henry had been taken ill again. I hope it's nothing serious?'

Lucinda's emotionless voice betrayed all the stoicism of her breed. 'He's had a second severe heart attack, Mrs. Miles. As a result we are not allowed to disturb him.'

Mary flinched and her voice turned small. 'I'm sorry. I hadn't known. . . . Only there was no one else I could turn to.'

'No, I suppose not.' There was a short pause, then Lucinda's voice changed in tone. 'I'll tell you what I'll do, my dear. I'll speak to my husband's secretary. If any news has come through recently, I'll call you back. If you don't hear from me, there is none.'

Mary gave the woman both her office and her home number and waited by one phone and then the other until seven o'clock that evening. When no call came she knew the worst.

229

She did not cry that night, the wells of her grief seemed to have gone dry. Instead she lay listening to the sounds of the night. A wind had blown up in the early evening and was rustling the trees and keening in the eaves. It brought to her the wail of a train whistle and she remembered listening to the same mournful sound when Harry had lain beside her before returning to France.

Grief came suddenly, as it so often did, with an impact that seemed to drive the air from her lungs. Had he really gone for ever, like her father? Never to be seen or touched or kissed again? Did people fully understand that terrible word *never* which was death? The agonies of remorse, the words that should have been said but now could only remain inside and haunt the mind for ever. Oh, Harry, I worshipped you but I could never tell you so because I was shy and inhibited. Sometimes I was even angry with you when I could not understand why you had to go back to France, or when I thought you too patient with Elizabeth or with Mother. Now I know that your conscience, your patience and kindness were as much a part of you as your blood and bone, and when you were given to me I was blessed beyond measure.

But now you might be gone from me for ever and I left with fifty years of loneliness. As she tossed about the bed in agony, the child in her womb kicked and kicked again in protest.

The movements calmed her. At least his seed was left in her and she must guard it as a treasure beyond price. Yet even as her hands moved down and cradled her swollen body, she felt that even a suckling baby could never replace the warmth and the arms of the only man she had ever loved.

Chapter 24

Towards the end of that week Mary found a handwritten letter in the postbox addressed to Ethel. It was in a military envelope and although her mother kept her face expressionless as she tore it open, her off-hand remark to Mary could not wholly disguise her pleasure. 'It's from Captain Watson. He says he's been posted back to some depot in Yorkshire and asks if he might visit us again.'

'I'm glad,' Mary said. 'When would he like to come?'

'He suggests next Thursday evening if it's convenient, although heaven knows what kind of meal we can give him.'

'He usually brings food. At least he did the last time.'

'I know that but we must have a meal ready for him.' Ethel did her best to keep her tone casual. 'Do you think Mr. Willis could help out again? With another leg of lamb perhaps?'

Mary's voice turned dry. 'I'm sure Willis can, provided he makes something out of it himself.'

For once Ethel made no protest at her criticism of the salesman. 'Then will you ask him? We can't let the poor man face an empty table.'

As Mary confidently expected, Willis returned with a large leg of lamb the following Wednesday, at the same time proclaiming his disgust at the price he'd had to pay. 'Five pounds, ten shillings, m'dear! Isn't it disgusting how people are making money out of the war? It's enough to destroy a man's faith in human nature.'

Ethel paid the money without complaint and after judicious hints to neighbours with vegetable plots that she was entertaining an American ally, she had a mouth-watering meal simmering in the oven when Watson arrived. As Mary had expected, he was carrying a food parcel, two bunches of flowers which he handed to Ethel and Mary in turn, and a large packet of sweets for Elizabeth. 'It's sure good to see you folks again. It seems a long, long time.' Then, turning his eyes back to Ethel: 'Mind you, those letters of yours helped, Ethel. They sure did.'

Ethel, who had never said a word to Mary about writing to the American, turned quickly to Elizabeth who was chattering away excitely. 'There, dear. Give Captain Watson a chance to get into the house. I'm sure he'll find time to talk to you later.'

It was only after she had led Watson to an armchair and was giving him a whisky that Mary noticed there was a small envelope among her flowers. Opening it she found a handwritten card. 'With my deepest sympathy. But don't give up hope and keep the home fires burning!'

Surprised, she then realised Ethel must have told him the news in one of her letters. The homespun genuineness of the message brought tears to her eyes and when supper was over she thanked him. 'It's a very sweet thought, Jack. I do appreciate it.'

His round face became serious. 'It sure hurt me to read it, Mary. It was like losing someone in the family, even though I'd never met him. But he'll come back. See if he doesn't.'

'Do you think it's possible for prison camp records to be lost?' she asked.

'In Germany today? Anything can be lost, honey. From the intelligence we get, they're in a real bad state over there. Food riots, looting, it's all happening. The only thing we can't understand is how they keep on fighting so hard. I guess it's because they keep an iron hand on their soldiers.'

She gave him a wan smile. 'So you really do think there could be hope?'

She did not miss his slight fidget as if his armchair had suddenly become uncomfortable. 'Of course there's hope, honey. There's always hope when they tell you they're only missing.'

Knowing Ethel wanted to be alone with him, she waited until he had told Elizabeth one of his stories, then took her daughter's hand. 'Come along, darling. It's past your bedtime. Say goodnight to Captain Watson, thank him for your sweets, and ask him to come again soon.'

The child pouted. 'Must I go now? I want to hear another story about America.'

'No, that's all tonight or you won't sleep.' She turned to the grinning American. 'I'll say goodnight too, Jack. Thanks for everything and visit us again soon.'

'I'll do that, honey,' Watson said, glancing at Ethel. 'At least I will if your mother will have me.' When Ethel smiled, he took Mary's hand. 'Now don't you worry, honey. Keep that British stiff upper lip and remember that inside every cloud there's a silver lining. Promise?'

She managed to smile back. 'I'll try, Jack. Goodnight.'

'Good night, honey. Sleep tight.'

Upstairs she undressed Elizabeth and then said her prayers with the girl. From the beginning she and Harry had agreed Elizabeth should be given a religious upbringing and these days she found comfort in prayer herself. After tucking the child into bed and reading to her for fifteen minutes, she turned off the light and retired to her own room.

She tried to read for a while but finding she could not concentrate she turned off the light. She could hear laughter downstairs and for a moment felt resentment that anyone, and particularly her mother, could laugh while she was living in such darkness. The feeling passed with the thought that if Ethel could find a man to take the place of her beloved William, her embittered behaviour might take a turn for the better.

It was nearly midnight and she was almost asleep when she heard movement and whispering in the hall below. When the sounds ceased for a moment, she wondered if the two of them were kissing. Then there was movement again, more whispering, and finally the sound of the front door closing. Fully awake now, Mary felt certain she could hear Ethel humming as she walked back into the sitting room. Finding comfort in the sound, Mary relaxed and was soon asleep.

The following afternoon, after she left school, Elizabeth came to the warehouse office. It was something she seldom did and Mary's curiosity grew when she saw the child had been crying. Closing the office door, she sat the girl in a chair and knelt beside her. 'What's happened, darling? Have you had trouble at school?'

Although the girl shook her head, her eyes filled with tears. Mary took her hand and pressed it. 'Then what is it, darling?'

Elizabeth brushed her eyes. 'Grannie's been talking about Daddy. She says he's dead, just like Grandpa, and that I'll never see him again.'

Mary took a deep steadying breath. 'When did she say this?'

234

'Just now. After I got home from school. I said I hoped Daddy would be home by Christmas so that I could buy him a present and she said it was wicked to go on hoping like this. Is she right, Mummy? Won't we ever see him again?'

To give herself time to think, Mary found a handkerchief and dried the girl's eyes. Wondering what to tell the child had been a problem from the beginning and in the end she and Ethel had agreed to warn her that she might never see her father again but equally that there was hope he might return when the war was over. After all, the girl was in daily contact with children who were losing their fathers and the news of Harry lacked the finality some of the others were receiving.

The reasoning had appeared to work. The girl had cried and fretted for a few days but then had seemed to accept the situation, leaving Mary with a sense of relief and a spark of resentment that her distress had not been longer lived. Conversation with other young mothers, however, had assured her that Elizabeth was no different to their children. Most had seen little of their fathers during the last three or four years and with death an incomprehensible state to the very young, there was little difference to them in having their fathers absent in France and absent in death. Men it seemed could lose more in war than just their health or their lives.

Yet Elizabeth was clearly distressed now and Mary loved her for it. She took hold of the child's hands and pressed them. 'I can't promise you we'll see Daddy again, darling. There is a chance that Grannie is right and we won't. But there's also hope he might have been taken prisoner and will come back to us when the war's over. I think we should cling to that hope, don't you?'

The moment she spoke she felt guilty. Was she right in advocating hope when she had almost given up hope

235

herself? Yet to tell the child her father was dead seemed at that moment to conspire his death.

Elizabeth's tearful voice gave her a chance to retract. 'But, Mummy, if he's a prisoner why haven't we been told? Peter Latimer's father's a prisoner and his Mummy was told.'

The opening was there but she could not take it. 'I don't know why, darling. Perhaps Daddy's records have been lost. There could be all kinds of reasons why we haven't heard.'

Another tear trickled down Elizabeth's cheek. 'But why doesn't God tell us, Mummy? You say God knows everything.'

Mary bit her lip. What was right? she thought. You bring them up to believe in God and every night you pray alongside her that God will bring him back. But what happens if God doesn't bring him back? Will it destroy her faith? I know it will mine. If I want her to go on believing, what words do I use?

She cleared her throat. 'We must have faith, darling. We must keep on praying for Daddy and if God is . . .' She paused for the non-committal word that would give God his loophole. It came and she went on gratefully: 'If God is willing, he will bring Daddy back to us.'

In the way of children, the girl's mood changed quickly. 'Then, that's all right, isn't it, Mummy? Daddy always taught us to trust in God, didn't he?'

Mary flinched. At one time, yes, she thought. But that was before the Somme. 'If God is willing,' she repeated. 'We'll just have to wait and pray. Now dry your eyes and try not to think about it any more today.'

Apparently satisfied, Elizabeth changed the subject. 'Has Grannie told you about our holiday, Mummy?'

'Holiday? What holiday?'

'The one in America. When the war's over, Captain

Watson wants her to visit him and she's promised to take me.' The girl's eyes were shining now. 'Isn't that wonderful?'

Mary stared at her. 'Grannie said that?'

'Yes. She promised just now, after she told me about Daddy. She said it would make up for things. Oh, Mummy, isn't it wonderful? America sounds such an exciting place.'

I don't believe this, Mary thought. Pulling herself together, she leaned forward and kissed the child. 'No, she hasn't said anything to me yet but I'll talk to her about it later. What do you want to do now? Stay with me until I lock up or go back to the house?'

The girl jumped from her chair. 'I'll go back, Mummy. Grannie said she'd read me a story before supper. You don't mind, do you?'

Seething with resentment, Mary turned away. 'No. Off you go then. I'll see you in about half an hour.'

The storm broke over supper that night. Afraid of Elizabeth's reaction, Mary had decided she must wait until the girl was tucked away in bed before she confronted Ethel. Inevitably, however, the excited Elizabeth mentioned the holiday almost before Mary had entered the sitting room. 'Grannie, Mummy says you haven't told her yet about our holiday in America.'

Rising to set the dinner table, Ethel froze for a moment. Mary, knowing there was no turning back now, gave her resentment full rein. 'That's right, Mother, you haven't. How can you make her such a promise without talking to me first? Have you forgotten I'm her mother?'

Although guilt was written all over Ethel's face, in her usual manner she went immediately on the offensive.

'So that's why you barely spoke to me when you came in. I wondered what was the matter.'

'Don't tell me that you're surprised! You promised Elizabeth a thing like that without even thinking about me! I don't know anyone else who could do such a thing.'

Ethel glanced at Elizabeth whose expression had changed from excitement to dismay at the consequence of her words. 'I've hardly had time to tell you, have I? It was only last night that Jack gave me his invitation.'

'Gave *you* his invitation. Where did Elizabeth come into it?'

Ethel gave the little defiant toss of her head that betrayed her discomfort. 'She's shown such interest in America that I thought how much she'd enjoy a holiday over there. So I asked Jack if she could come too.'

'Without a word to me first?'

Ethel gave a tut of irritation. 'You weren't there, were you? I was going to ask you tonight.'

'But only after you'd first made your promise to Elizabeth.'

Ethel's lips compressed. 'I don't know what you're making such a fuss about. The war isn't over yet. Anything could happen before then.'

There was an instant wail from Elizabeth. 'Does that mean you might not take me, Grannie?'

Ethel turned to her solicitously. 'I shall take you if I'm allowed to, dear. But not if your mother forbids it. After all, she is your mother.'

The child turned her appeal on Mary. 'You won't do that, will you, Mummy? You won't stop me going to America?'

Mary winced. 'Darling, I can't make promises at a time like this. What if Daddy comes back to us? You wouldn't want to be away in America then, would you? Think how hurt and upset he'd be.'

'But Daddy's not coming back. Grannie said so.' Disappointment was turning the child hysterical. 'I want to go to America with Grannie. Do you hear, Mummy? I want to.'

Mary's eyes moved to Ethel. 'You see what you've done? How could you make her such a promise?'

Before Ethel could reply, the child grabbed a book from the settee and hurled it to the floor. Then, sobbing bitterly, she ran towards the door. Running after her, Mary tried to catch her but the child struck at her hysterically. 'I hate you, Mummy! I hate you, I hate you!' With that she tore herself away and went screaming up the stairs.

Chapter 25

To Mary the last few weeks before her baby was born were full of anxiety and tension. By September the reports that the food shortage in Germany was acute and that widespread riots were sweeping the country were verified by neutral observers. The effect of these reports on Mary was double-edged. If Harry was a prisoner in some remote part of Germany and the social structure of that country was collapsing, then it seemed almost certain she would now have to wait for news of him until peace came and the Red Cross were able to search for missing men. On the other hand, how could the Germans be expected to feed prisoners if their kith and kin were starving?

She began having nightmares about it. In one of them the war went on until only a few survivors were left in an endless sea of mud. And even then their blood lust was undiminished. Wading, floundering, they still struggled to reach one another and to tear each others' throats out. The world had gone mad and soon there would be no one left to call a halt to the madness.

She carried these thoughts with her every day that autumn as she dragged her swelling body up the warehouse steps to her office. She also carried fear for her unborn baby, for she had not forgotten her fall in 1915 down those same steps that had resulted in a miscarriage. Yet precious though her burden was, she felt unable to hand over the running of the business to Ethel. With food growing scarcer by the week, the public were spending more and more of their wages in trying to augment their rations and shopkeepers and pharmacists were suffering accordingly.

The problem of Willis was also growing. His age had saved him from the last call-up but with the German resistance growing even fiercer as they were driven back towards their Fatherland and British casualties mounting accordingly, it was expected the next call-up would draw him into the net. Terrified by the prospect, he was already behaving as if his last days were near and taking more than his usual solace from the widows and married women he met on his rounds. As a result the orders he brought in were even fewer than the situation warranted and only Mary's knowledge of the markets kept him under some kind of control. Under Ethel he would be able to do as he pleased, with disastrous consequences for the business.

Although sentiment played its part in Mary's desire to keep the business afloat – she could never forget what it had meant to her father – her own independence was a more compelling factor by this time. If the business were to go bankrupt, she and her children would be entirely at Ethel's mercy, for without her getting another job she could see no hope of running a house and bringing up a family on the tiny pension she would receive if Harry were finally judged to be dead. And if she did go out to work, there would be only Ethel to look after both children and that was a future she could not contemplate.

It was necessity then that made he drag her swollen body from her bed at seven-thirty and plod her painful way to the warehouse after Elizabeth had gone off to school. At no time, she noted, did her mother protest and offer to take her place. At first she wondered if Ethel had at last accepted her lack of business sense. Then she had less charitable thoughts. Was it possible that Ethel did not care if she lost this child? Did she still harbour thoughts about Chadwick and feel that she, Mary, was a better prospect for him with one child instead of two? Or was it simply she did not want a second grandchild from the man she disliked so much?

Such thoughts made her ashamed at times but in her run-down condition they kept running round her mind like animals in a cage. Why did Ethel hate Harry so much? What had he ever done to her except come from a different social class and hold different political views?

She knew the futility of the questions even as her mind asked them. Who could ever hope to understand Ethel? Even her spite and malice seemed to have no consistency, for while she hated Harry she undoubtedly loved Elizabeth, his child. Could William have been right when he once said her menopause was to blame for her behaviour? Or had William's death embittered her against the whole world and made her jealous of any woman who loved as deeply as she had once loved?

Of one thing Mary was quite certain: Ethel hoped Harry was dead. Since that one moment of revelation in her daughter's bedroom Ethel had never by so much as a word or a glance hinted at it and yet Mary was as certain as if she had shouted it from the roof-tops. In marrying Harry Miles, her younger daughter had made an error that was beyond grace and absolution and yet by a miracle she was being given a second chance. She, Ethel, would move heaven and earth to make certain Mary did not make the same mistake twice.

Mary worked up to and on the very day of her labour. After the problems of her first delivery, she had almost expected one as lengthy and painful but in fact she was in labour only five hours. She felt her first pains in the evening, after arriving back from the office, and asked her mother to call for the Irish midwife who had delivered Elizabeth. Two hours later, when the pains began to quicken, she went to bed.

Her baby was born on the stroke of eleven that night. The Irish midwife, who had talked nonstop throughout the delivery and was something of a know-all in her field, had an immediate explanation for the relatively easy birth. 'It's because you wus workin' right through to the end, y'see, like we have to do in Oireland. It helps the little creatures on their way, if you get my meanin'.'

Mary, sweating and hoarse from her efforts, heard a slap and a sharp cry and tried to lift her head. 'What is it, Mrs. McInnes? Tell me!'

'Why, it's a boy, m'dear. Complete with all his bits and pieces. Aren't you the luckiest girl in the world?'

Ethel and Elizabeth were allowed into the room fifteen minutes later. After a few brief words to the midwife, Ethel crossed over to the cot, followed by the impatient and excited Elizabeth. Watching her mother, Mary saw her face was expressionless as she stared down. Beside her, Elizabeth tugged at her arm. 'Is it a boy, Grannie?'

The midwife answered her. 'Aye, it is. You've got a baby brother now.' Her eyes moved to Ethel. 'An' you're a grannie to a boy and a girl, Mrs. Your daughter's done well for you, hasn't she?'

Ethel gave her an irritable, haughty stare, then moved to Mary's bedside. 'How are you feeling, dear?'

Vulnerable in her exhaustion, Mary was longing for a kiss from her mother. She thought how weak and distant her voice sounded. 'I'm all right, thank you. It was quick this time, wasn't it?'

Ethel nodded. 'Very quick. Much quicker than my second one, thank goodness. I was nearly two days in labour that time. So you've been lucky.'

Mary's eyes closed for a moment. I was your second one, mother. And after my birth you had complications. Is that one of the reasons you've never loved me as much as Connie? Her eyes opened again. 'I know,' she whispered. 'I'm sorry, Mother.'

Ethel stared down at her. 'Sorry? What do you mean? You wanted a boy, didn't you?'

Suddenly the effort to explain seemed too much and she answered Ethel's question instead. 'Yes, I did. I suppose it's because of Harry.'

Something hardened in Ethel's expression. She half-opened her mouth to comment, then drew back. 'Well you've got your wish. Now you'd better get some rest. And I'd better get Elizabeth to bed. Come and say goodnight to your mummy, Elizabeth.'

The child, bright with excitement, ran to Mary's bedside. 'Will I be able to play with him, Mummy?'

Mary lifted a hand and stroked her long, plaited hair. 'Yes, of course, you will. When he's older.'

'But I can bathe and dress him before then, can't I?'

'Yes, darling, of course you can. When he's a little bigger.'

'How long will that be, Mummy?'

'Not long. Babies grow very quickly. How you must let Grannie take you to bed or you'll never get up in the morning.'

The girl planted a kiss on Mary's forehead, then scampered back to look into the cot again. Ethel took hold of her arm. 'Come along, dear. It's nearly midnight.'

Reluctantly the excited girl allowed Ethel to lead her from the room. As Mary sank back on her pillows she could hear their voices as they crossed the landing to Elizabeth's bedroom. 'Isn't it exciting, Grannie? Can I get up early in the morning to see him?'

'You can if you like, dear. But I think you'll be too tired after such a late night.'

'I won't, Grannie. Please call me early.'

'All right. I will.' Then Ethel's tone changed. 'But you mustn't get too excited, dear. A new baby makes a lot of changes in a family, you know.'

Elizabeth sounded curious. 'What sort of changes, Grannie?'

Ethel's voice was just audible now as she led the child into her room. 'Mummy has always wanted a boy, dear. So you must expect her to give him lots of attention in the future. But you mustn't let that upset you. You've always got Grannie to come to if sometimes you feel neglected, haven't you?'

The Irishwoman muttered something, crossed the room and closed the door. She said something to Mary as she returned to the cot but the girl did not hear her. At first her body had stiffened in outrage, then her emotion had turned into despair. The feeling grew until she felt herself drifting away into a grey and terrifying limbo.

She felt the midwife shaking her. 'What's the matter, dearie? You've gone as cold as ice.'

For a moment her eyes were blind with misery. Then, as the outline of the woman appeared above her, she made a great effort to speak. 'I'm all right,' she whispered. 'Really I am.'

The Irishwoman stared down at her, then turned to the cot. 'You'd better have your baby, dearie. He'll soon warm you up.'

A moment later the child was suckling at her breast. Yet even in that moment of symbiosis, her sense of despair remained. Oh, God, she prayed, bring Harry

245

back to me. End this hideous war, bring him back, and take away my loneliness.

Although to Mary and millions like her the constant ebb and flow of battles seemed to offer no hope of an armistice, in fact the beginning of the end was in sight. On the 8th of August, under the command of General Rawlinson, the British and French had launched an attack a few miles east of Amiens. Using tanks, and for once themselves aided by fog, they had smashed through the enemy lines with such effect that thousands of German soldiers had surrendered virtually without firing a shot. Ludendorff called it 'The black day of the German Army' and certainly no one had seen the grey-clad soldiers behave this way before. The effect on Ludendorff was shattering and he offered his resignation to the Kaiser who promptly refused it.

Three more Allied offensives were launched in September, the Americans in the Ardenne, the French in Champagne, and the British in Flanders. All were successful to a greater or lesser degree but with the Allies now encountering the Wotan, Siegfried, Alberich, and other defence lines that had been massively fortified during the last four years, their losses were as high or higher than at any other time of the war. It was these casuality lists, appearing with frightful regularity day after day in the newspapers that gave the Allied public the impression the war would go on into 1919 and beyond.

Instead, behind the scenes, the German High Command was making frantic efforts to conclude an armistice before its armies disintegrated, and a peace note was sent to the American President. Wilson's reply, which he made without consulting his Allies, appeared to the Germans to demand a transformation of all their institutions. The military factions that still ruled Germany refused his terms and for the moment the slaughter went on.

Chapter 26

Hearing Willis's heavy tread on the warehouse steps, Mary hastily adjusted her blouse and replaced her baby in its cot. She had just finished tucking the blankets around it when the door knob turned. With her cheeks red she ran to the door and unlocked it.

The baby began crying resentfully as Willis entered the office. He gave her a knowing look. 'Have I interrupted his meal?'

She was only too aware that the salesman found pleasure in making references to her breast-feeding the child. In fact she was convinced that he was hoping one day he would walk in and catch her in the act.

Her reply was curt. 'No. What kind of a day have you had?'

His avoidance of her question was an answer in itself. 'Have you decided on a name for him yet?'

'No, not yet. I asked what kind of a day you've had?'

He stalled a little longer by lowering his heavy body into a chair. By this time the baby was crying lustily, forcing her to bend over the cot to comfort him. With no other option she had recommenced work only three days after the child was born. Her doctor had been shocked but she had made her decision before her confinement and had found no reason to change it. Fortunately the office had a gas ring on which she could heat water and by bringing over the child's cot and the necessary linen she had somehow managed to combine business and motherhood, although the wear and tear on her nerves and body had been considerable. Now, three weeks into October, she liked to believe the worst was over, although the embarrassment of interviewing men with a crying baby in the office still remained. Fortunately most of the visiting salesmen and customers admired the determined way she was carrying on but Willis was a different proposition. There was a prurience in him that was clearly enjoying her physical problems.

She soothed the hungry child until its cries died down, then picked up Willis's order book from the desk. Opening it, she gave a start. 'Five orders! Is that all you've got?'

His fleshy face showed both embarrassment and defiance. 'Business is bad, m'dear. There's no money about. And what money there is people are spending on food.'

'I know all that, but five orders! We've got to do better than this, Mr. Willis. I can't keep the business going otherwise.'

He changed the subject by pulling a folded newspaper from his jacket pocket and laying it on the desk. 'Have you heard about Sir Henry Chadwick?'

She gave a start. 'No. What about him?'

'He's dead. It happened early this morning.' He nodded at the newspaper. 'It's at the bottom of the first page.'

She read the ringed paragraph. 'Sir Henry Chadwick, who was believed to have recovered from his heart attack earlier in the year, died suddenly at The Grange at 3 a.m. this morning. He is survived by his wife, Lady Lucinda Chadwick, and his only son, Michael. Major Michael Chadwick, DSO, MC is expected to be given

249

leave to attend his father's funeral next week.'

So Michael was still alive, she thought. Harry had been right: he was immortal. Willis' voice interrupted her thoughts. 'Weren't you hoping the old boy might find out something about your husband?'

She nodded. 'Four months ago, yes. But not any longer. I'll have to wait until the end of the war for that.' Then, as she returned the newspaper to the desk, she noticed that Willis' slightly protruding eyes were fastened on the neck of her blouse. Glancing down, she saw that in her haste to cover herself she had wrongly fastened two buttons and a crescent of flesh was showing between them. Turning hastily to the cot where the half-fed baby was showing its resentment again, she pretended to soothe it while she made the necessary adjustments. When she turned back to Willis her voice was curt again. 'We've got to do better than this, Mr. Willis. Five orders in a day just isn't good enough.'

He frowned. 'We can't make shopkeepers and warehouses give us orders, m'dear. They're like us, they can't buy if the money's not coming in.'

'I think we can try harder, Mr. Willis. Did you go to Ferriby today? Or to Brough?'

His sullen eyes avoided her. 'Remember I'm doing my rounds on a bicycle these days. If I could use the Ford, as I did when I started with you, it would be a different matter.'

The cries of the baby were stretching her nerves to breaking point. 'You're no worse off than all the other salesmen in the town. And it's not my fault petrol's so strictly rationed. I don't think you try hard enough, Mr. Willis. When my husband had to go round on a bicycle he covered twice as many shops as you do.'

Resentment coloured the man's florid cheeks. 'Your

husband was twenty-five years younger than me. Don't you think that makes a difference?'

'Age had nothing to do with it, Mr. Willis. My husband believed in giving proper value for his wages. I think you ought to do the same.'

She had never spoken so bluntly to the salesman before and was surprised at herself. As the baby's cries reached a new crescendo, Willis muttered something and slammed his leather cash bag on the desk. The act gave her nerves a final wire-snapping twist and she swung round on him.

'Don't think I don't know what's going on either! Mrs. Tyson's daughter isn't the only woman you've had an affair with since you've worked here. Well, it's going to stop! I'm not paying you wages to spend your time entertaining women whose husbands are fighting for us at the Front. You'll either have to work harder and bring in more orders or you'll have to go. And don't expect a reference from me either.'

She could read his thoughts as he stood gazing at her sullenly. With trade in the doldrums he was going to stand little if any chance of finding a similar job with such easy conditions. 'Who says all these things about me?' he muttered.

'I hear them from all sides. Not that I need to. I've known for a long time what's going on. Well, what's it going to be, Mr. Willis? Are you going to start pulling your weight or not?'

He gave her another stare of dislike, then turned away. 'I can't work miracles,' he muttered. 'All I can do is my best.'

She knew it was capitulation and relaxed. 'Then please do your best,' she said. 'From tomorrow!'

He threw her another glance, nodded his head sullenly, then left the office. She ran to the door, locked

251

it, then picked up the half-hysterical child. Sitting at the desk, she opened her blouse and put him to her breast.

For a minute she sat there uttering soothing words to the suckling baby. Then, like a flood barrage breaking, her tears came. They poured down her cheeks and fell like rain on the baby who, oblivious to her misery, continued to suckle.

The Armistice was declared two weeks later, after the Kaiser had abdicated and fled to Holland. On the eleventh hour of the eleventh day of the eleventh month, men would lay down their arms and hostilities would cease. In essence it was a peace pact between the military powers of both sides and in later years that proved to be a mistake. Germany had not yet been invaded, indeed she still occupied three quarters of Belgium and parts of France, and her industrial might remained intact. It was therefore hardly surprising that the German public believed their military leaders when they claimed their army had not been defeated but instead had agreed to an honourable settlement. It was a myth that was to feed another upsurge of German militarism twenty years later.

For the soldiers on both sides, however, the effects were immediate and startling. At dawn on the 11th they were given their orders. On the stroke of the eleventh hour their lives would no longer rest on luck or the vagaries of some general they had never seen. From that moment on they would be able to make plans for the future, a luxury that had been beyond their dreams even twenty-four hours earlier. It was the stuff of intoxication and some men did behave as if they were drunk.

Others found the order more difficult to assimilate. For years death had been their constant companion and had slaughtered friends before their eyes. This macabre

252

carnival was to continue until the stroke of eleven. Until then it remained their patriotic duty to kill every enemy within sight. A second past the hour and killing would be a murderous crime. It is small wonder that some men with sensitivity found the order more insane than the war itself.

On some fronts men put their weapons aside and peace came early. On others the killing reached a crescendo. On the sector where Pershing had his troops, the Germans, bitter at their impending defeat and with stocks of shells they would not need on the morrow, pounded the Americans with a barrage of unparalleled ferocity. Not surprisingly the Americans replied in kind and in the four hours before the guns died into sullen silence, the ground was littered with the bodies of men, who, in a sane world, might have lived to old age and wisdom.

Similar tragedies were occurring in the air where pilots, without radio and forgetting the time in their battle fever, fought to the death and came down like flaming meteors on to battlefields already still and silent. The Angel of Death was not giving up lightly its dominance over the lives and souls of men.

There was little wonder, then, that soldiers on both sides treated the eleventh hour with suspicion. The silence that suddenly fell reminded them too vividly of the hush that had so often preceded another bloody offensive. Soldiers exchanged cigarettes, talked in whispers, and waited. When the eerie silence remained unbroken a few men, either the brave or the foolish, took a quick glance over the sandbags. Seeing heads bobbing up from the trenches opposite, they called out and heard shouts in reply.

Confidence began to spread. One man took a deep breath, climbed over the parapet and stood upright.

When no shots rang out, other men took their courage in both hands and followed him. Although all men felt naked at first, the trickle turned into a flood and soon the two lines of men were advancing on one another.

They paused when only a few feet apart, a few of the younger men surprised to see that the uniformed figures opposite them had eyes, noses and mouths very simiiar to their own. Gruff uncertain voices were heard and a few cautious smiles appeared. Then, as suspicion finally died, the lines converged in a great outburst of relief and comradeship. Hands were grasped, cigarettes exchanged, and here and there ex-enemies were seen hugging one another.

The accord was not to last for long. Uncertain that the peace negotiations would be successfully concluded, the Allies issued a stern order against fraternisation and an armed picket was set up between the lines, from the Channel down to Switzerland. But with initial contact established, the common soldier on both sides was not to be denied paying his respects to his ex-enemy. The need for rockets, contact flares, star shells and the rest was over at last. Then let them be used to celebrate peace. That night, with singing coming from both lines of trenches, both sides gave the other a stupendous display of pyrotechnics.

Back in Britain the reaction to peace was more spontaneous. The moment church bells began ringing, people poured out into the streets in their thousands. Tramcars clanged their bells, taxis and lorries pipped their horns, and strangers hugged one another as if they were life-long friends.

In Hull the bedlam was further increased by the triumphant sirens of ships in the Humber Docks. Pubs on Hessle Road began offering free drinks to anyone in their vicinity. Women, some already drunk, cried, sang, and cried again. Children, some unsure of the cause of the festivity, waved flags, ran around under people's feet, and sang and shouted themselves hoarse.

When the early evening darkness fell, the gaiety increased instead of fading. With shop windows blazing with light again, eyes accustomed to privation became both dazzled and intoxicated. Bands playing in both East and West Parks, couples danced in the streets, groups of strangers joined hands, sang patriotic songs, and kissed one another. Private houses opened their doors to anyone unlucky enough not to gain entry into the pubs which stayed open all night. Four years of sorrow, anxiety and stress were releasing an outburst of emotion such as the city had never known in its long history.

Not everyone joined in the public merrymaking. Some preferred to attend the crowded churches to offer their thanksgiving to God. Others, like Mary, although grateful the years of suffering were over at last, found the revelries too bitter a reminder of their personal loss and remained indoors instead.

Mary's choice had not lacked opposition. Jack Watson's base had known about the forthcoming Armistice for two weeks and had given some of its officers leave to enjoy the occasion with their British friends. Watson had been one of the lucky ones. He had promptly made a beeline for No. 57 and persuaded Ethel to go out with him that evening. He had also tried to include Mary, whom he had now taken to calling 'kid'.

'I know how you must be feeling, kid, but it'll do you good to forget things for a while. How often do we have Armistice nights? Can't you get your friend Mabel to look after the children? We won't be that late back.'

Mabel had been a ready-made excuse. 'How can I ask her? She'll be having her own celebrations.'

Watson's face had shown genuine regret. 'But I don't

like leaving you on your own. Don't you know anyone who'll look after the children?'

'Jack, who'll want to baby-sit tonight? Go out with mother and enjoy yourselves.'

In the end they had gone without her. Ethel's willingness to go had surprised Mary. In the past she would have turned up a contemptuous nose at the revelry and drunkeness that had taken over the city. If Mary needed further proof that Ethel's intentions regarding Watson were serious, she received it that night.

It was a relief to her to be left alone. All day she had felt obliged to hide her feelings. Now, with Elizabeth playing with children three houses away, there was no longer the need to pretend emotions she did not share. She knew that the public response was a human one but at the same time felt a distaste for it. The war had been a prodigious betrayal of life and faith. Then should not the world be on its knees praying for forgiveness instead of drinking and toasting the end of its monstrous folly?

She knew these feelings were born of her loss but if anything they grew stronger as the evening wore on and the sounds outside grew louder as drink took its toll. She fed her baby, bathed him, and then rocked him to sleep in his cot. Then she slipped out to collect Elizabeth. Excited by the lights and atmosphere, the child was reluctant to go to bed and was talkative once she was put there. 'Is this really the end of the war, Mummy? The very end?'

'Yes, darling. It's over at last. Soon there'll be nice fruit to eat and pretty toys in the shops. Isn't that something to look forward to?'

Elizabeth nodded. Then her face, pink from soap and water, changed expression as she stared up at Mary. 'Does it mean Daddy might come home now? Or is Grannie right and he never will?'

Mary felt a spasm of hatred for Ethel. 'Don't listen to

256

Grannie. She doesn't know what she's talking about.' To keep her feelings in check, she changed the subject. 'Wasn't it kind of Captain Watson to bring you all those sweets.'

The girl nodded vigorously. 'Yes. They're nice too. I like the liquorice toffee ones best of all.' She continued without pausing: 'Captain Watson said more about Grannie going over to America. Did you know?'

'No. When was this?'

'When you went over to the warehouse to let the men off for the day. He said he expected to be home for the New Year and would like her to go over in the spring for a holiday. Then he said he might come back to England.'

'What did Grannie say?'

'She said she'd like to but would have to see.' The child's voice ran on without changing tone. 'When do you think you'll hear about Daddy? Will it be soon?'

The question sent a sudden chill through Mary. It took her a moment to reply. 'I don't know. It might be a week or it might be months. Why do you ask?'

The girl looked surprised at her words. 'I just want to know, that's all. How do you hear, Mummy? Do they write to you?'

'No. They usually send a telegram.'

'Then I'll watch out for it every day. And if I'm home I'll bring it over to you.'

Still feeling chilled, Mary gazed down at the girl's ingenuous face. 'Yes. Please do that, darling. Now I'm going to put the light out and let you go to sleep.'

As she rose from the bed, Elizabeth's voice checked her. 'Can I play with John and Maud tomorrow, Mummy?'

'If they've been given a school holiday too, yes, of course you can. But we'll talk about it in the morning, shall we?'

The child snuggled down in her bed as Mary crossed over to the light switch. Her voice sounded again as the room plunged into darkness. 'It's good the war's over, isn't it, Mummy?'

'Yes, it is,' Mary said. 'Goodnight, darling.'

Without knowing why, she paused outside the door. When the child made no further comment she went downstairs into the sitting room and drew up a chair in front of the coal fire. Watching the flames dancing and leaping, she felt cold again and held out her hands. She was being ridiculous, she thought. Elizabeth was still a child and what child would not find a trip to America exciting? In all probability there was no link between that and her questions about her father, but even if there was, could a child be blamed for asking them? She had seen little enough of Harry to date and the awesome matters of life and death were unreal to the very young. But she could not excuse her mother for the unhealthy fears and false hopes she had fed into the child.

It took the cry of her baby upstairs to drag her from her thoughts and by the time she had fed it, changed it, and wooed it back to sleep again, an hour and a half had passed. She thought about going downstairs to make herself a drink, then changed her mind. She did not want to face her mother again tonight and it was not likely that Ethel would allow Jack to keep her out late. Instead she undressed and slipped into bed.

She lay listening to the sounds outside and the quiet breathing of her baby. To divert her mind she tried to settle on a name for him. Although originally she had wanted to call him Harry, she had felt that a household with two men with the same forename might be confusing. Now, with the truth about his fate becoming imminent, she had the added fear that if she took Harry's name for the child, she might lose the father for

258

ever. She ridiculed her superstition but nevertheless decided that Harry would only be the child's second name.

But what forename would suit him? Frank? William? – yes, she could call him after her father. But then people would call him Bill and she had never liked Bill. What name would Harry like? Why not postpone a decision until he came back?

She was still wide awake when Ethel and Jack Watson returned. She heard their voices lower when they realised she had gone to bed and then diminish into a murmur as the sitting room door closed behind them. A clink of cups followed as Ethel made them a drink and then, some time afterwards, the soft creak of their footsteps on the stairs. They both appeared to enter Ethel's bedroom because she could still hear their low voices after the door closed.

Outside, the sounds of revelry were beginning to fade at last although she could hear occasional shouts, music, and a distant ship's siren. The world, she thought, would wake up on the morrow with a massive hangover to face the devastation its folly had wrought.

It was a thought that finally made her face the apprehension she had felt all day. Resigned after Sir Henry's death into believing she would hear no more about Harry's fate until the war ended, she had at first longed for that end with every fibre of her being. But now the day had come, her feelings had changed. Without any news, hope remained and a woman could live on hope. But with the Armistice here at last, the truth must soon come out and that truth might destroy hope for ever.

From now on time would be like the slow winding of a rack, notch by notch, day by day, while she waited for the brown envelope that would seal his fate and her own.

Feeling her heart thudding at the prospect, she won-

259

dered why she viewed it with such pessimism. The envelope could contain good news as well as bad. Then was some sympathetic power trying to break the facts to her gently? Frightened by the thought and by the superstitions that were plaguing her, she searched the recesses of her mind for comfort. But they were shadowy and full of ghosts that night and it was nearly dawn before she fell asleep.

Chapter 27

The phone in Mary's office rang just before three o'clock on the 12th of December. 'Mary?'

Recognising her mother's voice and the urgency in it, Mary felt her heart stop, then give a thud of apprehension. 'Yes, Mother. What is it?'

'A messenger's just delivered a letter. It's in a War Office envelope. Do you want me to open it.'

She felt her throat close. 'No. I'll come over for it. I'll come straight away.'

'There's no need for that, dear. I'll bring it over to you.'

Unable to argue. Mary lowered the receiver. Her heart was beating so fast she thought she would faint. Supporting herself against the desk, she turned to the window. The winter day was closing in and the trees that flanked the lane were threadbare scarecrows. A raw wind was seeking out the last of their leaves and as she watched half a dozen fluttered to the ground. The bleakness of the scene sank into her: the very elements were surely warning her of the news to come.

Then, afraid her pessimism might bring the news she feared, she willed herself to believe. 'Harry's alive! Harry's alive! He is, he is, he is . . .! Harry's alive!' She willed the belief with every atom of her being until she felt the veins of her mind would burst under the strain.

Ethel appeared in the lane a moment later. As her erect figure approached the warehouse yard, Mary saw she was wearing a high-collared coat but was bare-headed. The envelope was clutched in her right hand. As she opened the gate and crossed the yard, Mary could watch no longer and sank back into her chair.

She heard her mother reach the stairs and begin ascending them. Time seemed to slow down now but because it gave her a few seconds more of hope she welcomed its tardiness. When Ethel's footsteps reached the landing outside, she took a deep breath and held it.

Ethel appeared in the doorway. Seeing Mary's pallor as she sat at the desk, she gave a start. 'What's the matter, girl? Are you ill?'

Although her legs would barely support her, Mary managed to rise and hold out her hand. 'Give me the envelope, Mother. Please!'

Ethel hesitated, then handed it over. Bracing herself, Mary tore it open and drew out the buff-coloured letter inside.

In the silence that followed, a distant clock could be heard striking the hour. Seeing her daughter's face growing paler as she read, Ethel took a step forward. 'Well! What does it say?'

Moving as stiffly as a clockwork toy, Mary reached out to the desk to steady herself. As she scanned the letter again, Ethel's voice became urgent. 'Mary! What does it say?'

The girl lifted her ashen face. She looked dazed and uncomprehending and although her lips moved, no sound came from them.

Frowning, Ethel held out an impatient hand. 'For heaven's sake! Give it to me, girl!'

Mary found words at last. 'It says Harry's alive. That

he's in a hospital near London. And that I can go to see him.'

Ethel gave a violent start. 'Are you sure?'

Mary held out the letter. Unable to hide her disbelief, Ethel read it twice before handing it back. 'I can hardly believe it! So he's been a prisoner all this time?'

Unaware that when the tourniquet of grief is removed, joy takes time to reach the mind, Mary was frightened by her inability to feel any emotion. Her hushed voice repeated itself. 'Harry's alive, Mother. I can go and see him.'

Tears were trickling down her cheeks now but her expression was still that of a woman in shock. Ethel hesitated, then leaned forward and kissed her forehead. Mary was never to know whether the kiss and the words that followed were Ethel's attempt to disguise her disappointment or one of her rare moments of maternalism. 'Pull yourself together, dear. At least your son will see his father now. And that's what you've wanted, isn't it? I'll go and tell Elizabeth and in the meantime I think you should close the office and come home.'

She left Mary standing like a statue with the precious letter clutched in her hand. Then, as Ethel descended the stairs, the impact of her words exploded like a sunburst in the girl's mind. It was true! It was incredibly, miraculously true! Her son would know his father because her prayers had been answered and Harry was alive! With a cry that was pure joy, she ran to the cot, picked up the sleeping baby, and sobbed out her relief and gratitude.

The young nurse held out her hands. 'Let me take him, Mrs. Miles. It'll give you a chance to talk to your husband.'

Thanking her, Mary watched the nurse carry the crying child into the office at the end of the ward before turning back to Harry. 'What do you think of him?' she asked.

His gaunt face smiled up at her. 'He's beautiful. The finest present a man could have.'

'I'm sorry he's a bit irritable. The train journey must have upset him.'

'He's beautiful,' he said again. His eyes moved over her solicitous face and mass of golden hair. 'And so are you. I'd forgotten just how beautiful you are.'

She felt her cheeks burn and glanced round at the row of beds. 'Sssh,' she whispered. 'They'll hear you.'

He laughed. 'They'll all be thinking the same thing. So what does it matter?'

Although his prison pallor was fading, she could see strands of grey in his black hair. As she ran a hand over his hollow cheek and then to his shoulder, a shudder ran through her. 'You're so thin! Was the food that bad?'

'It wasn't their fault,' he said. 'They were nearly starving too.'

'What about the rest of your men? The ones you told me about in your letter before you were captured.'

He winced. 'Turnor went early. It was my fault. I should have known what would happen.'

Seeing his distress, she bent down and kissed him. 'I'm sorry. Don't talk about it now. Leave it until later.'

For a moment he seemed to be talking to himself rather than her. 'I must remember to see Turnor's wife. He was so worried about her.' Then his eyes lifted again. 'A young lad called Apps took his place and he and Dunn were killed in the last attack. Swanson and I were knocked out and ended up in the same POW camp together.'

'Did he survive?'

'Yes, although he said he'd volunteer to be a scarecrow when he got back to Blighty! Swanson could

264

laugh at anything, even the food they gave us.'

'Is he here in the hospital?'

'No. We got split up after the hospital ship docked. I think he went to a hospital in Folkestone. I don't suppose you know if Chadwick got through all right?'

Half-expecting the question, she gave nothing away. 'Yes, he survived. But his father died a few weeks ago.'

His mouth, the sensitive, expressive mouth that she had always loved, quirked humorously. 'I thought Chadwick would make it. He's bullet-proof. But I'm sorry about his father. He was a fair man and I liked him. Did Chadwick write to you after I was reported missing?'

From the way her mouth turned dry, she knew how careful she must be. 'Yes, I got a letter. And we also met.'

His gaunt face reflected his surprise. 'Met?'

'Yes. I heard he was on sick leave and I had to find out all I could about you. We met in town and he was quite helpful although he hadn't actually seen what happened.' Afraid Ethel might make some mention of Chadwick's visits, she went on: 'He promised to ask Sir Henry to find out all he could and he called round at No. 57 a few times afterwards. But no one could get any news about you.'

He nodded. 'That's Chadwick all right. He'd sacrifice men like pawns to gain a military target but he'd usually take care of their welfare when off duty.'

She could not hold back all her bitterness. 'He hardly took care of you and Gareth, did he?'

He gave a wry smile. 'I suppose he'd claim extenuating circumstances there. But I can't deny that on the whole he's a good officer.'

That's one way you haven't changed, she thought. You can still forgive people for the wrongs they do you. But I can't. Not Chadwick. I hate him, both for what he's done to you and done to me, and I hope to God he'll never cross our path again.'

'He's inherited the estate, of course,' she said. 'I just hope he doesn't treat his tenants the way he treated you.'

'Why? Are you thinking about the old couple?'

She knew he meant his grandparents. 'They both seem well,' she said. 'I've kept in touch with them by letter.'

He squeezed her hand appreciatively. 'That leaves only one question, doesn't it? How has Ethel been behaving?'

Determined before she left home that her mother should not spoil this day, she laughed. 'Mother's been mother. No better and no worse. You don't know she's found herself an admirer, do you?'

He gave a start. 'You're not serious!'

'She has. He's an American, an army captain called Jack Watson. He wants her to have a holiday with him in America next year.'

'I don't believe it,' he said. 'Is she going?'

'I think she might. She seems very fond of him.'

'I just can't believe it,' he repeated. 'I always thought she worshipped your father.'

'She did.' Shy as ever, Mary felt her cheeks grow warm as she lowered her voice. 'Underneath she's a very passionate woman, Harry. I think she needs a man. In fact I think they've already been sleeping together.'

This time his head rose from his pillow. 'Sleeping together? Ethel?'

His amazement that any man should want to sleep with Ethel or that Ethel should so demean herself made her suddenly want to giggle. 'I think so. There's no question that she's very fond of him.'

His comical expression told her that whatever else the war had done to him, it had not destroyed his sense of

266

humour. 'Ethel in bed with an American serviceman! My God it could be the end of the world.'

This time the giggle broke from her. Then she gazed hastily around. 'Be careful! Someone might hear you.'

His grin broadened. 'Mind you, if the sky doesn't fall down, it could be good news. Do you think she'll marry him?'

'I can't say that. It's too early.'

'But you think she might go over to America for a holiday? Do you know how long for?'

She did not need telling the way his thoughts were running. 'I don't suppose it would be worth her while to go for less than two months. It might even be longer.' For a moment her thoughts betrayed her. 'She can go for ten years as far as I'm concerned.'

He frowned. 'She has been up to her old games, hasn't she?'

'No,' she lied, wondering what he would say if he knew about Ethel's promise to Elizabeth. 'It's just it will be heaven to have the house to ourselves, that's all.'

He looked unconvinced but changed the subject. 'It'll give us time to look for a house of our own. I want us to start doing that the moment I get back.'

There was nothing she wanted to hear more but the cries from the office, growing louder and more impatient, forced her to rise. 'I'll have to go to him, darling. It'll be his feed time in a few minutes.'

He laughed. 'That's not why he's crying. It's because you told him this scarecrow is his father. I don't think even you recognised me at first, did you?'

'Of course I did.' Bending down, she whispered in his ear. You're the handsomest man in the hospital. Don't you realise that?' Then, quite suddenly, her breath caught in her throat. 'I thought I was never going to see you again, Harry. Do you realise how awful that was?'

He caught her hand and gripped it. 'It's all over now, love. We'll all be together again in a few more days.'

His face blurred as she gazed down at him. 'But this was the second time, Harry. Twice I thought I'd lost you for ever. You won't do it to me again, will you?'

He reached up and brushed away her tears. 'No, love. It really is over. I'm coming home to stay this time.'

Then it's all right, she thought, as she bent down and kissed him. No matter what Ethel might do, no matter what problems the future might hold, the war was over and Harry was back. For Mary Miles the future on that December day in 1918 seemed aglow with hope again.

5